ALMOST TRUE

A SMALL TOWN ROMANCE

THE BACK TO SILVER RIDGE SERIES

CLAIRE CAIN

Cover Photography by Ava Veater, @avajphoto

Cover design by Emma Robinson

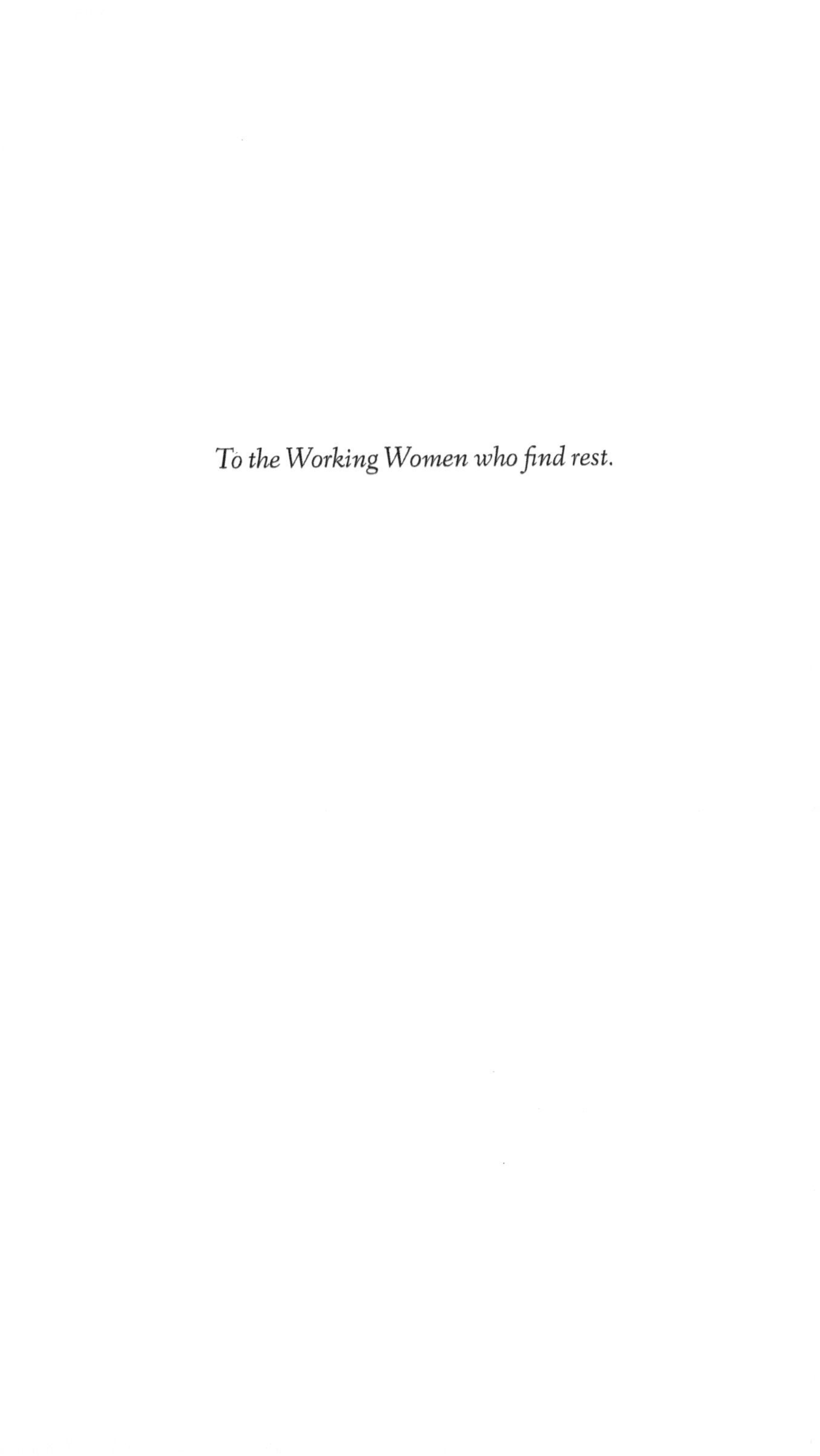

To the Working Women who find rest.

CONTENT WARNING

Dear reader,

Almost True is a closed door romance full of longing and heart that focuses on a widowed father. While the hero's grief isn't fresh, he does still think about his spouse. The heroine experiences a stalker and near-death experience (as written in *Almost Home*).

I mention this content in case any of those topics are ones you'd prefer to avoid. I want you to walk away with only happy, lovely feelings, and hope you'll feel safe proceeding with this information in mind.

My very best to you,
Claire

CHAPTER ONE

THEN

18 Months Ago

Maddie

The twenty-something guy slinging drinks nodded my way as I slumped into a seat at the polished wood bar.

"What can I get you, beautiful?" He winked and squared himself to me from across the bar top. His name tag said *Brandon*.

"G and T, please."

He couldn't have noticed my forced smile, busy as he was with my order and whatever else he was doing back there.

Did I even really want to be here? No. But had I

promised myself and my best friend that I'd leave my hotel room for a solid two hours and enjoy myself before returning to reality tomorrow? *Unfortunately yes.*

"You got it, lovely."

He spun away and began composing the drink, thankfully missing my eye roll. Not that I didn't appreciate that his job as a bartender made a certain amount of flirting necessary. It was just so... campy. And I had enough snark stored up after having to work nonstop on what should've been a nice little getaway that I had to keep my response locked down or I'd end up in the headlines for being an ungracious priss or who knew what else.

Bonus? He clearly didn't recognize me.

With a flourish, he set down a *Silver Ridge Resort – Welcome Home* coaster and nestled a crystal highball on top. "Alrighty, gorgeous. Here you are. Lemme know when I can get you a refill."

A snicker two seats over had me glancing to my right. *Whoa.* Tall, broad shoulders under a plaid shirt rolled at the forearms, all of which happened to be my kryptonite—but for some reason, especially those forearms. Dark hair longer on top and cut short on the sides, with almost startling contrast of salt-and-pepper gray that told me he must be at least a decade older than sweet Brandon, who was at most twenty-five.

No clear sign the gorgeous, towering man sitting there had laughed at the bartender's words, but apparently Brandon wasn't going to let it slide.

"What's so funny, Aid?"

The man's head popped up from studying his beer and pinned the bartender with a look. "Just wondering how many more endearments you were going to toss out."

"You saying this nice lady isn't beautiful, lovely, and

gorgeous?" Brandon asked, notching his chin in my direction.

Years of being impervious to comments about my appearance, at least in the moment and in front of the public, came to play as I didn't react to his words. I averted my eyes and sipped my drink—well made, though it was hard to screw up a gin and tonic.

Something pulled my eyes toward the man and when I glanced up, I met his gaze.

My stomach swooped low because *wow*, this man was handsome. What one might call a *specimen* of manhood, and even thinking that would make me roll my eyes if I wasn't sitting here *looking at him*. Not in the polished, Wall Street way I'd grown tired of. Not in the manicured look of Hollywood. In just a bone deep *this is how we keep the human race alive* kind of way. Some essential part of me recognized a gut-level attraction in an instant.

His eyes flicked over my face, and he shook his head ever so slightly. "I'd be a fool to say that."

Aidan

Brandon had the awareness to shoot me a smirk and walk to the other end of the bar, clearing the way for an interaction between me and the woman. Meanwhile, I internally scrambled for what to do. When was the last time I'd found myself in a situation like this?

Honestly? Never. I didn't just go out by myself. I didn't accidentally end up complimenting a gorgeous woman I'd never met but suddenly *really* wanted to get to know. *If I got* out, it was with my cousin and other male friends for the express purpose of being out of my house, or it was on a date with yet another woman I'd known too long and who already had me cast in her Tragic Hero Project. *No, thanks.*

"He wasn't going to let you off the hook, was he?" the woman said, reminding me I'd just overtly indicated I agreed she was beautiful. And obviously, she was. She had to know it just as well as I did, though I suspected it didn't punch her in the gut like it did me.

"No. Looks like he wasn't." I let my eyes find her again. My stomach dropped. "I didn't mean anything by it—not about you. I just..." Her expression didn't say she was mad, but I didn't want to insult her.

"I took no offense. And honestly, I'd been rolling my eyes at *lovely*, so by the time he got to *gorgeous*, you sort of took the words out of my mouth." Her lips pressed together in a pretty, amused smile.

Here's where I'd normally nod in agreement but stop talking. Let the conversation die with me and go back to sipping my beer and drowning in the frustrations of the day.

I couldn't say why, but I couldn't do that. So I nodded, and the next words slipped out. "Glad to hear it, though I'm sorry you didn't get a chance to say whatever you would've said."

She waved a hand. *Left hand. No ring.* Dang, I was worse than my cousin right about now. He was always on the prowl on my behalf. I'd been on a half dozen bad dates in the last three months thanks to him.

"I wouldn't have said anything—that's not a great way to get a clean drink."

"Fair point. He knows my name and where I live, so I have no hope," I joked, like some alternate-world version of myself.

She tilted her head. "You're a local?"

I stifled a grin and looked down at my beer, but nodded. She said *a local* like being from Silverton was charming and idyllic. Not a surprise given she was most definitely *not* a local and therefore had likely chosen to come visit for vacation.

"And? What's it like to live in Silverton full time?" She crossed her legs in my direction.

At some point in the last few years, in a stupid article John had probably foisted on me, I'd read that was a sign of interest.

"It's nice." But that didn't even touch it. It was beautiful and stifling and freeing and difficult and heartbreaking and lonely as all get out. But maybe that wasn't just Silverton.

"Wow. Don't sell me too hard." She laughed lightly and turned back to her drink.

My instinct to leave after the misstep, that brittle part of me I didn't exercise or air out in public, didn't chime in. It stayed strangely silent, and that left me with nothing to do or say but, "It's not so bad. Just... small, sometimes."

Her gaze climbed back up to mine. "Everybody knows all your secrets?"

Not exactly secrets, but I nodded.

"And? What are they?"

A rough laugh shot out of me, but it came sharper than I would've liked. Something in her demeanor shifted and she looked away.

A pulse of alarm shot through me. I hadn't meant to shut her down. But I didn't do this. I didn't make small talk with beautiful women at bars on a Sunday night. I didn't share my *secrets*, but maybe that was because it didn't feel like I had any around here. Everyone knew just about every-thing. When I walked into a room, it wasn't just me showing up. It was me and the baggage of my story—what my life had become. I couldn't just sit here and chat with this woman like I didn't have that dark cloud of history hanging over me.

And why not?

The voice rang loud and clear and sounded a little bit too much like my meddling cousin. But the point hit *why not?* Why couldn't I be that guy, just for tonight?

The idea solidified so rapidly, I took a drink to buy time. But my pulse had kicked up, and I already knew what I'd do. This was my chance to be a man talking to a beautiful woman and nothing more. Not poor Aidan Wallace, single father and widower. Not pitiable Aidan, who hadn't found another woman in the seven years since his wife had tragically perished in a car accident. Not broken Aidan Wallace, who just needed a good woman to fix him.

No. Tonight I could simply be... a man.

In a move I'd never know who to thank for, I stood and moved to the empty stool between us. I set down my beer and leaned an arm on the bar. She watched me do all this, studying my movements.

And then I did it. The most un-Aidan-like thing I'd done in memory.

I dipped my head down, eyes on hers, and said, "I'll tell you mine if you tell me yours."

CHAPTER TWO

THEN

18 Months Ago

Maddie

A thrill spiraled through me, followed by a note of warning. Was he trying to get me to tell him who I was? Did he already know?

But in those brown eyes smoldering at me, now closer than ever, I didn't see anything but genuine interest. Not that eagle-eyed searching, waiting for me to offer something, become a connection, do something newsworthy, whatever. Normally, that's when my shields came down hard and I extricated myself as quickly as possible—unless that person had something to offer me, too.

I could easily shut this down right now. I could have Brandon charge my room and duck out. But the fluttering in my chest, the accelerated pulse, and the way this man was looking at me?

I didn't want to.

For the first time in I honestly couldn't tell when, I wanted to stay.

So I returned his gaze, my stomach somersaulting at his proximity and the steadiness in his whole demeanor, and I smiled. "I have no secrets."

His brow rose. "What you see is what you get, huh?"

Well, no. Not for this guy, anyway, since he apparently didn't see me like people usually did. And yes, in the circles I ran, many people recognized me rather quickly. They immediately knew me as Madeline Reynolds. Thirty-five-year-old multi-millionaire CEO of a flourishing tech company. Those were the basics, and then of course depending on the magazine or tabloid, you might stumble upon more specific information on my net worth, my real estate holdings, my wealthy parents, my famous friends, my soldier brother, or my terrible track record with love.

I would argue that seeing any of those things would be difficult and there was no chance this handsome man would guess any of that. But I didn't have to be her tonight. I didn't have to demur and wait for the inevitable "How did you do it?" or "Do you have any advice?" or "I should set you up with my son/grandson/brother/husband's friend."

Embracing that revelation and the rarity that was sitting down with someone who didn't know me in a place where I had a taste of anonymity after a week of disappointments, I relaxed somewhat. "Yes. And you?"

He sat up and extended a hand. "I'm Aidan."

I suppressed the smile that would give me away as

completely charmed, and a little relieved he hadn't given a last name. "Maddie."

Our hands clasped in a firm, warm grip, and we shook without breaking eye contact.

He grinned. "It's nice to meet you, Maddie."

"Nice to meet you, too, Aidan," I said, completely transfixed and also wondering what world I was living in, because I'd never had as strong of a reaction to someone in a matter of minutes as I was having to this guy. But I wasn't about to ruin the thrill of that sizzling first contact or risk ending the conversation, so I asked, "What do you do here in Silverton?"

His eyes narrowed for a second, but then his brow smoothed out. "I run a tree farm, mostly."

"A tree farm? Like Christmas trees?"

He swallowed a sip of his drink, the long column of his throat working in a way that was stupidly attractive. I didn't particularly have a thing for throats or Adam's apples or anything, but just now it struck me as supremely and unavoidably alluring.

"We do have Christmas trees. We also do a few other kinds, mostly working with the local landscape. It's an interesting place to grow trees, especially since it's been so dry. It presents challenges for us as growers, but also for—"

His head dropped and he shook it before looking up again. If I wasn't sitting a foot from him, I never would've believed this man could blush. *Seriously?* But he sported a bona fide blush on his high cheekbones, and it took all I had in me not to run a finger along the line of his beard, where his cheek reddened.

"Sorry. *Sorry.*"

What in the what? "Why are you sorry?"

He raised a brow. "Because I was droning on about my work?"

A slice of pain paired with a weird sense of kinship twisted through me. "You don't ever have to apologize to me for talking about your work. Plus, you weren't 'droning on,' you were explaining some of the challenges. You hadn't even been talking for two minutes."

He blinked, then again. "Uh, right. It's just..." He cleared his throat.

Ah. "Women don't normally like to hear about your work?"

He took a swig of his drink, then set the empty glass on the bar. "You could say that."

"I would say, 'I'm not like those women,' but I couldn't tell you. I'm a pretty typical woman. But I can tell you that I love talking business, and work is a huge if not unhealthily large part of my life, so I relate to the tendency to think about and talk about your job constantly."

"Well, then it's your turn. What's your job? Lay it on me."

Aidan

Instead of answering, she ducked her head and took a drink.

Even that pulled me in—that almost shy little dip of her head. She set her glass back onto the counter with a manicured hand—I'd bet twenty bucks she didn't work with her hands.

"I'm in tech."

I waited for more while she studied the contents of her glass—now just ice and a spent slice of lime.

"Tech. Like... computers? Smartphones? Or, uh... self-driving cars?"

She chuckled and bit her lip, grinning back at me. My heart flipped in my chest because that was a very lovely look, and I didn't mind it directed toward me *at all*.

But, was it pitying? I shifted in my seat, suddenly realizing maybe I was so wrong she thought I was pathetic for not knowing. "Am I way off?"

Brandon set a new beer down next to me and another drink in front of her, and though I hadn't ordered it, I reached for my glass gratefully and took a long pull.

"It's not anything exciting, actually. I just like your list of possible things. Were you one of those kids who always dreamed of traveling in a self-driving car?"

Her smile and the way she tilted her head to one side made any trace of embarrassment evaporate. *Crap, I need to work on being more confident.* Not an easy ask, but I'd gotten so used to misstepping on dates or saying something that suddenly shifted the conversation into this awkward, saccharine pity-fest, I didn't know how to just sit here and have a conversation with someone who wasn't about to bring up my dead wife.

"Of course. Who wasn't?"

She grinned again. "I wasn't. But that was only because my big brother told me my self-driving car would get tired of me bossing it around and crash on purpose."

A laugh shot out of me, and we chuckled together at her statement. "Wow. That's cold."

She nodded. "He is the best brother of all time, but he had his moments. I blame him for the fact that my company isn't the one leading the self-driving car movement."

"That's unfortunate. But hey, I'm sure you've got some other cool tech thing that'll blow his mind someday."

With a smile, she took a sip of her drink again.

"Can I ask about something you said?"

She nodded since she was still swallowing.

"You said work is a 'huge if not unhealthy' part of your life. Why do you say that?"

She winced. "Mostly because it's true."

"How so?"

"Well, for example, I came here for a week. This is the first time I've come to this bar. I have not walked around downtown. I didn't take the gondola up to the peak. I have done nothing on the list my friend gave me to do."

Dang, she looked so disappointed with herself. I had to console her. "But here you are, at the bar."

She gave me a chagrined smile. "Yes. And not a moment too soon."

"Oh?"

"I leave in a few hours."

Illogically, disappointment shot through me. I hadn't thought past *right now* since the beginning of the conversation, but the thought of her leaving tonight was bad news. "That's a shame."

Her eyes met mine, and she set her hand on my wrist. "Well, we've got some time before I go."

CHAPTER THREE

THEN

18 Months Ago

Maddie

We didn't stop talking until I got an alert on my phone. An obnoxious alarm that blared and startled both of us.

Regret hit immediately. I didn't want to leave. I hadn't talked to someone like this in years. Maybe ever. I hadn't clicked like this with a man in my entire life.

"Does that mean you have to go?" he asked, flagging Brandon, who nodded at him.

"Yes. But please, I'll get my bill. Really, I—"

"Maddie, come on. It's not like I'm expecting anything here, but we've had a nice time, right?"

I nodded, pleased to hear my name on his lips and his assertion about our evening. The last two hours had absolutely flown. "We have. I've loved talking to you. But why don't I buy?"

He squinted at me, a similar look he'd given only once or twice over the course of the night, but it made my stomach twist. He was so handsome, and that expression made him seem so serious and just... irresistible.

This was both a kind of test I'd grown used to giving and also just the right thing. I didn't know what he made in his tree farm business, but it couldn't be much. We hadn't talked in depth about what our day-to-day lives were like— maybe we both had things we were keeping close and didn't want the other person to know. I didn't like that thought— that I didn't really know him. It felt like I did. But I couldn't let him pay for my drinks and the appetizer I'd ordered an hour after sitting down.

"If it's important to you that you pay, then please do," he said with a small nod just as Brandon dropped the check.

I quickly signed to my room, scribbled my name as best I could *just in case*, and signed with a flourish and a giant tip, then flipped the booklet closed and slid it away.

"Done. Thank you."

"Thank *you*." He stood and held out a hand. "Can I walk you to the elevators?"

A cage of butterflies dumped over in my chest and had their way with my insides as I took his hand and stood from the seat. We'd touched on and off since I broke first contact with my hand on his wrist earlier, and every time sent a little thrill chasing through me. Now that he'd initiated, I didn't want to let go.

Regrettably, he released me before I could slide our palms close and link our fingers.

"Yes. Please." *And come upstairs.*

But no. I couldn't ask him that. I wouldn't. Maybe if I really was this woman—this person who was some anonymous businesswoman meeting a nice guy at a bar... but still no. My heart had never been casual about relationships or love, and it still wasn't. Despite the tempting slide toward cynicism lately, I wouldn't have been able to do something like that in any version of my story.

We walked slowly, arms brushing, out of the bar. At just before ten on a Sunday, the place was nearly empty. Brandon would be turning out the lights and closing up. I'd be boarding a plane back to New York. Aidan would find his way home.

The evening would be over.

My heartbeat accelerated steadily as we padded down the carpeted hallway. No one else was around, thankfully, so by the time we got within ten feet of the elevators, we were completely alone.

"Thank you for talking with me tonight. I—I can't tell you when I've enjoyed a conversation more."

His earnest tone urged me closer.

"Same for me. I don't do this often, but I'm so glad you said something to Brandon." I grinned, still relishing the memory of how we'd started talking hours ago.

"I am, too."

"Will you—"

"Can I—"

We both laughed, the first awkward simultaneous attempt to say more beating back the boldness I'd almost had when asking if I could get his number. I couldn't actually do this. I wasn't actually this woman.

My phone alarm blared again, and I fumbled to silence it, the invasive sound pushing my pulse to a race. "Sorry. I'm a little weird about staying on schedule."

He grabbed my hand then, slowing everything in me to a steady thud. The contact lit my nerves in a new way—a twinge of actual nervous energy, and more.

"Don't apologize. You're a woman who gets things done. I like that."

Of all the things he'd said to me tonight, this one made me blush. There was no sense in it considering I'd been complimented in that exact way most of my life, but the fact that this man didn't know who I was or what I'd done and yet still sensed that about me made the statement feel particularly rewarding.

More than that, it was this connection. Like in the last two hours, he'd listened and shared of himself.

Walking away felt so stupid. How often did a person encounter someone like this—someone handsome and charming and adorably shy at times while also being assertive enough to keep the conversation and connection rolling.

And because of that, I tugged at his hand and he inched closer, eyes spearing down into mine like he wasn't certain I meant for him to get closer. But I did.

"Thank you," I said, the strange crush of regret and desire driving me forward.

He blinked as if startled when my hand reached the warm skin of his neck. But as he'd demonstrated plenty so far tonight, he was a smart man, so even as he started to thank me in return with words, he leaned down and met my lips with his.

The light touch, just like our meeting, slid into something more in a matter of seconds. Soon, we were pressed close, our bodies pulling at each other as he devoured me, and I him.

The elevator's ding broke our connection, and I stumbled back. He steadied me by the shoulders, his face as much a ravenous reflection of pleasure and want as mine felt.

"That..."

"Yeah," I said, all breath and disbelief and longing. But instead of going back for more, I stepped away and caught the sliding doors before they shut. I leaned against the back, holding onto the railing with both hands, and watched as they slid shut again, Aidan's gorgeous face and one hand raised in farewell the image I'd keep in my mind until the last second.

And for a long, long time after.

The memory of this night, of that kiss, would have to hold me through the long winter coming, the longer nights of New York City winter. They'd have to keep me close through my brother's wedding and the utter bliss I'd see and love for them but be so far from for myself.

It might have to tide me over forever.

CHAPTER FOUR

NOW

Maddie

The air tasted sweeter after a near-death experience.

I laughed under my breath at that ridiculous statement but couldn't deny the truth of it. Before, I wouldn't have noticed the touch of vanilla on the breeze or how the trees planted at regular intervals along the street were starting to bud. I likely wouldn't have even been outside, first from the need to be inside working, and more recently, for fear of being seen, found, or harmed.

And now, I was finally walking down Elk Street in Silverton, the small town where I'd come to take my sabbatical. And by *sabbatical*, I really meant *the time I needed to run away from a full-on stalker*. I'd arrived what felt like weeks ago but had only been days, and I'd done almost nothing but cower in my sparsely furnished, unlandscaped new vacation home.

But that's kind of what you do when someone's stalking you. Or what I'd resorted to. After leaving me creepy signs that he'd "found me" in New York and LA, where I usually spent time, I'd fled here, but not without a plan. I'd hoped that would mean he'd lose track of me, lose interest. I know —a foolish line of thought in retrospect, and to their credit, none of the authorities who'd consulted on the case had suggested that would happen. It'd just been me living in la-la Land.

He didn't forget, and we didn't shake him, thanks to an epic security leak *yet again* in my personal team. I'd hired Wilder Saint's company, a local Silverton security outfit, and he'd done everything he could, but a guy could only do so much when my own people were hampering his every move. But now that the creep had been apprehended and caught, I felt like I was taking a full breath for the first time in months.

Honestly? Maybe years.

I'd been in survival mode the last few months especially, but it'd never been more clear than now. Outside, in the open, continually reminding myself it was okay to be here. If someone saw me, recognized me, that was just fine. It'd take time to ease off the constant vigilance, and even now, knowing I was technically safe in this small town, it took purposeful mental unwinding of the tension in my head and heart to enjoy the moment.

The air here in the mountains of Silverton was thinner than back in LA or New York, but it felt fresh—crisp, almost, even though it was nearly June. I'd been warned by friends who'd spent some of the summer in different mountain towns that I'd be more likely to burn and thus needed to pack sunscreen.

It struck me as the oddest thing. I hadn't put sunscreen on anything other than my face, neck, and hands as part of my skincare routine in years. I hadn't taken a break from my life long enough to go outside and risk getting burned by the sun.

Well, my last time here didn't count. Not really. Eighteen months ago, shortly after a brief visit with my brother and family at our house in Italy, I'd taken what I'd called a "holiday" in Silverton. My best friend, Juliet, had been raving about it for years as a beautiful, peaceful spot for an escape. We couldn't ever coordinate our schedules for long, and the closer I'd gotten to my brother's wedding, the more I'd needed a minute. I'd taken it... and had ended up spending all week holed up in my hotel room doing work. The idea that I'd let myself relax enough to spend time outside and need sunscreen?

And yet, the sun on my face felt amazing. I truly loved it. Of course, I occasionally felt it in New York, though coming out of winter, it didn't seem like it, especially with the hours I kept. After the stress of the stalker, then the terror of him actually finding me—

Fear and nausea hit me like a slap in the face, a hand going to my stomach as if in reflex. I exhaled slowly and swallowed, willing away the sick, hunted feeling I'd lived with for months.

He's not going to find you, because he's in jail. It's over. You're free.

You're free.

My heart slowed and I centered myself with a glance to the Silver Ridge Peak. It was truly beautiful, and even now, the very top still had a snowy peak, as it'd been unseasonably cool for late May. I savored the different view—not the rooftops of New York or glimpse of green space that was Central Park like my office and apartment offered. Not the parking lot from LA. Not the wisps of clouds streaming by my jet as I moved from one place to another.

I was back here in Silverton. In a place I'd *almost* missed entirely, and yet, in the last two hours of that first visit, I'd found a tether to a dream I hadn't realized could exist.

The night I met Aidan. The night I'd met the first and only man to captivate me completely and need nothing from me. The night I left a little piece of myself here, though I didn't realize it for months and months.

I'd crawled out of my hotel room at the Silver Ridge Resort because I'd promised Juliet I'd at least go get a drink at the gorgeous bar downstairs. I had gotten that drink, and before I knew what was happening, I was chatting with the handsome bearded local sitting next to me. He hadn't been hitting on me—he'd been making fun of the bartender's cheesy lines. It'd charmed me as much as it'd surprised me, much like the ensuing hours we spent perched on our barstools talking.

He hadn't recognized me. I'd only given him my first name, and the lack of recognition had been what'd drawn me in initially almost as much as his pure, masculine beauty. Because truly, the man was stunning and so positively un-New York or LA, it'd sent a wave of longing through me I'd *never* experienced.

So many things I'd never experienced hit me that night —thoughts, fleeting dreams, questions asked.

Though I hadn't told him everything about me, I'd been honest. More honest than I'd been with anyone other than my closest friend in a long, long time. Maybe even more honest because there was a certain kind of fleeting anonymity to our night. It'd been a fantasy, and so had the kiss at the end of the night before I'd returned to my life, not knowing how much those two hours would change me.

I'd learned to block the memory of this place, of the time with that man, from my mind during the workday. But as the intensity with the stalker had increased, my mind had run back here. And so, ultimately, had I.

For some strange reason, Silverton and Aidan had become a safe place for my mind. The combination of chemistry and connection, and honestly, probably the fact that I hadn't known about the stalker yet, made the memory a reprieve. But as time pushed me farther from the reality of him and made those fleeting hours more and more of a distant fantasy, I fell further into work and, eventually, into fearing my life would ever return to normal. By the time I'd rung in the New Year from a hotel room in LA this year, I'd known I needed to truly escape. Things escalated, my mind returned here, here, here, to *him*, and without much more than hope to guide me, I bought a house as an investment— an excuse—and made a plan.

And though this was where Korry Taggart had eventually found me, I couldn't be angry about it. I mean, I was one hundred percent angry about it since stalking wasn't something I was just going to chalk up to being moderately famous for a while, but more than anything else, I felt relief. It came in waves, almost like grief, and washed around me at intervals.

I shut my eyes and inhaled another deep, grateful breath and—

"Shoot, I'm sorry, ma'am. I'm—Maddie?"

The physical jolt of running into someone with my eyes closed in the middle of the sidewalk was nothing compared to hearing that voice again. Butterflies exploded in my belly, and anticipation lit every nerve.

His voice.

I'd missed it. I'd longed to hear it despite only having spent a few hours with him the one and only time we'd met. It made no sense how good it felt, before I'd even set eyes on him, but my pulse pounded deep and satisfied at just being near him again.

"Aidan?"

I didn't need to ask. Because when I opened my eyes, there he stood in the flesh, handsome as ever—more so. I hadn't imagined that, at least. His dark hair was still a bit longer on top and closer-cropped on the sides with more of that salt-and-pepper look above his ears. He seemed taller, maybe, but we'd been sitting most of the first time we'd spent time together.

Goodness, the man was better than I'd remembered. And I'd remembered him a lot.

His brown gaze surveyed me head to toe, then he spoke. "Are you in town again? Or, that's a stupid question, but are you here for a while?"

Adorable and charming and disarming. I hadn't imagined that either. Or how good his dark beard looked. Or how his eyes were both kind and demanding, like they'd found something they'd lost when they looked at me.

"I am, yes." I couldn't help the blazing smile on my face because this was absolutely one of the things I'd hoped for when I'd originally planned to come back to Silver Ridge Resort and the small town of Silverton. It had called to me, the memory, this feeling, and now that I was back, something shifted into place. Not a piece into a puzzle or a key into a lock, but the brush of just the right color on a canvas.

"That's good," he said, a small half-smile playing on his lips.

Lips I've kissed. Heat flashed through me at the memory I'd revisited a hundred times since our first meeting. Completely out of character for me, but after talking for two hours straight, we'd shared that mind-melting kiss.

I'd started it, but he'd met me without hesitation. And like our hours together, what began as easy and casual became something devouring and delicious. It'd been astounding, and we'd failed to say a proper goodbye because of it. We'd kissed like our stars were dying and then we went our separate ways.

Most of me had, anyway. I'd often felt like I'd left a piece of me here—just a sliver. And I'd been compelled to come back and retrieve it.

"Yes. I'm glad to be back." What an understatement.

Despite everything that'd happened, walking down this sunny little street, passing shops I couldn't wait to duck into for the first time, I felt what I always did when something good was beginning. A jolt of adrenaline hit my veins and disseminated a sparkling, ready feeling through me. I had the urge to clap my hands together and dive into a big project I knew I could conquer, but today, the conquering wasn't for work. It was for something entirely new.

"Would you—"

"Could I—"

We grinned at each other, and I gestured for him to go first.

"I was just going to ask if you'd want a tour. But maybe you'd already been exploring, so that would be redundant."

Even if I'd spent hours in every shop on the block, I wouldn't have turned him down. I'd waited for this moment for a year and a half, through the hardest months of my life.

Nothing would keep me from accepting an offer for time with him. "No, actually. This is the first chance I've gotten to wander around."

And though he hadn't known the whole truth last time, he'd known I'd spent my whole trip inside working and not enjoying the mountain town.

"It's a perfect day for it," he said, another small smile on his handsome face.

My stomach flipped for the first time in eighteen months. No, make that second, because it flipped when I saw him again just a few moments ago, alive and strong in front of me. "It is."

His brow furrowed right as ringing burst through the air, and he pulled his phone out of the back pocket of his worn-in jeans. "Shoot, sorry. I actually have to run. But can we get coffee sometime soon? We'll grab something to go and wander around, if you want."

"That sounds perfect. I'd love it." *So much. It's stupid how much.*

"Good. Do you want my number? Or we can just meet at Rise and Shine on Saturday, if that's easier?" He glanced down at his phone again. "Sorry. I have to take this. Would ten work?"

"Yes. I'll see you there. Looking forward to it." I waved as he moved away, and his gaze lingered even as his body retreated in the direction of wherever he needed to be. Finally, he turned completely and jogged ahead a bit, then slipped around a corner and went out of sight.

I smiled to myself, probably wider than I should've considering I was standing in the middle of the sidewalk. If the paparazzi could see me now, who knew what they'd write.

Madeline Reynolds has officially lost her mind.

Madeline Reynolds' close call with her stalker has sent her into a mental spiral.

Madeline Reynolds has a crush on local Silverton tree farmer, Aidan, and don't mind if we do, he looks great in those jeans.

I chuckled under my breath. Maybe not that last one. Hopefully, not any of them. The story of getting held at gunpoint by my stalker of over a year shouldn't get out. My assistant and security team had everything on lockdown—at least in theory. But I'd been around long enough to know that didn't always keep things from hitting the press. Thanks to the rise in public awareness of me these last few years after my book and some very public interviews, people wanted to know about me. Instead of being known just in the financial and tech world, I'd become something close to a household name.

Working Woman wasn't a name I would've chosen, but the treatise at its heart was my own. Sometimes, it still struck me as crazy, but after years in the business and tech worlds, I'd felt the need to say it "out loud" and so everyone could hear slash read it. What complex, life-changing thing might I have penned a book about?

It's okay for women to like work. That was the gist of it, honestly. The thesis that women who love to work are happiest working seemed so obvious to me, and yet how many times had people insisted on my taking breaks over the years? How many times had my ambition made others uncomfortable or seemed like an accusation or a suggestion of laziness when all it did was have me reaching for the things that made me most satisfied?

Somehow, I'd managed to do what the world expected of women in positions of power. I'd made it look easy. Or so

I'd been told. So often, that was the praise that followed my bio. "*How do you do it? How do you make it look so easy?*"

Well, spoiler alert, it wasn't easy. But even as often as I said that, people refused to accept it, as though my working hard and long hours and sacrificing my social life and any real relationships beyond my oldest friends and family was something that soured my success.

Maybe it did. I'd wondered if maybe that was true—and in my heart of hearts, I'd felt a resounding yes. Two years after I'd written the book, I found myself a Working Woman who was not, in fact, working. And I had to admit, I'd sacrificed so much, right up to and including my personal safety and nearly my sanity in the last year. I'd tried to hide it, to keep up this façade that any amount of fame or success required, but I wasn't sure if I could go back into the spotlight and pick up where I'd left off.

I'd have to, though. I'd taken the sabbatical to get my head on straight, and especially now that the stalker wasn't an issue, I would get back to managing things better. I would learn how to rest while I was here and soak up this time, and then I'd get back to work.

And in the meantime, I'd look forward to seeing the one man who'd held my attention and made me forget about pretending I had it all together to begin with.

CHAPTER FIVE

Aidan

My son squinted up at me. "Dad? Did you hear me?" I shook myself from the whirlwind blowing through my brain. And let's be honest, my body. I'd never been so surprised, excited, weirdly sad, relieved, and... just... *wow* as I had in the moment I'd registered Maddie's gorgeous face a few minutes ago.

"Sorry, bud. What were you saying?" I'd let him stay at All Booked Up to browse while I ran an errand, and on my way back, *bam*, there she was. Unfortunately, the bam had been literally, but I couldn't regret that too much because it'd let me touch her, just for a second, and know for certain she was real. I hadn't dreamed her up.

Like I had so many nights since our first meeting.

"I *said*, am I staying at Grandma and Grandpa's or Gig and Doodle's tonight?"

He'd started thumbing his way toward the marked page

in one of the books he'd gotten. We'd *just* bought the book, and he'd read a third of it. His reading speed never failed to startle me, but then Luca tended to be a constant source of amazement in these small ways.

"Grandma and Grandpa's tonight. You'll hang with Gig and Doodle soon, though," I reassured him.

For some insane reason, my aunt and uncle were referred to as Gig and Doodle. Something to do with my cousin's oldest child calling them that and them accepting the kid's birthright to name them or something... who knew. What it meant was that I was a grown man left referring to my relatives as Gig and Doodle like it was a perfectly normal thing to say out loud.

"Sounds good. And what are you doing?" he asked, head in his book, placing one foot in front of the other with his shoulder lightly brushing my arm. He'd mastered this positioning, as it let me steer him, if needed, but avoided holding my hand or hooking his arm in mine because *the horror*.

What would I be doing? Thinking about Maddie. This wasn't altogether different than any other night of the last eighteen months, but it would certainly take a different tone. Rather than a mildly hopeless sense of longing, I'd be looking forward to something real. We had plans to meet on Saturday. No, I didn't have her number, but I had an appointment with her. *A date.*

That was the first time I'd thought those words without a hefty amount of dread coating them in I didn't know how long. A date with Maddie sounded like a dream—yes, I'd had actual dreams about it.

Her voice. Her eyes when they'd dip down to my lips and flicker with desire. The way she looked at me like a man —just a normal, red-blooded man who was talking and flirting with her, and not damaged goods. *That kiss.* How I'd dreamed of it.

But would I tell my sweet summer child that? No. And in reality, I did have a few other things to do. "I'll be at the farm, which is part of the reason you're going with the grands, especially since you're feeling better. Right?"

I reached up and pressed my hand to his forehead. He jerked away like I'd scalded him with my touch, a dramatic scoffing sound issuing from his formerly strep-infected throat.

"No, I'm not still sick. I've felt fine all day. I can go."

I waited for him to register the words. For our discussion this morning when he rolled out of bed and looked so deeply pitiful when he said, "I just can't go back yet" to come to him. To recall me saying, "You haven't had a fever for more than twenty-four hours. You're going to get behind. I shouldn't have let you skip a grade and take advanced math if you were going to miss school for no reason."

I saw the moment when he did, and his eyes slid to mine. I blinked slowly and, had we been standing in the kitchen where most of these types of conversations tended to occur, I would've crossed my arms and leaned against the counter, perfectly at my leisure. But just now, since I had a number of other things to do before returning to work and finishing up all manner of things before sending Luca to my in-laws' house, I simply waited as we walked.

He snapped the book in his hands closed. "Fine. I'm sorry. I should've gone to school. But you were finally coming into town, and I've gotten every bit of work done that they've sent home."

I didn't bother stifling my sigh. Eleven-year-old going on twenty logic sometimes wore on me. I couldn't blame him for wanting a change in the routine, but school would be out inside the month. We were almost there. "The issue is never whether you can complete the work. You and I both know you're smart enough and you're diligent. But part of the issue with skipping a grade, especially as we're about to end seventh grade and you're going into eighth before you even turn twelve, is maturity. And showing up, doing the thing you say you'll do... that's part of the equation here."

Somehow, he managed to avoid rolling his eyes, though I would've bet a month's farm revenue he wanted to at my use of *equation*.

He exhaled loudly, the flair for the dramatic never far from reach. "I get it. I'm sorry."

My heart squeezed. Damn, he was such a good kid and I loved him. And because I loved him, it was my duty as his father to publicly humiliate him at times like this. So I reached around and hugged him to me, my arm smashing him against my side.

"Dad!" He pulled back, shoving me away lightly, but I caught his grin as he brushed off his sleeves.

"Just doing my job," I said.

He shook his head like he was so fed up, but he glanced my way with a look I knew well. It wasn't humiliation or frustration, which I certainly got often enough these days. This one was love, and knowing I could still harass him and get such a response reminded me yet again how thankful I was for him.

I eased the storm door shut, hoping Luca was passed out on the couch. When I saw Martha, who was sitting at the small kitchen table with her book, raise her finger to her lips to keep me quiet, I had my confirmation.

"He went down around nine," she said in the same way we used to when he was little.

"Good. Thank you."

She nodded. "You know we love it."

I did. "Still. I'm sorry it's so late."

She sighed. "I'm sorry there's so much for you to do."

Her eyes tracked past me as though she could see the farm office from her seat. She couldn't, but knowing the way Rich had worked all their lives, I wondered how often she'd sat right here like this and waited for him on late nights.

"Get those reports in?" Rich asked as he entered the kitchen.

"Yep. All set." I'd submitted our water usage for April, which was monitored and partially subsidized by a grant. Then I'd done a handful of other total drudgery tasks that had to be done, and in the last few years, they'd fallen to me. When Rich's office administrator moved away and the work got too much for him alone, I'd stepped in even more than I had been after Vivienne's death. And there'd been no going back.

"Good. 'Preciate ya, son. You're a natural with all that."

After decades with the man, I knew this was a genuine compliment from him. It also often felt a lot like when people say they're not good at something and then expect someone else to do it because they do it better. Like men saying women cook better, so they should do it. "*Honey, you do the dishes and laundry and cleaning so much better than I do, so it just makes sense for you to do it all.*"

I couldn't help hearing it that way from Rich, but I knew that wasn't right or in any way fair. I'd stepped in. I'd taken over. It was my actual job, and yes, I was good at it, even if I wasn't great at simultaneously managing the actual tree farm and workers and paperwork and parenting my son and trying not to lose my mind—*oh* and making some feeble stab at my own business. My sustainable landscaping firm had come dead last in recent years, and though I picked up a job here and there, it simply couldn't get as much of my time as I wanted it to *and* make sure things were covered at Templeton Tree Farm.

"Thanks, Rich. Mind if I grab him?" I nodded toward the living room where Luca would be sprawled.

He dropped his chin and Martha smiled. Minutes later, I had my almost-too-old-for-this son buckled into his seat behind me, his head lolling to the side, and we headed home. Tonight, I didn't have that same restless feeling I usually did after hours buried in farm business and ending with a typical farewell meant to keep me focused on just that and not my own work.

Tonight, I wasn't just driving cautiously toward home with my son and anticipating the lonely routine of pouring him into bed and waiting for sleep to take me in a few hours.

Tonight, I was counting down to Saturday. *Thirty-six hours and counting.*

CHAPTER SIX

Aidan

F riday morning, my truck rumbled over the gravel of the tree farm's rear exit, and I merged onto the road that would lead me right out of my league.

You gotta stop thinking that way.

The internal reprimand came in the voice of my cousin, John. Even though he spent ninety percent of his time heading up the brewing and legal end of Silver Ridge Brewing, he'd practiced law at his family's firm here in Silverton for just under a decade before that. The guy had a huge brain, a nice nest egg, and a family who stood behind him no matter what.

Granted, they stood behind me, too. My parents may have fled the wild winters of Silverton for the perpetual sunny thickness of Florida, but John's parents—Gig and Doodle—were stalwart supporters of mine. I couldn't complain.

But I could damn sure feel out of my league as I pulled into the neighborhood locally known as The Ridge. So far, no fewer than eight celebrities had made their homes in the fancy area, but it'd all started as born and bred Silverton local turned mega rock star Jamie Morris' pet project. Well, his and billionaire Julian Grenier's. Both were good men, and I'd done their landscaping—or, I'd fixed a few issues with Jamie's after Julian attempted to do the design himself. He had good ideas, but he was missing a few key pieces like sustainability and forgot about some basic properties of physics a time or two.

I'd worked in this area before, but it'd been a few years since I'd been able to take on much in the way of land-scaping work. I loved landscape architecture—I'd studied it in school and I was skilled at it. But when my in-laws needed me, I stepped in.

Like I always did.

And what was meant to be a few months of me bridging the gap for them became over three years. I hadn't done any landscape work in over eight months. Finally, a while back, I'd put my foot down in the most "Aidan way" possible, as John would say.

Speak of the devil, my phone rang and his doofy face popped up on the screen.

"Yeah?"

A cheery laugh rang out. "Well, hello to you, too, dear cousin."

"I'm almost to this job. What did you need?"

"The one at The Ridge?"

I grunted, nerves swirling in my gut.

"Whose house is it?"

"You know I sign all kinds of confidentiality paperwork

for these kind of things," I said, knowing that wouldn't stop him.

"So? Who am I going to tell? My latest spreadsheet on cost projections?"

As social a guy as John could be, he did have a real workaholic streak in him. We were both good and bad for each other in that way—we both needed to take breaks and get out. But at the same time, we both tended not to take breaks or go out. Even if we'd been brothers, we wouldn't have been so alike.

"In this case, I don't know the name. Anthony Shelton was the signing agent on behalf of some other entity. You know how these people layer their stuff for privacy."

"Oooh, so it's definitely a celebrity. One of Jamie's friends?" He gasped. An actual, full-out gasp. "Is it Jack McKean? I heard he likes Utah mountain towns."

"You *heard* that Jack McKean, A-list Oscar-winning celebrity, likes mountain towns? Where did you hear this?"

"Shut up."

John's dirty little secret just happened to be that he loved celebrity gossip. I was pretty sure his life was made when Jamie Morris moved back here and started bringing all his fancy, wealthy friends with him. So far, only he and Callaway Rice were really big names, but we had a resident reality star and at least one former soap star turned makeup person. The others were quieter or C-listers who'd invested well. Could I tell them apart from Joe Shmoe on the street? Heck no.

"Listen, I'm here. Gotta go."

"You've got this, man. You're brilliant and awesome and I'm proud of you. Go kill it."

He clicked off, leaving me with those kind words and a reminder of what a gift he was.

He drove me nuts half the time, like the little brother I never had, but he was a truly good man.

I parked in front of the lot after the security guy out here waved me off as if he'd been expecting me. The house was situated well away from the main road, and thankfully, Jamie and Julian's developer had done whatever she could to work with the existing landscape. On the front end of the neighborhood, this meant very few mature trees, as that had been a small pasture before they'd bought it out, but farther in, like this lot, were towering pines, a little copse of aspens, and a ridiculous amount of scrub oak.

Guaranteed, they'd want the scrub oak gone. I'd set up three versions of my design, each with differing levels of maintaining the existing trees. Of course, I hadn't seen much of the back yard in person, and they'd hired me on reputation alone, which was always terrifying. Apparently, Julian Grenier had strongly recommended me and that was that.

Nice, except now I had to wow them, and I was long past rusty.

Channeling John's words, I straightened my shoulders and slung my bag over one of them, hoping the strap wouldn't irrevocably wrinkle my button-down. I much preferred the part where I got to oversee and implement the landscaping—one thing that made my company both unique and impossible to grow. But for now? I'd keep my crap together and get this done and hope they'd like my ideas.

I rang the bell a few minutes early on the oversized wood-carved door, then stepped back. Even though it was likely reinforced with steel inside for security, I admired the natural look of the materials. The house, like so many in this area, was truly gargantuan. Just... more house than anyone actually needed. But I supposed once your net worth climbed into eight and nine figures, the idea of *need* became moot.

"Ah, Mr. Wallace. Right this way. I'm Anthony, Ms. Reynolds' assistant. I'll have you step inside there and she'll be with you—" He stepped around two large, sleek-looking bags in the hallway. "After finishing a call. Forgive the clutter, please."

"This the meeting you mentioned?" A tall man with a blond swath of hair combed back from his face extended a hand even as he asked Anthony the question, then switched his focus to me. "Chadwick Brantley, but you can call me Chadwick."

Huh. I took his hand and shook, but my eyes slid to Anthony. His were narrowed at Brantley and his whole welcoming, bubbly, friendly energy had closed up shop and moved to the woods.

"Aidan Wallace."

"Right. So, let's see if I can help you while she's finishing up." He paced a few feet farther inside and gestured to a dining room with upholstered chairs and a giant polished wood table, then sat.

Anthony's eyes flared. "No, that's not necessary. Ms. Reynolds will be right in."

Just then a voice in the far room said, "I don't appreciate it, but I'll speak with you about it later, Mother." Followed by an exasperated groan I didn't imagine we were meant to hear.

John will get a kick out of this. At least I'll have a good story to tell him.

I took the seat across from Chadwick after Anthony nodded as though to say *ignore that idiot but yes, have a seat,* and flipped open my notebook. I hesitated, wondering if I should wait for Ms. Reynolds, who was apparently the person I was supposed to meet with. The assistant, Anthony, had to be Anthony Shelton, the signing agent and person I'd been communicating with, so if he'd allowed this Chadwick the go-ahead to join the meeting, even reluctantly, I supposed we should move ahead with things.

I passed Anthony a few pages that would show a proposal or two but also tapped into my tablet to bring up the digital rendering. Seeing things in color always helped, especially if the person wasn't versed in looking at landscape plans in black and white.

This project had already fallen behind by quite a few days after our meeting last week had been canceled, and I was eager not to lose the window of opportunity originally laid out in the contract.

"You can get started. She'll join us in a few," Chadwick said, an irritated edge to his voice.

No one was stopping me, and did I really want to stay here any longer? Deciding to just go for it and get this weird meeting over with, I dove in. "You'll see here we'll keep the existing trees and shrubs. We'll work to bring in local rock and as much found material as possible—I've got a decent supply for paths and other—"

"Is this grass?"

He pointed to a stretch of space that fell at the front of the lot.

"It can be, if that's what the client wants. I like to suggest alternatives because most grasses people have in mind tend to be very demanding in terms of water consumption and in a drought-prone environment—"

"Trust me, paying the water bill won't be an issue here. Now, let's talk about—"

Footsteps sounded in the hall. "I'm so sorry to keep you, Mr. Wallace. I—"

A feminine voice interrupted Chadwick, and my stomach swooped low.

I stood on reflex, my gut tightening, knowing.

The woman had frozen, not unlike I had once I confirmed with my eyes what I knew by sound, standing here in her multi-million-dollar home. *Her.*

"Aidan?"

CHAPTER SEVEN

Maddie

"You two know each other? How?" Chad asked, goggling his giant, thick skull back and forth like my knowing Aidan was the most unbelievable thing he'd ever heard.

Aidan didn't speak. He was still looking at me with an unreadable expression, though I did detect some surprise. Not shock, exactly, but definitely surprise.

Welcome to the club.

Seeing him again so soon, so unexpectedly, sent my heart racing. It took every bit of composure to hide the way my hands shook, and I said a prayer of thanks that I'd long mastered the vocal quaver that used to hit when I got nervous.

I kept my eyes locked with Aidan's even though it was well past time I got rid of Chad. "We do. We met last time I was in Silverton."

My heart kicked as I said it—the only sign our meeting had been monumental and what I'd often thought of as life-changing. Simple and straightforward, our *meeting* had traveled with me across the country, had slept next to me in the dark as I worried over what I couldn't control, had held my hand when I didn't know what to do. Of course, he'd never know it, and yet...

Chad's head swiveled so dramatically, it pulled my focus.

"You've been here before? When? I don't remember that." He glanced at Anthony, like my beloved assistant would tell this man *anything*.

"It's been a while," I said, uninterested in him knowing details. Why was he still here? He hadn't been invited, and my tolerance for his unwelcomed visit had run out. His barging into my life like he owned it? Hell no. He didn't get anything from me. Of me. *Anything.* Especially when there was a man here who I'd often thought about giving everything.

"Eighteen months."

Those words came from Aidan, who still stood stock-still and transfixed, until Chad slapped him on the back aggressively hard.

"Sample some local flavor, huh? Good for you, Mads. But I can't blame you for leveling up." Chad winked at me and gave Anthony an *Am I right?* grin.

My stomach rolled and nausea hit. *Local flavor? Leveling up?* As in *he* was the level-up in question? Who in the? What? Who would even say something like that? It was all I could do not to give Anthony the look that said, *Get Brad to toss him to the curb.* If holding Aidan's attention and wading through this awkwardness hadn't taken first priority, I would've. And in a few minutes, I absolutely would invite Chad to meet with the street.

Anthony attempted to save me, likely reading my face, when he said, "Ms. Reynolds, I believe Mr. Wallace was explaining some of his plans, if you wanted to join the meeting. I'm sure Mr. Brantley has other things to... attend to."

If my heart hadn't been pumping with so much adrenaline, I might've laughed at the disgust lacing Anthony's words. He made no secret of his opinion of Chad, and I couldn't deny I agreed with him.

"It's no trouble for me to stay. I'll help you decide." Chad pulled out the chair next to him as Anthony gestured to the one at the head of the table.

My skin crawled at his proximity, and how little I wanted *him* near me, and I happily took the seat at the end where Anthony stood. But my brain had locked up at Aidan's presence. Everything was happening so quickly. I'd acquiesced and let Chad come to the house rather than having him cause a scene with security at the gate, but then my frustration escalated with the call to my mother and the utter lack of acknowledgment that she'd overstepped by a mile in sending Chad here, and now this. *This man.*

"So Wallace here was saying grass will drive up your water bill, and I was just letting him know, if he couldn't tell by the house itself, that paying that little tab won't be an issue." He leaned onto the table with one arm and ducked his head like he was whispering to Aidan. "You're in one of the wealthiest women in America's homes, bud. Not sure if you missed that last time you were with Mads, but girl can pay her own bills."

Inhaling and counting to ten as I did, calm descended. It required persistent summoning with jerkface Chad around, and his subtle-as-an-asteroid approach to telling

Aidan about my financial circumstances made the challenge burn brighter.

Not that it wouldn't have been obvious by the house, the meeting, the entire circumstance, but something about *Chad* being the one to blow the top off the reality that I was... me... lit a simmer of fury on the back burner of my mind.

Before I could speak and put an end to Chad's presence altogether, Aidan spoke up and all my mental energy returned to him

"I was less concerned with the water bill and more with the natural resource itself during an unprecedented drought." Aidan's voice held notes of calm and confidence and betrayed no irritation, which was, frankly, remarkable.

And also, for some stupid reason, insanely appealing. A man who could hold his own against the Chads of the world? Win in my book.

"Sure, sure, sure, but when you're living in a place like this, do you really need to think like that?" Chad directed this question and a satisfied little smirk in my direction.

"I would hope so. I assume that's part of the reason Ms. Reynolds hired me."

Aidan's staunch position only made me like him more. Julian had raved about his company—little did I know it was *my* Aidan's company. And yet seeing him unbendable, unwilling to cow to a man so blasé, made me want to applaud.

It shouldn't have sent heat and longing through me, but it did. Every little thing about him did, even in the midst of knowing this was just shy of a train wreck.

Anthony spoke up from where he stood a few feet from the table. "Mr. Wallace has a reputation for designing sustainable, responsibly-sourced gardens and outdoor spaces. He comes highly recommended by many, including Julian Grenier."

Pride filled me at hearing just a few of Aidan's accolades. It hit differently to know it was Aidan, of course, even though I'd been eager to meet the man behind the recommendation long before this moment.

Chad slow-blinked. "Good for you."

Ah, there it was. One of many, *many* reasons I couldn't wait to get rid of this person. The only thing that could wow a man like Chad? More zeroes on the end of a paycheck. Julian Grenier had us all beat, and God bless him for it.

"Thank you." Aidan's eyes flicked to mine. "Would you like to reschedule?"

Warmth and goodness bloomed in my chest at his direct question.

"Please." I managed not to continue and say, *let's leave here together and be alone.* That wouldn't be professional, and based on how things had proceeded, we were sticking with the formal meeting set up. We'd have much to discuss, and I only prayed he'd still give me the chance to do it tomorrow at coffee.

Nodding just slightly, he began gathering his things. Chad's continued existence paired with the general frisson lighting up my entire body because *it's Aidan!* meant I hadn't managed any of this well, not at all like I normally would've, and I couldn't stand it.

"Thank you so much for coming, Aidan. I appreciate your time, and I apologize for this." I couldn't pretend treating him like a business associate came naturally. All I wanted to do was hug him. Be close enough to him to assure myself we were, in fact, standing next to each other in real life and not during some midnight conjuring my exhausted, lonely mind had dreamed up.

Or, you know, I'd also like to kiss him. Like I'd never wanted to kiss anyone else in my entire life. And that made little sense in the real world considering we were acquaintances at best and strangers at worst.

That thought made my shoulders tighten with tension and regret. We weren't anything right now. But that magnetic pull toward him hadn't gone anywhere since yesterday or the last eighteen months.

"Of course. No problem."

He left the portfolio on the table as he shoved a few things back into his bag. He had this purposeful, slow methodology about him, but something about the way he hadn't looked me in the eye for the last half hour made it feel like he was in a rush.

"I think you sent them digitally as well. Is that correct?" Anthony asked.

"Yes. You should have everything. I'll look forward to your call."

Still no eye contact.

I stood and pushed past Chad as he tried to slide his seat back, rushing toward Aidan, who'd already made it to the door. Unable to stand the thought of him leaving without another word, without some kind of conversation to address what'd happened, how he'd found out who I was, *anything*, I reached for him. "Aidan, I'm—"

"Baby, let the man go! It's a Friday afternoon and he's been working all week!" Chad threw his hands out wide like everyone in his invisible audience would understand his perspective.

"Have a good afternoon," Aidan said, and left, the door shutting firmly behind him.

"I am not, nor have I ever been, your baby." My body hummed with so many conflicting feelings—regret to see

Aidan go, irritation that Chad had said anything at all or was even here. But the baby, and the presumption, and the fact that he'd shown his face at all, meant my fuse was far shorter than it should've been. Maybe because I'd missed a chance to talk to Aidan, to really reconnect and help us past this crazy realization.

Anthony appeared out of nowhere, as he often did, and shut the door firmly behind him while giving me a meaningful look.

I revisited my well of *don't make a scene or you'll end up on CNN* and smiled at Chad. Then I threw that out the window because I should've said all this minutes ago, but my brain had been wading through the sludgy matter created by an upsetting phone call with my very misguided mother after Chad's surprise arrival right as my meeting was about to begin, and *Aidan*. "You can leave, Chad. I didn't invite you and you are not welcome here. Please get your bags—they're waiting in the hallway, so you won't have any trouble finding them on the way out."

His lower lip jutted out. "Really? You won't even have dinner with me?"

Okay. No. The lip. The pout. None of it was going to work and I was just... done. "No. Since I had no idea you were coming and I didn't invite you, I won't. Add to that I don't want you here, and I see no reason on earth why I'd bother having a meal with you."

He reared back. "Didn't *invite* me? Your own mother invited me. She knows what I have to offer you."

Goodness gracious, the man had fire in his eyes like this was truly a personal insult and he hadn't weaseled his way into my house by showing up unannounced and playing on my desire to go without a public scene. It was only right that I turned him away myself rather than having security do it.

My ghosting him for weeks clearly hadn't penetrated his miraculously thick skull.

And though I knew it was a mistake to laugh at the man when his ego was the issue, I couldn't resist the short chuckle. "What could you possibly have to offer *me*, Chad? You don't like me. You like my portfolio. And I certainly don't like you. Go, be free to find your dream woman. May she be even wealthier than me."

He scoffed and looked genuinely horrified, but I just waved him off, totally done with him. "You can grab your things. I'll have a car waiting for you whenever you're ready."

He shook his head, clearly disgusted with me. *Oh darn.*

I turned to find Anthony, but Chad's voice cut through the air. "You know, you wouldn't be such a lonely, work-obsessed shrew if you'd admit you need someone in your life."

I straightened my spine and stopped just shy of flipping my ponytail over my shoulder because *good riddance to you, sir.*

If his parting shot had a tiny ring of truth in it, so what? I already knew that. Chadwick Brantley wasn't telling me anything I didn't already know.

And now I had to figure out how to get ahold of Aidan and get him to talk to me, because the unsettled, anxious feeling in my chest wasn't about dumping Chad to the curb. It had everything to do with realizing Aidan truly had no idea who I was and suspecting that now that he did, he wouldn't want anything to do with me.

CHAPTER EIGHT

Aidan

John slid into the seat next to me. "Madeline *Reynolds?*"

I glared at him.

"Seriously though? *Madeline Reynolds!?*"

"Can you not broadcast that? And why would I know who she is or what she looks like?" I caged my beer with my forearms and stared at the light layer of foam.

"Oh, I don't know. She's only been on *Forbes, Time,* and every morning TV show promoting her book in the last few years." Then he nodded. "Thanks, man."

Kieran slid a beer across the bar to him. John brewed beer for a living—his stated dream job—but he always got a Guinness here, the weirdo.

"Have you ever known me to watch a morning television program?"

John scoffed. "Do you mean to sound like you're ninety, or is this a joke?"

I grumbled and took a drink.

He snickered. "Television program."

We sat, sipping beers, the buzz of Craic's happy hour around us. I'd have to get Luca soon, but I needed a minute after the afternoon I'd had.

"So... how'd she look?"

I shot him a glare.

He held up a hand. "I'm not being weird, I'm just asking. You said you saw her yesterday and she looked good but kind of different, right? Like, different hair and stuff? So did she look different again? Like, does standing inside a multi-millionaire's house automatically give you rose-colored glasses or something?"

"You are an idiot."

He chuckled. "But seriously. Was *she* upset? Or was it all on your end?"

I hadn't even told him the worst part. "She was calm. Maybe slightly ruffled when she first saw me, but I'm not sure I can even assess that because I was freaking out."

John grinned. "Now that's not something I'd ever expect to hear you say."

I glared at him again.

He beamed back at me like he'd never wanted anything more than to irritate me. Moments like this drove home our closeness more than anything else. They also made me pity his actual older brother.

He nudged me with his elbow until I gave him my full attention.

"You liked her a lot."

"Based on two hours of interaction." But enough that I'd ended up telling him about it a few weeks later when I couldn't think about anything else. I hadn't decided if it was better or worse that I wasn't alone in knowing she'd never looked me up. I'd had nothing on her. You couldn't exactly search "Maddie in Tech in New York" and find someone. But maybe "Aidan Tree Farm Silverton" would've gotten her somewhere.

"Yeah, but you were practically glowing when you texted me that you saw her and made plans."

"I was *glowing*? How did you detect that through a text message?"

"Come on, man. When you're happy, it's the best thing in the world. All of Silver Ridge Peak lights up when Aidan Wallace smiles."

I cringed. "What is happening right now?"

"Shut up." He shoved me full out, and beer sloshed over the side of my pint glass. "I'm just saying, you being happy is good. And I know you just got thrown a crazy-huge curveball about who this mystery Maddie is, but if she's into you, why the heck do you care?"

"I really need to elaborate this for you?"

He pursed his lips and nodded. "Yep. Because I'm betting all your reasons are BS."

I leaned on the bar with an elbow and ticked off the most obvious points with my opposite fingers. "One, she's in a different socioeconomic universe than me. Second, I am damaged goods with a child she knows nothing about. Three, I'm contracted to work for her, so she's off-limits anyway. Four—"

"Wait, stop. First. You own your business and she's a grown up. If she wants to date her landscape architect slash dream guy she kissed last time she visited Silverton, she can! And don't let me hear you say you're damaged goods again because I will call Alan and we will beat you up."

I blinked, unconcerned with this threat. His older brother Alan was basically the sweetest person on the planet with the possible exception of their father. That said, he became genuinely upset if he heard me say anything negative about myself, and John did, too. Almost like I was insulting *them* instead of saying something true about myself.

"I see your blinky face and raise you this: you're not broken. You might've been through hell, but you healed. Different than before, yes. I kind of think your night out with Maddie was the first sign of that healing, and since then, you've been on... how many dates?"

"A thousand?"

He choked on the swig of beer he'd just taken and coughed before shaking his head at me. "In the last eighteen months, you've gone on a thousand dates? So what, like two to three a day?"

"Feels like it," I grumbled.

"This is my point, though—you've been out there. And I think you realized that night that you might actually connect with someone new. And now she's back. And yes, you have some baggage, but what person in their late thirties doesn't?"

Someone new. Internally, I cringed at the phrasing. I hated the reference to the connection I'd lost. Seven years and small moments like this still hurt like hell when facing the gaping hole my life had become without my best friend. And she was—Viv was my absolute best friend and partner.

I hadn't met anyone who came even remotely close to her or how we interacted. Not that I wanted to find that. I understood both logically and emotionally that there was no replacing what I'd lost. But to find *someone new*...

And Maddie? She was definitely different.

I shrugged. "It's irrelevant."

"Good grief, you're crusty tonight. I'm here making a great case, and you—"

"Her boyfriend, *Chadwick*, was the one who started off the meeting. The guy called her 'baby.'"

He made a disgusted sound. "Ew. No. He called her a pet name during a meeting?"

My face must've confirmed it for him.

He sighed. "Well. Forget everything I said. If she's to the point of putting up with someone like that, then you're out of luck." He clinked his glass with mine. "Drink up, cuz. Here's to finding someone who isn't dating a guy who sounds like he probably uses a little too much hair gel."

I chuckled but obeyed his order and took a long pull of my beer. My phone buzzed and I took it from my pocket, fully prepared to see a message from Luca asking when I'd be picking him up.

Instead, I had a message from an unknown number.

"Aidan, this is Maddie. Can we still get coffee tomorrow?"

I sighed, and John zeroed in and read the screen. "Innnnteresting."

I tapped out my response. *"How would Chadwick feel about that?"*

The responding dots popped up immediately, and I'd be a liar if I said my pulse didn't tick up at the same time. This would tell me a lot about her.

John leaned back like he was impressed. "Ooh, Aidan with the sass."

"I'm not worried about how he feels. He invited himself here and I invited him to leave. He isn't a friend or anything else in my life. I'd advise avoiding Silver Ridge Resort tonight since he's definitely not staying here."

"Let me see! I can't read all that upside down." John pulled at my arm and read, then gave me the biggest cheeseball grin ever. "Oh heck yes."

I laughed, but no denying I felt the same. The answer was definitive and clear. Granted, he *had* called her baby, but she hadn't reciprocated—in truth, I'd shut the door right after so maybe she'd smacked him upside the head. He needed it. In fact, I'd noticed she hadn't touched him the entire meeting and had seemed annoyed every time he'd tried to speak for her. Maybe he really had invited himself.

"Do I really want to do this?" I asked John, but more truthfully, myself.

"Yes. You do. Because even if the story is she just broke up with him and he's a d-bag and she's not ready for a relationship, you won't spend your time wandering around thinking about what might've been. And if not?"

I tapped out my response, agreeing to meet the next morning, and braced myself for whatever was coming because the look on his face told me I'd need it. "If not?"

He smirked. "Then you'll land yourself a millionaire sugar mama."

CHAPTER NINE

Maddie

S adie, the owner of Rise and Shine, greeted me when I entered the adorable little coffee shop and bakery. "Welcome back."

"Thank you. Is it okay if I wait for a few? I'm meeting someone."

Though there were a handful of other people, Aidan hadn't arrived yet. He didn't strike me as the kind of man to just not show up, but the nerves twisting through me wouldn't stop hounding me. He'd been thrown at the meeting yesterday, and based on his response to my messages last night, he'd clearly thought Chad was my boyfriend. *Gross.* I'd set that straight, and I hoped he could take the reality of my life in stride. *Please, please take it in stride.*

Sadie smiled. "Of course. No rush."

I eyed the two open tables, unsure which would be

better. The one I wanted was tucked right next to the window and offered a view of the towering mountain peaks, the resort up on the bench, and Main Street. The other would be less likely to draw attention.

Then I remembered I didn't have to be secretive. I didn't have to hide anymore, and I didn't have to be afraid. Sure, it was possible someone else could choose to stalk me, but the odds were low. My book had hit all the best-seller lists thanks to the tireless work of my own publicity team and the publisher's and the million and one interviews I'd done around the country, but it'd been almost eight months since the last one of those. And so far, if anyone noticed me in town, they didn't care who I was. It probably helped there were much more famous people milling around both as residents and visitors. In any case, the rigid set to my shoulders softened with the reminder.

I slipped into the chair facing the north end of Main Street, and my stomach flipped at the sight of the man checking his watch as he approached the coffee shop. He frowned down at his wrist, no easy charm or smile to be found. Granted, he hadn't really been that way with me the first time we'd met either. It'd been more intense—sweet heat and the focus of his attention like a spotlight on me but in the unfamiliar way I didn't mind since it was *his*.

He didn't notice me as he turned into the entrance and pulled the door. As the bell rang, I internally debated whether to stand. Waste of time, so I squashed the trepidatious feeling and simply met his gaze when his found me a moment after entering the bright shop.

I stood and stepped forward, eager to simply be near him again. The self-control I'd normally have, that part of me that stood tall and strong and implacable, had gone

MIA. I inched forward, drawn toward him like he'd beckoned me.

He didn't say anything, and that threw me. I hadn't deluded myself into thinking he'd be happy to have discovered who I was in the real world, but I certainly hadn't expected the standoffish set of his shoulders. He'd agreed to come and had seemed to believe that Chad was nothing to me, but maybe this was just humoring me for some reason. Granted, he'd never struck me as someone who'd do that in the past, but I didn't really know him.

Just like he didn't really know me.

And yet he did. In some ways, it felt like my conversation with him was the first one I'd ever had with a man where I'd been myself. With almost every other man I'd dated, I'd been Madeline Reynolds, CEO. They'd wanted to date that side of me, but not the daughter and little sister. Not the reader and podcast nerd. Not the woman who could eat pasta every night of the week for the rest of her life and never tire of it.

It'd been freeing, but suddenly, his lack of smile or hug or *anything*, so different from our first meeting two days ago, sent ice into my veins. I felt stripped down and vulnerable in a way I didn't ever feel as Madeline. And there, apparently, was one more twist in this dream. That openness I'd loved had also left me without anything between me and this potential disaster of an encounter.

"Ready to order?" Sadie said from behind the counter.

"Yes. I'll have a half-caf flat-white with skim, if you have it. Aidan?"

His eyes flicked down to me. "Coffee. Black."

"Is that together or—"

"Together."

"Separate."

My eyes jumped to him, awkwardness shooting through me. "Oh, right. Sorry. Separate."

I wasn't a blusher, but there it came, a creeping heat at my neck and climbing to my cheeks. Apparently, my body didn't follow my orders when it came to Aidan Wallace.

Thankfully, Sadie breezed over the weirdness and nodded. "I'm heading into the back, but Garrett will be right out with your drinks."

I nodded, and Aidan said, "Thanks, Sadie," so he did know her. Of course he did. He probably knew everyone in the shop right now, though no one else had greeted him.

"Do you mind sitting there by the window?" I asked him, realizing he might not want to be seen with me so publicly—at least not on the street. Again, in the other version of my life, I made the decisions, no question. People looked to me and expected me to dictate these details by my body language or patterns. With Aidan, I had no established patterns, no way to read what *he* wanted, and worse, I cared very much about that.

"That's fine."

I realized the mistake of this tiny window-side table the minute he took his seat across from me. Our knees knocked, and even when we both sat up completely straight, he had to inch his chair away to avoid our legs threading together under the table. I'd remembered he was tall, but had he grown taller since we saw each other even yesterday?

I liked that. I liked it so freaking much. I liked pretty much everything about him, and I had to get a handle on that before I started blushing again. Why was my pulse still fluttering at my neck, my wrist? Why did everything sound muted except for the scrape of the chair as I inched it forward?

I'd mastered nervous energy a thousand times, and as

much as I liked Aidan Wallace and had admitted that to myself, I wasn't about to let this go south because of those nerves. I launched in. "So, how are you?"

He looked back at me for a beat, those dark eyes giving me nothing. "Fine. You?"

"I'm well. But I do want to explain a few things. I'm assuming that since you're here, you'd be interested in that?"

He settled into his seat. "I'm here because you made clear you aren't dating Chadwick whatever his name is. If my interpretation of that text was wrong, tell me upfront and we'll be done here. If I'm right, then yes. I wouldn't mind... understanding."

A tall redhead set down a saucer with my flat white complete with a little mountain design in the tight foam on top and Aidan's black coffee, both in bright robin's egg blue cups. *Adorable.*

"Here we go, folks. Let me know if you need anything else." The man grinned and we happily reached for our drinks.

We both thanked the guy with a nod, and I held up my cup. "To second first impressions."

He let out what sounded like a reluctant, clipped laugh. "To second first impressions."

We both sipped, and I ran through the many points I wanted to make to ensure he didn't think I was... anything other than who I was.

"Okay, so first. I am not with Chadwick. We went out twice about four months ago at my mother's request, and it was very clear we didn't work. He heard about something that happened recently and just showed up." I didn't want to get into the fact that my mother had instigated that whole mess.

Aidan didn't respond verbally, but his steady eye contact and quiet patience urged me on, so I kept going. "I was on the phone with a family member when you arrived. I'm very sorry about that. Chad had just walked in and took over while I was in the other room, and I hope I don't need to tell you that he did so without my permission and that anything he suggested was not speaking for me or what I want."

"Good to know."

Still that calm, tight beat to his tone. Okay, fine—I could do this.

"I also want to make clear that I see no issue with us interacting outside of the landscaping contract unless you do." My heart beat wildly in my chest. That was me putting it out there. That was me just... going for it.

He sipped his coffee, still giving me nothing. Dang, this man should consider negotiating as a side gig because he could hold his expression so still and sober, I couldn't tell whether he agreed or wanted to flip tables in protest.

Why did it feel like the onus was on me?

More, why did that *not* bother me?

"And I suppose we should address the fact that I didn't tell you who I am," I said, but my shoulders deflated a touch.

He immediately sensed that, and as though to prove I hadn't imagined everything about him, he spoke. "No apology necessary. I didn't give you my last name. I didn't tell you everything about myself either."

That cut. As much as I didn't want to feel it, his words sliced along the tips of my fingers, papercuts that'd take a while to heal even though the action of creating them seemed like a throw away.

I didn't tell you everything about myself either. Why

would that hurt me? How did I care about this man so much?

My best friend would likely say it was because I'd been dreaming of him for so long, he'd become this larger than life, complete person based on a mountaintop evening together.

Still, it hurt. But I didn't want to let him know that, of course. Times like these sent me right back to when my dad stumbled upon me crying over a guy who'd been a total jerk in high school. I'd sat with our cat, who had the habit of stretching out on his back, paws in opposite directions, and welcoming belly rubs. Unlike other cats, he never hit that overstimulated attack mode. He just lay there, completely vulnerable, letting me nuzzle his head and stroke the softness. My father had studied us both for what might've been the longest he'd given me attention outside of a meal. He rarely dispensed anything but mildly approving nods to us kids, but that night, he'd said, *"Never show them your underbelly."*

I'd carried that with me a long time. Sometimes, I wondered if maybe I'd curled up too far in the opposite direction. But in this moment, I saw the wisdom again, and I pressed forward. "No, you didn't."

We drank in the quiet moment. I wouldn't have called it awkward, but I didn't want to stay in this taut, unfeeling space. I wanted that warmth between us, but maybe it'd been too long. Or maybe he was with someone?

Or maybe, knowing who I was in reality changed everything for him.

"So... you don't do the tree farm anymore?" I tried, hoping to break through.

"That's still my primary focus. I've worked to add in

more landscape work, but—" He glanced out the window sharply. "But I'm obligated to my in-laws."

Stones dropped down into the pit of my stomach, piling up so quickly, my chest felt heavy, my torso rooted to the spot even though the restless energy in me wanted to send me springing from my seat. "In-laws?"

He heaved a large sigh. "In the same way you didn't mention your last name and everything that entails, I didn't share everything about me. I—I'm sorry."

I spoke slowly, ignoring the tumbling, tossing sensation, and channeling calm like the boss I was. "You're married?"

He blinked slowly, so slowly I would've thought he was embarrassed or ashamed of himself, except when his gaze hit mine upon opening his eyes, an ache twisted its way through me. That wasn't shame or guilt.

That was something else entirely.

"I was married. Now I'm not."

My heart rate picked up. I knew what this was, and I didn't understand why it made me feel a little sick to my stomach, but I had to be certain. I'd been manipulated enough to know you had to hear the words, whatever they were, however horrible they'd be, or in the end it was only yourself you could blame when things went wrong or the truth came out and you weren't expecting it.

"You're divorced?"

Only a slight sideways jerk of his head, and he said it. "Not divorced. Widowed."

CHAPTER TEN

Aidan

Everything was going wrong. Every damn thing, and there wasn't a way to get this back on track. I saw the pity. The shade of her cheeks blanch. Her throat work to swallow, her brilliant mind scrambling for something to say.

"I'm sorry."

I shook my head, internally raging at the situation. Why couldn't it have stayed simple? Hadn't we both enjoyed it when it'd just been Maddie and Aidan, not Madeline Reynolds, CEO and out of my league, and Aidan Wallace, widowed father of one—and she didn't even know about Luca yet.

"Truly, I am." She reached out but pulled her hand back before she touched me. "But I'm also sorry that you've felt in any way deceived by me. That night..."

Staring into the darkness of my half-consumed coffee, I finished for her. "It was a fantasy."

A smile flashed, but it looked more pained than pleased. "It was. And I didn't realize it was like that for you, too. But now I'm glad it was for both of us, at least."

I nodded, not sure I understood completely, but getting it on some level. We'd both been escaping.

But the reality of that meant something very clear now, in the light of day, in the minutes that ticked by during this version of life. The smooth tabletop of the café under my hand. The glittering sun outside. The responsibilities waiting for me around every corner. *The real world.* "I don't regret it. But I think that's probably it."

What good would it do me to pretend this could go anywhere? I'd had the thought a thousand times since I'd agreed to show up yesterday, but it wasn't going anywhere. No amount of normalcy—sipping coffee at the local café or chatting about mundane parts of our lives—would erase the disparity between us.

She dipped her chin, a physical acceptance, but didn't speak for a moment. When I stood, she did, too, knocking the table and making a loud enough clatter that everyone looked in our direction. She ducked her head and focused out the window, shielding herself from embarrassment, I supposed.

I reached the door and held it open for her. She slipped past me and glanced up. "You'll keep the contract?"

My heart lurched, but I couldn't tell whether it was for fear she didn't want me to or fear she did. I was counting on this contract, though. I needed it.

"If you still want me."

Her lashes fluttered, until I realized how that might sound and abruptly continued with, "To do the job. If you still want me to do the job, I mean."

"I do. I chose you based on your recommendations and portfolio, and there's no one else I want to do the job."

Relief swept in. "Then I'm in."

"Maddie! I'm so glad to see you!" Sarah James came out of nowhere and wrapped Maddie in a surprisingly familiar hug.

"Hey, same." She glanced at me from over Sarah's shoulder, her face somehow strained and unsure. Did she not want me witnessing who her friends were? Or maybe she didn't want Sarah to realize we had any connection?

"How do you know Aidan?" Sarah said, patting my shoulder in the friendly way she had.

Maddie smiled at Sarah and nodded to me. "Aidan is one of the first people I ever met in Silverton."

"Really? I love that. You couldn't find anyone better, I don't think. How did you meet?"

Sarah beamed, like she really meant it. I didn't know her all that well, so the idea that she'd recommend me so highly came as a bit of a shock, though her group of mutual friends were all at least friendly acquaintances with me, so perhaps that was why.

It didn't make much sense, but the thought of Maddie telling Sarah we'd met at the lounge up at the resort made something in me chafe, so I quickly explained. "I'm doing the landscape design for her home."

Sarah grinned. "I'm so glad you're adding clients. I told Wilder we need to beg you to do some work for Saint Security. The curb appeal is not up to snuff for our clientele." She winked at Maddie.

Of course. That was how these two knew each other. Sarah worked at Saint Security and Maddie was very likely a client.

"It didn't scare me away," Maddie said, confirming.

But then, something shifted. Both of them seemed to slip into another mood entirely.

"How are you feeling? After—"

"Fine. Um, do you have a minute? Aidan and I were just wrapping up, but I'd love to chat if you're free?"

Maddie's rushed shut down of Sarah's question had me curious. Sarah stepped back, assuring her she could take her time with me.

"Sorry. I—she's been so nice since I got to town and..."

I waved away her apology. "Say no more. I've taken enough of your time. I'll be in touch with the plans. You can review them digitally, and we'll correspond via e-mail while you get settled in. If you still want it completed next month, we'll need to get started soon. Just... let me know if you have any questions."

Maddie blinked and gave a tight nod. She stepped away, leaving more, then more space between us. And just like that, we were done. She knew the truth of me and wouldn't be able to do anything more than see me as a project to fix, and I was so far out of her league, so far into another universe of existence, there was nothing for it. My life had enough complications and challenges. This wasn't one I could navigate right now, even if I wanted to.

After more than a year and a half of pining for a woman I had never known, I put the walls back up around myself and headed home. I'd done what I'd promised myself—I'd come to hear her out, I'd been honest with her about my own situation, at least mostly, and that was all that needed to be done.

Now I just had to figure out how to oversee the project at her house without having to actually see her, because this spiraling cut of disappointment and regret was bound to improve if I had a little space.

I rubbed a hand over my chest above my heart and nodded, certain it would. Even the worst things improved with time, and this would, too.

It had to.

CHAPTER ELEVEN

Maddie

"How are you doing, after everything?"

Sarah's expression and tone were full of concern, but my heart jolted at her words. I glanced around, fully aware Aidan hadn't turned the corner yet. Thankfully, no one else was nearby. I didn't know her very well, but she'd been astute and thoughtful every time I'd interacted with her, and this time was no different.

"I'm sorry. I shouldn't be speaking so loudly. I've just been thinking about you but didn't want to invade your privacy by calling."

I gave her a smile. "Please don't apologize. I appreciate your concern. Other than Anthony and Brad, I haven't had a chance to talk with anyone in person. I told Juliet and my family via video call, which was not great."

It wasn't that I wanted to pretend it hadn't happened. But something like shame rose up in me at the thought of

Aidan knowing. I couldn't explain that in any way other than thinking of receiving his pity *now*, after he'd cracked the gavel and adjudicated our future so cleanly and without faltering, made me cringe.

She grimaced. "I'm sure they were so upset. Is Juliet still going to come visit?"

Warmth and hope and all good things flooded my mind at the mention of my closest friend. "Yes. She'll be here in a week or so. She got delayed, but she'll be here. And I'm so happy to have a familiar face coming to see me."

Sarah clapped before folding her arms in what looked like an effort to quell the outward enthusiasm. She was endearing and I already liked her. Plus, being held at gunpoint with someone kind of bonded you to them for life.

"Well listen, if you need something to do before she arrives, we're having a girls' night in at my friend Quinn's. We'd love for you to join us if you want to meet a few locals who are trustworthy and, in my opinion, the very best people on earth."

"Wow. That's a hard sell."

She grinned. "You have a full life and a ton of people who love you, I'm sure. But I know what it's like to come to Silverton and feel like it's a new beginning, but also a kind of... reckoning. Those kinds of moments are best served with guacamole, margaritas, and friends."

I chuckled and she took a step back, continuing before I could say anything.

"I won't take any more of your time, but I'm going to text Anthony the details and you can let me know if you're up for it or not. Your call. And no pressure, ever. Good to see you!" She turned and speed-walked away.

And speak of the devil, Anthony was calling. Since he

was my right-hand man and a dear friend, too, I always answered.

"I'm heading back soon. He didn't try to murder me."

The silent beat before he spoke told me just how much he'd liked my joke. "Ha. Look at you with your humor. But I'm actually calling to say I just received all the information for your landscaping via e-mail."

His question came through loud and clear. I answered with a little ache in my chest. "Yeah. He... suggested that." I didn't want to say Aidan had rejected me or the possibility of anything. But there it was, clear enough even without my spelling it out.

"Ah. Well. I'll send these on to you, and you can review them. He proposed starting Wednesday if we can approve at least forty-eight hours ahead. Mentioned knowing you were anxious to get the project completed."

I thanked him for calling and wandered back toward my car. I rarely drove in LA and never did in New York, but I'd made Brad promise me that when all of the stalker business was resolved, I'd be allowed to drive.

Allowed to drive. With a huff and more than a little disappointment, I crossed the street to my car and slumped inside. I stared unseeing out the front window until someone walked past, and I came back to myself.

Sarah's words hit me. *It's a new beginning... and a reckoning.* Wasn't that the truth. Add to that getting held at gunpoint and seeing your life melt away in a meaningless work-obsessed haze, and I'd had a full-on life-changing event.

I supposed the after-action review here *was* the reckoning. Here I sat in the middle of it. And as much as I'd typically failed to summon even the slightest interest at meeting new people in a truly social capacity versus professional networking, right about now, talking about my personal crisis and getting to know some other locals over margaritas sounded... perfect. How else would I change the way I'd been thinking and feeling about my life, the reality that'd been forced into my consciousness thanks to Korry Taggart, if I didn't do something different?

I rang the bell and glanced back at my car. I could still escape. I could also go in there, decide I hated it, and leave immediately. No problem. This was no problem. I had an escape hatch, and it wasn't as if I didn't know someone in there. I knew Sarah. She wasn't psycho, wasn't going to treat me like I was some oddity to be observed, wasn't about to ask me for a job.

"Hey, Maddie, right?" A vaguely familiar blond-haired woman gave me an easy smile as she swung the door open wide. She wore jeans, a cropped T-shirt, and looked to be about my age. "I'm Quinn Darling."

"Of course. I knew I recognized you."

She arched a brow. "*You* recognized *me?*"

I shrugged. "I heard about you from a friend, and then my assistant kind of fell down a rabbit hole and became obsessed with you. We watched the video of you and Miss Mayhem singing like twenty times. Big fans."

She grinned. "Well, please contain yourself, because Mayhem herself is in residence tonight."

I couldn't help the chuckle that escaped. This woman was one hundred percent not impressed with her very fancy friend and certainly not with me either. Then again, who would be impressed with anyone if they were engaged to a billionaire?

I hung out with what many might call "high society" often—growing up at family events, and now as an adult in my own capacity. The feeling of wanting to be connected to —that someone wanted to add you to a harem of contacts they could use when the time was right—never ended. Of course, some places were safe. Usually, Juliet managed to host less mercenary things full of nice people. I'd managed it a time or two but still never felt comfortable.

Quinn Darling's up front, unimpressed vibe proved refreshing. It was genuine, and not put-on like she wanted to make a *point* about not being impressed. She was simply herself, in her home, with her friends.

For fear of being silent too long, I said, "I think we may have met once, but as long as you don't mind me crashing your girls' night—"

"Please, we've been dying to meet you since you blew through town years ago and didn't show your face. I'm just glad you're okay." She gave me a meaningful look.

Somehow, I'd forgotten that her fiancé would've told her everything because he, too, had been held at gunpoint. Granted, he'd put himself in that situation, but it'd been rather heroic.

"Thanks. I'm..." What was I? "I guess that's partly why I'm here."

Both her brows rose this time. "Well, I'm thinking that's a story you're going to need to tell us with a margarita in hand and only one time. Dahlia's running late, so come get yourself a drink and some food while we wait."

Inside, I saw Sarah's familiar face, Callaway Rice-Saint AKA Miss Mayhem's very pregnant form on the couch, and Sadie. *Huh.* Weirdly, I kind of knew all of them. I mean, of course I didn't *know* any of them, but it was more than a small relief to see that they were familiar faces. In a time when so much felt foreign and unknown, this tiny discovery brought me a wealth of comfort.

And maybe it was that low-level sense of safety and comfort that allowed me to get so comfortable so quickly. I didn't feel like a guest when Quinn simply nodded to the table laden with a glorious selection of snacks or when Sarah smiled over at me and raised a pitcher full of lime green liquid. I felt right at home, in fact, when everyone piled into the living room with plates stacked with chips, guacamole, taquitos, tacos, salad, and of course, glasses frosty with iced margaritas. Maybe more than home, because I so rarely felt relaxed in my home in New York anymore. Maybe this was the version of home I'd enjoy here in Silverton.

And after sipping said drink until Dahlia Price arrived to great cheers from her friends, that same sense of what I could only call comfort must've been why, when Quinn turned her bright green gaze to mine and said, "Okay, Reynolds, you're up," I told them everything.

Well, that, and the fact that I'd come here tonight to break the pattern I'd created. That big fat blank I'd drawn when Taggart had his gun pressed against my back? That's what I was changing. I'd fill in that void only by trying, and the combination of warmth, welcome, and tequila worked perfectly.

I flew past the summary of having a stalker since I knew just by being around them the last half hour that Sarah and Quinn had told them every possible detail of what happened days ago. Instead, I focused in on me... what I hadn't been able to tell Juliet yet thanks to time zones and her work obligations, and what I'd likely never be able to tell my parents.

"I was standing there drawing a blank. Instead of freaking out that I'd never see my parents again, I was just calm. Unsure whether I'd live to see tomorrow, but kind of… fine with it." I took a long drink of my margarita, hoping they wouldn't think me a horrible person.

"I'm so sorry," Sarah said, and Sadie nodded. "Me, too."

Calla studied me, her dark eyes weighty. "I have to say, I've kind of been there. Not so much the stalker situation, but feeling like my life didn't have much meaning."

She got it. "Yes. That's it. I probably sound insanely ungrateful, but I just had this sinking feeling when it was all over. I wanted to see my best friend and hug my brother and sister-in-law, snuggle their baby, but I didn't have someone I was desperate to see." I gestured to Sarah. "Like you and Wilder. I mean, he was crawling out of his skin to get to you. And Julian mentioned getting home to you more than three times while he debriefed, and that's more agitation than I've seen from him times a factor of ten."

A smile flashed across Quinn's face, but she smothered it by pressing her lips together, her brow furrowing. "So you want a boyfriend?"

CHAPTER TWELVE

Maddie

I laughed softly, but Dahlia was the one who spoke up. "Not just a *boyfriend*. A partner. Someone to go home to. Someone to give those moments gravity and meaning. Not that having a partner is all that gives someone meaning or anything. I'm not saying that. I'm single and my life is awesome, and I don't mean to sound like it's not, but... I get it."

Quinn nodded. "That's it for me, for sure. I love Julian. I never thought I'd care about someone the way I do him. I loved my life without him, but I think that was because I didn't know how much better it could be with him."

Calla and Sadie both agreed in their own way, and Sarah's blush grew deeper by the minute. Quinn called her out, which was clearly her role in the group.

"Go ahead. Tell us all about your actual action hero of a man, Sarah."

She laughed, all good naturedly, and toasted the room. "He is that. But I was also thinking about how much I relate to that. I felt so ungrateful for my life, for all of you, for being back here. It took me some time to accept that I could want a life with Wilder, that I could feel happy and full because of it, and still be deeply grateful for what I already had."

Hearing them all talk about how much they loved their partners made something in my chest cinch tight. I wanted it. I'd never wanted someone like that—not really. I'd always felt that was far away for me. Or maybe when I found it, it'd be more like an actual partnership—mutually beneficial versus something founded on love and trust. When my brother Nate got engaged to Ariel just a few months before my first trip out here, it started. I'd given up on the serial relationships I'd done for years, always certain the next one would be the one to make me think, "This will work."

And then Nate got married to the love of his life and it made it clear. I wanted *that*. I wanted someone I could share every bit of myself with, not just the upper crust, CEO girl. Not the woman people looked at and thought, "She makes it look so easy." I wanted to be a goof with that person like I was with my brother and be soft and romantic like I could be with Juliet. I wanted to be organized and thoughtful like I was with Anthony and loyal like I was with my parents.

I wanted to be all of myself and to know all of someone else.

Ironic that the one and only time I'd felt anything close to that had been with Aidan, and he hadn't even known my last name. That thought, and where my last interaction with the man had ended, sent an ache winding through me.

"Do you date? Or anything?" Sadie asked, clearly a little uncomfortable with the question.

I gave myself a moment to compose a response. The difference between the truth—I did, kind of, in an obligatory way—and what I wanted to be true—yes, the man of my dreams—brushed up against my tongue in uncomfortable ways.

"I went from one relationship to the next for years but stopped dating altogether a while ago because I was just tired and sad. Then a few months ago, I agreed to see someone my mom set me up with." I widened my eyes to illustrate just what a mistake that had been.

"Ohhh, so that went well," Calla said.

"Yep. He wanted to *check out my portfolio* on the second date. When I told him that wasn't a great discussion point for a date, nor was it an appropriate thing to say to a person he'd basically just met, he got offended and then asked if I wanted a third date after trying to kiss me."

"What the *what?* Talk about clueless," Quinn said, disgusted.

I'd known the woman less than an hour, and she was already in my corner. Was this what real friendships were like? The only one I really had was Juliet, and we'd known each other since we were born. Aside from Ariel, my sister-in-law, I wouldn't say I had many friends who weren't also in my employ. That didn't make them fake by any means. Anthony would take a bullet for me just as soon as Brad would. But it was just different.

"Well, the worst thing was, he showed up yesterday morning acting like he was so worried about me because somehow, he'd heard about the stalker. I hate to say it, but my mom let him know. So he jets out here, acts all territorial in front of Aidan, and—"

"Wait. Aidan Wallace?" Dahlia's question had everyone leaning in.

And again, where before I wouldn't have shared anything personal with women I'd just met, tonight, I wanted to. I wanted to lay every stupid, messy feeling from the last few days out on the table and let them help me sort through it. Juliet was in South Africa at a WHO conference, and she wouldn't be available for any lengthy downloads until she was back in the EU, at least. I needed a minute to process through this, and everything they'd said tonight told me I could trust them. Plus, Calla was a thousand times more famous than I was, and she clearly trusted them implicitly. That would've been as good a sign as any, even if my gut hadn't told me I was safe with these women.

"I hired him to design my yard."

Dahlia beamed. "Oh, he's so good at it! I'm glad you did."

I inspected her for... anything. Any hint that she had feelings for the man who felt like he should be mine even though *what?* Why did I feel that way? I had no right to him, no claim on him. Still, I didn't like the idea of getting attached to this group of women just to find out one of them had a thing for the same man I did.

My stomach twisted a bit at the thought. One thing that had become odiously clear over time? Women did compete with women, and sometimes it got nasty. As much as I wished we'd all support each other in a world that tried particularly hard to oppress us, we so often failed at lifting each other up. These women seemed like the best sort from what I could tell, and yet...

"Oh, but you *like* him, don't you. I see that little blush. He is super handsome," Quinn said, a wry smile on her lips.

"Oh, it's, uh—"

"You were having coffee with him earlier, right? You

seemed friendly enough. Did the weirdo guy who invited himself mess something up?" Sarah's innocent question saved me from directly answering Quinn's, bless her.

But how to respond? I sucked in a breath, letting it out slowly and deciding I might as well surrender. "Okay, so the full story?"

"Yes, obviously," Calla said, shaking her head like this was obvious.

"Of course," Sadie said, her words more encouragement than demand.

Sarah, Dahlia, and Quinn all nodded, and Quinn added a little "out with it" gesture to egg me on.

"So when I came eighteen months ago, I met him the last night of my trip. And it was... I mean, not to sound like a total idiot, but it was borderline *magical*."

Calla's mouth dropped open. Quinn grinned. Sarah and Sadie looked at each other, and Dahlia made a sound that was something between a squeal and a laugh.

"So you've kept in touch all this time? You've been dating long distance? What? More! Keep going!" Quinn's impatience had everyone chuckling.

"No. We didn't share last names. I was in this totally burnt-out place, where I just wanted a break. I'd been on the book tour and all over the press—largely good, except for the inconvenient reality of people hating a woman for being wildly financially successful *and* having a uterus."

More than one of them burst out laughing, and I reveled in that, too. It'd been too long since I'd just kind of ranted. The small buzz coming on from the margarita didn't hurt my honesty quotient.

"So I didn't tell him my last name because he didn't seem to recognize me. And he didn't tell me his, though that wouldn't have meant anything to me at the time. When we parted ways later that night…"

"Oh. *Ohhh.* How much later are we talking?" Quinn asked.

"Quinn! That's so nosy!" Sarah reprimanded.

"Not *that* much later. We sat at the bar for two hours, and then he walked me to the elevator and left me there."

Quinn slumped. "Oh."

"But he did kiss me."

"Now you're talking." She grinned.

Dahlia, who'd been smiling the entire time and not acting jealous or weird or anything other than like she wished she had some popcorn for the story time, asked, "How was it?"

I thought about demurring. But again, I didn't want to. And I sensed I didn't *have* to. "It was the best."

Truly. The best ever. The best first kiss. The best last kiss. The best kiss goodbye and hello and *let's start something*. Simply the best.

"And then?" Sarah prompted.

"And then nothing. We didn't exchange numbers or anything. But I thought about him nonstop. And then I ran into him on the street a few days ago. We made plans for coffee. And *then* he showed up at my house as my contractor for the landscaping. It never even occurred to me because he said he was a tree farmer. But Chadwick was being all possessive and awful and… yeah. He agreed to see me today when I made clear I am not with Chad."

Quinn snorted but pressed her lips together. I would've bet a thousand bucks she wanted to crack a joke about his name.

"But you both looked kind of bummed when I saw you."

I nodded. "We decided that staying focused on the professional side of things was best."

"We?" Sadie asked.

I shrugged, though the movement was about as natural as synthetic oil. "Well. I think once he realized who I am, it was… too much."

Quinn grumbled, and everyone else was quiet. After a moment, she spoke up. "But what about you? You want to give it a shot with him? Do you feel like that connection you had was something worth trying out for longer than a few hours?"

I swallowed the last bit of my margarita. "Honestly? Yes. I'm really disappointed that the whole *Madeline Reynolds* thing is what scared him away. I get it, but I kind of thought he'd be able to see past that."

Calla stood up. "Sorry, I just can't sit for all that long without my leg going numb. But also, you know I get this."

I nodded. She got it better than I did. My fame was isolated to certain circles. Yes, the book tour and all that publicity from it had put me out there to more people outside of the business world, but still. Not like her. Nothing would ever compare to being an international popstar.

"My advice is this: go for it. Make him see past that."

"But be careful. He's… he's been through a lot." Dahlia's eyes reflected her concern. Again, I worried maybe there was something there, but she wasn't warning me away.

And what he'd told me—that he was a widower. Someone who'd been through something so awful deserved to be cared for.

It was Quinn who had the last word. "I say screw careful. I'm guessing you've had your fair share of being careful with all this creepy stalker dude stuff and lying low for months while you figured it out. You're a public figure. You've got all kinds of obligations and all that."

She nailed it. That was it exactly. "True."

She grinned. "Then I say be done with careful. I say get a little reckless and show Aidan you're worth the risk, whether he wants to see it or not."

CHAPTER THIRTEEN

Aidan

J ake looked at Madeline with hearts in his eyes. "Thank you so much, ma'am."

"No problem, Jake. Thanks for being here early." She smiled at him, all warm and welcoming and trying to torture me.

That's right. She was hell-bent on torturing me, and I couldn't be convinced otherwise. Would she be here serving up coffees and pastries to my crew if she wasn't? Answer: no. I'd held my tongue about it, hadn't even mentioned it to John because I felt like such a fool for thinking it, but this morning, I was convinced. She'd come out every day since we started, and since ending up with two crew out sick this week, I'd joined in to help get things moving. I couldn't afford to fall behind on this project since we'd already started two days later thanks to Chadwick's helpful insights derailing the decision-making last week.

Even that—the fee she was paying to rush the job—made the difference between us, the impossibility of *anything* between us, feel more vivid. And it made this whole situation that much worse.

Each morning, she'd arrived looking pretty enough I knew I couldn't look directly at her. She'd offered coffees and food, and the first day we said no. We weren't in the habit of refusing gestures like water or coffee—it wasn't forbidden, necessarily. But I'd warned the men we shouldn't abuse the situation. We didn't want to seem like we were taking advantage. Sure, she had more money than anyone could spend in a lifetime, but somehow, that made me more uncomfortable taking something from her than if she'd been a more typical client.

The second day, Jake said yes, and Chris and Todd did, too. They couldn't resist her smile and that persistent generosity. Today, everyone snagged their orders with thanks and smiles and general adoration, and I held my breath as she approached with one last cup in her hand. One thing I didn't need was to take a deep inhale of her million-dollar perfume and have it stick with me like it had for so long. Before, I hadn't known anything but that it smelled amazing on her. Now, I knew it had to be some kind of custom scent formulated just for her using diamond dust and rare orchids from yet-undiscovered islands or something. Whatever it was, it was one more thing to high-light her status.

"Black coffee for you, Aidan?"

Of course she said my name. I'd made a point to think of her as Madeline instead of Maddie simply so I wouldn't feel the rush of anticipation just thinking her name created, and here she was saying mine.

Not fair.

"I'm good, thank you." I nodded to the thermos I'd very purposefully brought this morning.

"This was just brewed. Nice and steamy."

I glanced toward her and—*warning! Look away!* She wore tight spandex pants and a short T-shirt. Nothing unusual about a woman wearing workout clothes in her own home, but did she have to do it in front of me? Did she realize what she was doing to me and how hard it was to keep my eyes away from her? Hair, face, body, *all of it*. I liked it all, wanted to gulp down the images of her, inhale her scent and stuff my ears with her voice, but I wouldn't.

Because this wasn't Maddie who I'd met a year and a half ago. This was Madeline Reynolds. Technically my employer. Actually out of my league. Definitely not an option.

Not for the first time, the slimy film of embarrassment and foolishness filtered over my vision. I'd been such an ignorant bumpkin that night, hadn't I? Thinking she was just another regular woman who I could, outside of this fantasy, stand a chance with. And how many nights after our time together had I dreamed of her or lain awake missing her? Missing a woman I didn't even know.

Jake must've shot the coffee instead of sipped it, because he jogged over seconds later. "Thank you so much, Ms. Reynolds. And I hope it's not completely out of place to say, but I'm really glad that stalker didn't kill you. I'm glad you're okay."

At his heart, Jake was a sweetie. Always wanting to —*wait*. What? Stalker? *Killed her!?*

A strangled sound came right as I looked up at her. Her face had lost all color.

"Who told you about that?" she asked, still sounding calm despite the shift in her demeanor.

"It's on the local news channels. Popped up on my phone, too. I'm seriously so glad you weren't hurt."

Maddie smiled, something graceful but somehow forced. "Thanks for saying that, Jake. I am, too."

I couldn't stand there and not say something. My embarrassment and frustration could take a hike for a minute. "What? What happened?"

Jake dove right in to explain. "You didn't see the news? This stalker guy attacked her a few days ago. Held her and Sarah James at gunpoint. Wilder Saint took the guy down, and he's being held without bail until they can take him to trial. From what I heard, he's—"

My head was exploding, and everything came out in a rush. "This is insane. Are you okay? I'm so sorry. What can I—"

"Excuse me. I can't stay to talk just now. I've got to get to a meeting." Maddie gave a tight nod and turned on her heel, disappearing inside before Jake or I could say another word.

He turned his big eyes toward me. "I guess maybe she didn't want me to recap it. Whoops."

"It'll be fine. Let's get some work done." The sentiment rang hollow, though. She didn't seem fine. She seemed rattled to have Jake even talking about it, and she certainly didn't want to discuss it with me.

I'd been so dismissive of her the last few days. I'd been a jerk, as though I had no other way to protect myself from the stupid leaping feeling in my chest every time someone mentioned her or I thought about her. I'd tried to put distance between us physically, emotionally, just like I felt the distance between us in terms of our net worths and social circles and the sting of that reality.

But this was her reality, too. Not just mansions and

private jets and book deals and fame but pressure and danger. Incredible, terrible danger.

I'd put up a wall to keep myself safe from the small, impossible feeling being near her gave me, but look what I'd done.

Was that her fault? Was she to be blamed for my unmanageable feelings? No. And now that I knew she'd been through something awful, all I could think of was going to her and begging her to tell me she was truly okay. Well, that, and asking her to forgive me.

So I spent the day working as hard as I could physically stand. When the heat hit, we broke for lunch. She'd been coming out to offer us ice water all week, but today I didn't see her again. I knew I wouldn't, and yet the absence drove home what I needed to do.

By the end of the day, I was covered in dirt and sweat, having found some absolution in making as much progress for her as I could. Working the land had always given me solace. Maybe that was why I could never seem to stay on the business and design side of things for too long.

We'd leveled ground in one place, worked on mucking the little stream that ran through her yard and widened it for a small pond, and we'd transplanted a few shrubs to their final locations. Most of the larger-level surface work was done, and that meant we were technically on schedule even with the later start.

I said goodbye to the guys and wiped my face with a towel. I debated going home and showering, but there was a decent chance I'd shower and sit down with Luca and never get up again.

Not that I was unfamiliar with physical labor, but I didn't normally do it for this long—not days in a row, at least. I liked getting into the dirt, though. It was good for me to forget the burden of my in-laws' business and how stressful the year had been or how much work would need to be done to get their farm ready to sell. Knowing how getting that done would free up a lot of time and energy was about the only thing keeping me going.

With my gloves in the dirt and sweat on my brow, sometimes I could forget the obligation I felt to them. I could cast away the guilt for resenting that obligation, the frustration that seemed to grow larger by the day at the sensation that I was losing time to do what I really wanted. And this connection to the earth helped conjure up inspiration, which was so rare and lovely these days that I couldn't help but savor the time, even if it did often qualify as "back-breaking work."

Today, I'd thought of nothing but Maddie. Realistically, that'd been the case since we'd arrived on site, but I'd known working in her yard would do that, and her frequent visits had made sure of it. Until this morning, when her visits halted abruptly, and I felt like the biggest jerk on the planet for everything that'd happened.

So instead of going home and getting cleaned up, I tromped to the front door. My shirt had soaked through to my chest and back. My arms, neck, and legs were coated in a fine layer of dirt that would take some time to scrub off. I was essentially a little pig pen standing there in front of her welcome mat.

"Oh. Mr. Wallace. Um, let me see if she's available." Anthony's eyes ran over me, clearly taking in the utter dishevelment. "Feel free to come in. We've got the AC cranking."

"No. I'm a mess. I'll wait out here. And please call me Aidan."

He pursed his lips like he didn't like the invitation but nodded to accept it. "Okay, Aidan. I'll be right back."

He shut the door gently and I waited, tempted to pull out my phone and busy myself, but knowing there was nothing on it I cared about. My son was safe with a friend. My cousin was still at work, and I'd see him at some point this weekend if not tonight. And the woman I'd been pining for all these long months was on the other side of this door.

Yeah. Nothing on the phone would distract me from that reality.

Another minute or two passed and with them came the creeping exhaustion that often hit by the end of the week these days. Though this time, it wasn't all physical. I didn't see how Maddie's mere presence in Silverton could do damage to me, but it also felt like I'd gone ten rounds with an unnamed opponent.

The door swung open and she stepped out. My heart kicked at the sight of her. Inevitably, she looked amazing. She wore black heels and a black cocktail dress that fit her perfectly and accentuated her form while looking polished and sleek. Her hair was styled so one side was pulled back and showed an ear with a glinting diamond adorning it, and the other side hung long and shiny and soft-looking over her shoulder. I liked it darker like this—dark at the top and tapering to wavy lighter streaks. It'd been blond last time I saw her—the first time. She looked good no matter what.

"Hi," she said, standing tall and facing me like I was anyone else.

"I came to say I'm sorry." No sense putting that off.

"What for?" Her brows pulled together as though my statement truly puzzled her, but the way her gaze found mine and hooked into me gave me a sliver of hope.

"Quite a few things. First, that Jake said what he said.

He doesn't have a filter and can be a little oblivious. Clearly, you didn't want to discuss what happened, and I apologize that it even came up."

Her lips curved into a fond smile. "He's harmless."

"Agreed. But I gathered you didn't want him sharing all the details of what happened." And damn, but that was really why I'd come. To apologize, yes, but also to see for myself that she was okay. I had no right to that, among so many other things, but I needed to hear her say it. I'd deliberately chosen not to read the article I'd found on my phone during lunch. It'd taken every bit of restraint, but something in me felt it wouldn't be right.

"I didn't. I prefer not to talk about it."

Message received. I didn't need her to tell me all the gory details. "I get that."

She shook her head and let out a breath. "I didn't realize the story had broken. We've been doing damage control, but it's a little late. The story leaked and of course, it's sensational and will get clicks, so there you have it."

No wonder she'd seemed shaken by Jake's comment. "I'm sorry. That must feel like a terrible invasion."

She nodded, and slowly, her eyes lifted to meet mine. "Well, I've got to get going."

Crap. This wasn't how I wanted this to go. But what could I do? Clearly, she had plans and standing with her dirt-covered yard guy wasn't one of them.

"Of course. Right. I'll just..."

"Okay. Well. Have a good evening."

She turned for the door, but I had to know. So I grabbed her wrist with my giant, doubtless still dirty hand. Her inhale came on a gasp as she turned to look at me, then down at where I clasped her golden skin.

"Are you okay? You don't have to say anything more, but please tell me that."

Thoughts must've been flying through her mind with the way she stared down at our point of contact, lashes fluttering for a few seconds, before she gave me her face. "I'll be okay."

My heart thundered in my chest, the belated and completely futile need to protect her from this unseen and now irrelevant threat rising in me so sharply, I stepped closer. "I'm sorry that happened. I wish…"

What? That I'd been there? That I'd somehow kept her safe when Wilder Saint barely managed to? *Not likely.*

"It's fine. I'll be fine. Thank you for your concern."

I dropped her arm immediately, sensing the dismissal. She did that well—chose her words so specifically that they communicated more than one thing. The face-value sentiment and the other one—the one I read loud and clear.

The one that said we were done. My choice to stay away from her, to reject whatever she had in mind last weekend, and to treat her like an employer or even something forbidden… that'd closed all the doors between us.

I'd wanted to draw thick lines and not feel like a fool, but as the actual door shut behind her, I saw it clearly: I hadn't saved my pride, and I'd ruined any chance with Maddie Reynolds I might've had.

CHAPTER FOURTEEN

Maddie

Juliet wrapped me in her arms and held me tight enough my breaths grew shallow thanks to her brute emotion-fueled strength. We breathed in the comfort of each other's nearness and even though I knew what I'd find when she released me, my heart still ached with love and gratitude when I saw her tearstained face.

"I'm so glad you're okay, and I'm never leaving you again." She shook me where she held my shoulders.

I laughed through the tightness in my chest and nodded. "That's fine with me."

She grinned, then winced. "Okay, actually, I will have to leave you in a few days to go prep for my next UN trip, so I'm going to need the full download and everything stat."

I waved her inside. "Stat? Who are you right now?"

"I'm channeling you, probably. 'Bossy Boardroom Maven' as I think I recently saw a paper refer to you." She set her purse on the chair next to her and stood with a hand braced on the high bar top.

I groaned. "Maven? Who writes this stuff?"

She welcomed the glass of sparkling iced water I slid toward her and sipped before quipping, "Well, they can't use the alliterative option in that paper, so they had to get creative."

Ah, yes. How often had I been called the b-word in either a complimentary or accusatory way? Too many to count. I never took offense and didn't particularly mind the moniker, but it got old. I was not, in fact, all that bossy. I was assertive, firm in my convictions, and really good at my job. I did it without showing them I was sweating, and that let everyone say I did it without breaking one. Apparently, this made me a... *maven*.

As for the reason she was really here, Juliet didn't dive right in immediately. She kept it to surface-level chatting about her travels even though I knew what was coming, and finally, she pinned me down like I knew she would eventually. We'd snuggled into the couches, alone in the house aside from whatever security guard was stationed out front. Now that Taggart was in jail without bail, I actually got privacy fairly regularly.

"Any ideas who leaked the story?" she asked.

"Oh yeah. It was Chad."

Her jaw dropped. "Seriously? Why would he do that?"

I gave her a look. "You expected better of him?"

She chuckled. "No, of course not. But it's not like he needs the money from selling a story like that. It just seems so..."

"Vindictive? Juvenile? Selfish? Stupid?"

She sighed. "All fair. And I guess there's no sense in getting upset now, is there?"

I admired this about her—her innate ability to accept when things happened. It was like her brain just took the information and adapted. She seemed so sweet and soft, but anyone who truly knew her saw the layers of intelligence and strategic thinking underneath. I would never consider myself a particularly flexible person, so this quality of Juliet's always inspired me.

And this time, I agreed. "No. Can't take it back. Wilder warned me we'll be getting an influx of press, so they're going to shut down the neighborhood and I'll need security in town now." Frustrating, but having been through the madness of the last few months, I'd rather play it safe.

"Good plan, though I'm sorry. I know you were hoping this would be an escape from all of that." She sipped her wine, her kind eyes studying me.

"I was, but such is life." I *really* was, but again, no point wishing it hadn't happened, and I'd always known it was a possibility. Hopefully, being here in Silverton, the locals wouldn't feed into it, and the tourists wouldn't be around long enough to care. If I gave a few interviews or whatever I had to do to get people off my back, maybe they wouldn't be camped out in front of my house and hounding me constantly.

I'd still get my little vacation from real life and recover in time to return to reality and remember who I was and what life before all this mess looked like.

She gave a small grin and continued watching me, waiting for something. Finally, she prompted me. "So you saw him? Catch me up."

She'd been traveling the last few days and with family for a few before that. She didn't like being tethered to her phone, so when she spent time with loved ones, she usually got as close to *offline* as a person could be these days. All of that meant she knew little of what'd happened with Aidan since our coffee last weekend.

"He's been working with his crew in the back yard since Wednesday. I guess he doesn't normally do the grunt work, but since he has two guys out sick, he's right in there with them."

"Sounds like a good leader."

I gave her an unimpressed glare. "He's been ignoring me."

She gasped and her hand shot to her chest. "How is that possible? *You!?*"

I stuck my tongue out at her. "Rude. But seriously. I've been putting myself out there—taking them all ice water, coffee, snacks... honestly, whatever Anthony and I could come up with that didn't make me look pathetic."

"Can we just agree right now that having a crush on someone doesn't make you pathetic?" She did that little tilt of her head that meant she was actually a little concerned and not just joking.

Discomfort rippled through me. Admitting having a crush felt a lot like the whole underbelly situation. "Sure."

Her gaze didn't waver, nor did she take my dismissal of her point, and she let me continue. I huffed, loving her for pushing me even though it was easier when she didn't. But that was why I needed *her* here. Anthony couldn't do this for me, and neither could anyone else. Quinn Darling was the first person other than Juliet and my brother to do something like that in ages, and even then, it'd been different.

"Fine. I get it. But I feel stupid because he said we should keep it to work. But after the girls' night, I thought maybe they were right. And then he ignored me, right up until his chatty man Jake mentioned the whole stalker mess, and then he suddenly cared, and I wasn't having it so I went inside. Well, that and I hadn't seen that the story was out, so I did legitimately need to go deal with that." My heart raced, trying to block out what came next.

"And? I can tell there's more so just tell me, love."

Why did I feel like crying? Why did her gentleness always do this? It wasn't like I was starved for it. *She* was gentle and kind to me and always had been. It had to be the still mixed-up feelings surrounding his check-in last Friday that had me off-kilter.

"He came to apologize. Grabbed my arm and asked if I was okay. It felt..."

My eyes shut at the memory of his touch on my arm. I'd gone inside and held my forearm in front of me and just stared at the smudge of dirt he'd left on the soft skin of my inner wrist. Shouldn't it have bothered me he'd touched me? Shouldn't it have sent me running to the sink and scrubbing furiously to remove the evidence of someone so clearly uninterested in me?

But I hadn't. I'd walked around another twenty minutes before reluctantly wiping away the thumb print like it was the only proof I had of him. After that, I'd turned on my smile to go socialize in Salt Lake with a small group of donors to a foundation I championed and prayed they didn't all get hung up on the whole stalker issue. Since it was the only work I'd committed to doing during this "sabbatical," I hadn't been able to cancel and just stay home with those messy thoughts.

"How did it feel?"

I exhaled loudly, exhausted by the fact that I couldn't get this man out of my head. "It felt like he cared. And I spent the next forty-eight hours reprimanding myself for even thinking that. I'm still annoyed, but I've decided it's all because I haven't dated anyone decent in years, and he's the closest thing to decent I've encountered. It's not that he's special. It's just that I have a super low bar and I'm starved for affection."

She nodded. "Yes. I'm certain that's it, and it has nothing to do with the fact that you've been cultivating a hardcore crush on the man for well over a year."

My mouth dropped open. "Aren't you supposed to be sweet? Supportive?"

"Hmm. I believe the line is, 'beautiful, rich, and dumb as rocks.'"

We laughed at the same time, cackling over what one man had told her father. It hadn't gone over so well. If my dad was a poster child for absentee workaholic with expectations too high for anyone to reach, Juliet's was like Mr. Rogers if he'd been a billionaire genius. The man was so kind it seemed impossible. He was also fiercely protective of his daughters, and so the foolish failure of a date who'd dared report on Juliet's intelligence was essentially destroyed. Kind, loving, and ruthlessly loyal were Mr. Christensen's best and worst qualities.

Once the hilarity died down, Juliet got that pensive air again. "I guess I think you need to keep trying, but I don't want to be one of those people that assumes you just have to wear a low-cut top and your womanly wiles will change his mind."

I sighed, tired and tired again. When was the last time I'd felt rested? Refreshed? "I'm not going to chase him. I don't have it in me."

She reached for my hand and held it, evidently recognizing the severity of things based on that. A fair response considering that until the last year or so, I'd always *had it in me*. I was a go-getter. I made things happen. I worked hard and work fueled me, so working hard made me work harder.

Even the last time I'd been here, I hadn't felt so exhausted. Everything had spun out of control and I hated it. The bright spot to Silverton, aside from the stunning beauty of the mountains and charm of the town and the so far ridiculously nice, likeable townsfolk? Aidan. I'd come back hoping to see him. And now I had.

And he'd seen me and turned on his heel.

"You don't have to chase him. He'll be here tomorrow, right?"

They'd taken Sunday off, and Saturday, he hadn't been with the rest of his crew. But I doubted I'd get another reprieve. "Yes. They're trying to wrap this up by end of June, and he wanted to get a few things done early in the month for reasons I don't recall. So yes. Unless his guys are well, he'll probably be here."

Juliet flashed a bright grin. "Perfect. I'll get a feel for him."

I sat up, floored by the determination I saw in her expression. "And how would that work? You saunter out there in all your goddess-like glory and ask him if he has a crush on me because I've been talking about him for eighteen months?"

She stood and winked. "Absolutely."

CHAPTER FIFTEEN

Aidan

I parked in front of the driveway, but before we got out of the truck, I turned to Luca. "Let's talk rules."

He groaned. "Dad. Come on. I'm eleven. I shouldn't even be here, much less need the rules talk."

The glare he shot me should've withered a thousand oaks. Unfortunately for him, I was immune to his preteen irritation, and I also wasn't about to leave him at home alone. He'd been sick last week and had finally recovered, but now school was out, and I didn't trust that he would tell me if he was feeling bad so I could go home and help him. When he hit double digits, he'd declared himself a man and found any attempt to "baby him"—his words—repellant.

"Even Jake and the other guys need rules. This client is important and—"

"And I need to respect their property. I need to stay safe

and off the work site. I should stay in the shade. Yes, I brought sunscreen. Yes, my water bottle is full. Yes, I peed before we left. No, I do not still feel sick."

I exhaled slowly and as silently as I could. As much as I understood his irritation with me for repeating the same questions over and over again, they came from a place of experience. Add to that the fact that he hadn't come to a work site in over a year, and here we were.

If my nerves were a bit more present than normal for a regular Monday where I got to "play in the dirt" as my in-laws put it, then I only had myself to blame.

"Okay. You're all set. Did you bring your Gameboy?"

He gave me the dead-eyed stare I'd come to refer to as the *Really, Dad?* look.

"You know it hasn't been called a Gameboy for like thirty years, right?"

I exited the truck without addressing that little quip and rounded to the bed, where I handed him a few things and tossed some shovels over my shoulder. The easiest route to the back was along an access pathway shrouded in trees. I had to hand it to the developers—they'd kept as much original foliage as possible, and they'd done it well. Across the driveway, Wilder Saint gave me a little nod after doing a chin-point thing toward my son. Guess we had the security go-ahead. I'd heard he'd gotten his security firm up and running but hadn't realized he already had such high-profile clients. Good for him.

"This is pretty," Luca said as we walked along the weedy dirt pathway.

"It is. You'll like this project." Despite his irritability, the kid loved the outdoors. Thank God, because I didn't know what I'd do with him half the time if he didn't. Granted, he didn't want to work it with me, but he'd be content to read under a tree all day every day if I'd let him.

"Who's the owner? Someone fancy, right?"

I hid my wince at that. "A businesswoman. Ms. Reynolds. I doubt we'll see her." I'd done my job of scaring her away too effectively.

"Is that her?"

My heart kicked as I followed his gaze to a tall blonde woman. Even if Maddie had dyed her hair back, that wasn't her. This was someone else. Another assistant, maybe? "Uh, no. Not sure who that is."

"Aid! This is Juliet, Mad—er, Ms. Reynolds' best friend! She's taking our coffee order this morning."

Jake sent me an oblivious wave, and I willed my cheeks not to heat with the crush of embarrassment that hit.

I loved the kid. He was a hard worker. But never before had a person so embodied the Golden Retriever energy of friendly, adorable, and clueless as well as Jake did.

When we neared them enough so I didn't have to yell, I greeted her. "Hello, ma'am. Nice to meet you."

She smiled something so genuine, it almost blinded me.

"Please, call me Juliet. You must be Aidan Wallace." She stuck out her hand for a shake.

Thankful I hadn't already been digging and that my hands were relatively clean, I accepted. Though she looked like she might have one of those handshakes that sat limp at the fingers, she clasped mine firmly and gave a purposeful shake.

"Nice to meet you," I said, at a loss for what to do with myself. Again, my lack of interaction with beautiful, likely extremely wealthy women knocked me over the head.

"I was just getting orders, and then I'm going to run into town. Coffee?"

And the disarming bat of her lashes had me saying, "That'd be great. Just black."

Next, she looked down and to my right, where the son I'd temporarily forgotten about thanks to my spiking pulse and the repeated glances back to Maddie's house in an attempt to see if she was anywhere within view stood quietly.

"And you?"

"Sure. Are you going to Rise and Shine?"

Juliet smiled. "Yes. I hear it's the best."

"It is. Sadie's smart and she's expanded her business a lot in the last year. You should get some bread, too. But I'll take a raspberry whip if they're doing them. If not, that's okay."

Juliet's smile was charmed and not shocked by my son's presumption, thankfully. She watched Luca trot off to a spot under a tree and turned back to me. "That's your son?"

A wash of something—dread? Fear? God help me but was it embarrassment again?—slipped over me head to toe. Telling her meant telling Maddie, and this wasn't the right way to do that. Then again, we weren't involved anymore, so what did it matter?

That was a bunch of bull, and I knew it. "Yes. But I... we never talked about him."

She studied me as though deciding what she thought of me. "She's told me a bit about you."

I swallowed, desperate to know what Maddie had shared. Our first meeting? The kiss? My fumbling of every interaction since? "I'm not sure that's a good thing."

She tilted her head to one side. "It's good... depending."

I shifted, restless at that. "Depending on what?"

Juliet smiled again, a bright beaming thing that should probably be weaponized. "You, of course."

And with that, she spun and left without a backward glance. I watched her go, desperate for a sight of her friend, a woman I couldn't get out of my head no matter how I tried, but finally pushed on with work when she slipped inside and Maddie was nowhere to be seen.

For the rest of the day, Juliet's words floated around my head. What did that mean? What could she be insinuating with the suggestion that what she'd heard about me was good... depending on me?

As everyone packed up, I lost track of Luca. He might've taken a load of supplies to the truck, but we'd likely leave most of our gear at the site since we'd be back tomorrow. Maybe he was just packing up his stuff.

Since nothing had come easily lately, I rounded the corner and caught sight of him talking with Juliet and Maddie.

Of course.

My pulse spiked and my mind scrambled for how to manage this as I neared the small group. Juliet burst out laughing, and Maddie sent Luca an endeared smile. Who knew what he'd said, but the kid was precocious as all get out, and apparently, he'd left the moody pre-teen behind in the dirt.

"There's your dad now, Luca." Juliet touched Maddie on the arm. To give her strength? Warn her?

"Oh. Okay. Thanks for the invitation, Ms. Reynolds. Nice to talk to you again, Juliet." He nodded at them in a way that told me he'd reveled in talking to the two women, then headed to the truck.

Who would blame him? He was starved for attention this summer as it was, and aside from his grandmother, great-aunt, and occasionally Dahlia Price, he didn't actually speak to women. He got a face full of me, John, and all the people who worked the tree farm. Our neighbors only had boys, too.

A pang hit. Smaller and smaller each year, but lately, entering this preteen phase made me wish I wasn't doing it alone. What a stupid thing to feel as I faced down these two.

"Luca was telling us about his latest read. We told him he should feel free to come hang out inside tomorrow, if he has to come back." Juliet took a large step back. "I think I... left something in the oven. I'm going to run and check it. See you tomorrow, Aidan."

I nodded to her, but my eyes wouldn't leave Maddie's, especially since hers were pinned on me. Looking into their hazel depths had me feeling like I'd lost my footing.

She spoke first. "You have a son."

"Yes. Luca."

"He... looks like you."

I couldn't read her tone, but it wasn't angry or negative. Maybe not leaping for joy at this discovery, but what did I expect?

"Thanks. Yeah. He's got his mom's lighter eyes, but yeah."

We breathed through the awkwardness of another truth uncovered. Instead of waiting for her to ask why I hadn't told her, I offered it up. "I didn't mention him before for the same reasons both of us held things back."

We hadn't discussed those reasons, but we knew they existed between us. She nodded, waiting for more.

"I didn't say anything last weekend because it just... I didn't see what difference it made. You knowing I had a son. It just..." It made people's pity swell larger than when they found out I'd lost my wife. It made me an object to be coddled and cared for instead of a man who had obligations to his family and himself. I hadn't wanted to submit myself to her pity any more than the truths I'd admitted already did.

"Okay," she said, giving absolutely nothing away.

Was she masking pity? Was she embarrassed for me, that I'd kept this from her? Dread and guilt and all manner of nastiness swirled in my gut. Maybe the heat of the afternoon and a long day after little sleep pushed me to say it. Maybe it was the knowledge I still had to go home and work on the accounts for the farm.

Maybe it was something in me that needed to provoke her—to get something other than this blank space between us.

"Don't pity me. If that's what you're thinking, what you're hiding. I don't—"

"I don't pity you, Aidan."

I swallowed and ran a hand over my face. "No?"

Something in her shifted. I couldn't have said what, but it was like her *energy* shifted from standoffish to almost predatory. Her eyes slipped from my neck, where I swallowed again, down to my chest, where my shirt stuck to me like a second skin, and continued their path right down to my dirt-covered shoes.

When her gaze returned to mine, fire lit low in my gut. My breath came in odd, uneven gusts. She took a step back, hands laced behind her. "No. There's nothing pitiful about you."

With that, she turned and left, confirming that these women loved to make an exit. And more importantly, leaving me more confused than I'd been since she'd interrupted her houseguest and revealed herself as Madeline Reynolds.

CHAPTER SIXTEEN

Maddie

Aidan Wallace's mini-me furrowed his brow as he read his book on the couch of my living room. It'd taken no small amount of insisting on Juliet's part to get him inside, but Aidan had finally acquiesced when she'd promised to send him back when he wore out his welcome.

It'd been two hours and the kid had done nothing but sit there and read. Truly. He'd be finished with the book before the day was done. I would bet a thousand dollars he had at least one more book in his pack.

"Do you need a snack or anything?" I asked him, antsy for... something.

He looked up, taking a minute to find and focus on me like he'd been so engrossed in his reading he couldn't quite reconcile the reality of his surroundings. "No, thank you. I appreciate the offer, though."

I stifled a grin at his manners and even the way he

spoke. He really was a mini-Aidan—consummately polite and well-spoken. Granted, the small Wallace didn't have that thread of something rough and gritty underneath that made my stomach clutch, but that would be weird for a kid, so that was probably good. In Luca, this gangly bookworm made me want to tuck him into my pocket and make sure no one was ever mean to him.

Um. Okay, weirdo.

I shook off that oddly protective thought. "Okay. Just let me know. I'll be around."

"Thank you. I think I'm supposed to go meet my great-aunt out front in thirty minutes, so I'll be out of your way soon."

I wiped a rag across the immaculate counter. "You're not in the way. You should feel free to come in if you're back tomorrow."

He looked uneasy. "I'm not sure if I will be. I think I'll be at the Night in Bloom meeting with my dad tomorrow, but I'll check."

I smiled even as an annoying little streak of *Aidan won't be here either?* shot through me. "No problem. Offer stands."

He nodded briskly. "Okay. Cool. Thanks."

I waited, wondering if there was anything I could say that would draw him out. Then I saw it. His book. "Is that *The Two Towers?*"

His head shot up. "Have you read it?"

I grinned. "You're talking to a true-blue Tolkien lover. Is this your first time reading it?"

He outright beamed at me and launched into an explanation of his reading experience thus far. How he'd read the full series several times, but every read through brought him more insight, more detail, and he couldn't get enough. Then he basically blew my mind with his interpretation of how Tolkien casts good and evil, the decision to journey alone versus with a group, and how prejudice influences the choices of so many of the characters.

It was the most interesting discussion I'd ever had with a kid, and probably one of the best about the books themselves. *Wow.*

A knock on the back door interrupted us. Aidan stood outside the glass pane, hat pulled low and the man himself looking sweaty and earthy and frankly delicious. I had never realized how appealing I found men who weren't afraid to get dirty or hands-on, but my attraction to Aidan seemed only to grow every time I saw him working in the back.

I popped up and ran to open the door. "Hey, sorry. We got caught up talking about *Lord of the Rings.* Come in." I gestured for him to enter, but he inched back.

"No, my boots are a mess. My aunt will be here in a few, so I thought I'd grab him, get him out of your hair." His eyes flicked to my ponytail, my neck, then back to my eyes.

"Uh, okay. Why don't I have him meet you out front?"

He nodded, stepping all the way back. Luca had already grabbed his bag, so I shut the back door and led him to the front.

"This is a huge house, but it's nice. It's not sterile or cold."

Sterile? I'd already been impressed with him based on our book chat and the way he spoke, but more and more, I was getting the sense that he might be advanced in some way. Just in the way he said things more than the words themselves. I walked him out, not even pretending I didn't want to talk to Aidan and meet his aunt.

Somehow, Aidan had beaten us out front despite the route around the house being much longer than cutting through like we had. He leaned down and spoke into the driver's side window, his back and... other assets facing us since the driver had stopped across the street. I gave my full attention to Luca as we approached, reassuring him I wanted him to come in again tomorrow and telling him we'd have another book chat soon.

"Bye! Thanks, Maddie!" He trotted around the car and slumped into the back.

Aidan stepped away and patted the top of the car, ducking to wave at Luca. I made sure my eyes were safely removed from his person when he turned around, but they were pulled right back to him as he walked across the street.

Oddly, I hadn't seen him walk much. I was constantly turning and walking away from him. I'd seen him shoveling, crouching to pull weeds, sawing branches, and helping with planting. I'd seen him standing and surveying parts of the yard or directing the backhoe or nodding as he listened to his crew.

The walk? It got me. It did.

Nate had once told me that I only ever dated suit-wearing vampires and that was why I'd always found his best friend and Army buddy, Eric Wolfe, to be so hot. Truly, I'd had a crush on Eric from the minute I'd seen him, but he'd been married then, so it wasn't like I'd ever had a prayer. He was just such a strong, capable man, and he didn't saunter or swagger around. He didn't need to. Nate's point about the vampires wasn't wrong, though I doubted Chadwick or any of the men from my string of bad dates and failed relationships really hunched over their computers all that much. They were Wall Street types, always interested in me for my business connections and considerable wealth. They had the designer suits and shoes, and the attitude to match.

Aidan had that thing Eric had. He seemed completely capable of anything. He probably knew how to change his own oil and fix his furnace, and he clearly knew how to keep things alive. All skills I couldn't even begin to attempt.

My parents would scoff at the idea of doing any of that, save *maybe* gardening. But they'd want a garden full of things other people mostly took care of with a small section for roses or a greenhouse with orchids that required minimal effort beyond occasional attention and clear instructions from a paid housekeeper or gardener.

Aidan stopped a few feet from me and set his hands just above the worn-in utility pants riding his hips. "I know it looks a mess right now, but we're getting there. We'll have the terraces done today, and we'll begin building the rock wall. It should be shaping up by late next week, and you'll have your space to yourself again soon enough."

"I'm not worried."

"Good. And I hope Luca wasn't a bother. It was very kind of you to invite him in."

"He's great. He seems very smart."

A smile flashed but his eyes widened. "Yes. I'm just trying to keep up."

I chuckled at the chagrin on his face. "I doubt that. You seem like a good dad."

His brow furrowed. "You think?"

"I do. He seems very comfortable in his own skin. Happy." That wasn't a given for all kids, and I imagined all the more so for a child who'd lost one of his parents.

His eyes caught mine, our gazes locking. I wasn't sure how, but we stood only a foot or so away now. Had I moved closer, or had he?

"Thank you for saying that. I hope it's the case."

I nodded, my heart fluttering for no good reason except

I was finally standing closer to him. Not close enough, but the distance between us had beat out a low-level pulse of disappointment since the second time I'd seen him. I wanted to erase all of it. To start over.

And that's what I decided. No more of this tiptoeing. Maybe we couldn't dive in and date—maybe he wouldn't have done that anyway, now that I knew he had a son to think about. But we could be friends, couldn't we?

"Can we start over?"

His eyes narrowed. "How so?"

I huffed out a breath to calm my racing heart. "It's been weird since we had coffee. I'm so glad to see you after so long. And even if it's not what I'd want, I would like for us to at least be friends. We're going to see each other every day for the next few weeks at least, and it just seems silly to be at odds like this. Don't you think?"

He squinted back, all seriousness on that gorgeous face, but nodded. "Sure. Yes. I do agree."

I pressed my lips together to stay the grin. He didn't seem completely pleased by this, but frankly, I wasn't either. It was only a better option than nothing.

"Good." I held out a hand, like we needed a handshake to seal the deal.

His eyes practically burned into my own, but he slipped his hand in mine. My heart jumped and twisted as butter-flies took wing as his palm slipped against mine. His strong fingers, roughened with work and the labor of his job, brushed against my wrist before we both raised and lowered the connection between us.

And then we let go. And I knew very well that friend-ship wouldn't ever be enough for me.

CHAPTER SEVENTEEN

Aidan

The Night in Bloom planning meeting wrapped up at just after one. Today, we had the fire chief, sheriff, and a few people from the mayor's office in to make sure our designs were up to code. Since the event was outdoor at a park to begin with, we rarely had issues, but always best to get buy-in before we actually began assembling pieces.

"That went better than I expected," Dahlia said quietly as she piled her things into a large purse.

"That it did. Not sure who we should thank for Carolyn being in a generous mood, but we'll take it."

The usually persnickety staff member from the mayor's office typically fought us on everything. Half the reason we had the chief and sheriff come was to make sure she heard them say they approved our plans in tandem with their actual signatures—this way, there'd be no claims of coercion. And would one normally think coercion was involved in getting approval for floral displays at a local park for a fundraising event? No. No one would not.

Unless one's name was Carolyn Carney. Then all bets were off.

"You two make a good team. Any chance we'll see you tie the knot sometime soon?" The woman in question wiggled her brows at me and Dahlia.

I inhaled slowly, buying time before I said something insulting. I just wasn't in the mood for this nonsense. We'd made clear time and time again that Dahlia and I were not only *not* romantically linked but had never been and never planned to be. And yet, Carolyn loved to continue insinuating that our friendship and cooperation meant we were secretly lovers.

"Funny you should ask, but we're heading to Vegas for a shotgun wedding in about an hour." Dahlia grinned and hooked her arm through mine.

Carolyn clasped her hands in front of her chest like this was a prize. "Really?"

Dahlia dropped my arm and crossed hers. "No. Carolyn, no. Aidan's got his eye on someone else, and me? I've formed a love affair with several fictional men sure to never disappoint."

The woman straightened. "There's no need to be rude about it. It was only a compliment."

She whipped out of the room, heels clacking down the hallway. We'd set up the meeting in the Convention and Visitor's Bureau since they had a meeting room they generously let us use, and it was a more convenient space than having everyone come to the tree farm and more spacious than everyone cramming into the back of Dahlia's shop.

"You're having a love affair with *multiple* men?" I asked, appreciating her handling it this time. Very often, my protests fell on willingly obtuse ears who simply couldn't believe I didn't like—insert woman I worked with or stood near at any given time—or didn't want to be set up with their daughter/niece/granddaughter/hairdresser/sister. Or themselves, if they happened to be one of the four divorced moms in Luca's school who just couldn't take no for an answer.

Dahlia grinned. "Oh, yes. All tall, dark, handsome, and independently wealthy, of course. Some *quite* a bit older than me. It's rather scandalous."

"Sounds it. And now I have to ask, who is it I have my eye on?" I waited for her to grab her last notebook and followed her out of the building.

"Really? You're going to be shy about this? I know you're not exactly a chatterbox, but come on." She frowned enough that it looked like she might actually be disappointed.

"What do you mean?"

Her eyes widened. "Maddie Reynolds?"

My heart kicked. "You know about Maddie?"

She beamed. "Ha!"

I sighed and shook my head, realizing the mistake. "Seriously? I haven't said anything. Who did?"

Dahlia was well-connected in town, so she often had the scoop before anyone else. Fortunately, she didn't tend to perpetuate whatever news or rumors came her way.

"I guess you didn't hear that Maddie came to our girls' night Saturday before last."

This hit me... strangely. It didn't make sense, but I liked knowing this. "Why?"

She swatted me with her notebook. "Because we're amazing and she's new! Why else? Sarah invited her. They know each other from the—" She cleared her throat. "From

Sarah's work. And she fit in with us perfectly, I'll have you know."

A swirl of dread swept through me at the reference to Sarah's work, Saint Security, which meant the whole stalker mess. As much as she'd assured me she was fine, I wanted to hear more about it. Maybe now that we were officially friends, I could bring it up again.

"I'm glad. And I think anyone who's lucky enough to fold in with you all is genuinely blessed."

She blinked a few times, then exhaled. "You know, you are kind of ridiculous. You're exactly the hot single dad trope, with more than a little bit of cinnamon roll."

My turn to blink at her. "I have no idea what that means."

She waved me away. "Whatever. Point is, I know you like Maddie. I know she liked you, and she told us a bit about how you two met. But now seeing your reaction? Totally obvious. So? Are you taking her to Night in Bloom?"

I pulled out my phone and studied it, willing Luca or John or *anyone* to call me. I didn't want to say that I wasn't taking her, because just the suggestion made my stomach twist with anticipation. Stupid, completely misguided anticipation, sure, but that didn't stop my mind from racing toward the idea like it was made for me. Never mind the fact that she'd just asked me to be her friend.

Miraculously, my phone did buzz, so I gleefully held it up. "Sorry. Gotta run."

Her mouth dropped open. "Oh, that's mean."

But she smiled, showing my evasive maneuvers were forgiven, and slipped into her car as I pulled the phone to my ear. "Hey, Rich."

"Need you to sign some paperwork. We've got two guys out the rest of the week, so I'll need you to—"

"I'm on it. I'm just leaving my meeting, and so I'll be there soon."

"Good man."

I ended the call and exhaled slowly, pushing away the frustration that cropped up every time he called. I loved the man. He'd been my father-in-law for eight years before we lost Vivienne and another eight since. But the call was unnecessary. I'd told him we were missing men. I'd told him I'd be there to run through the cutting we had scheduled tomorrow and would do the prep today.

I'd been managing his business full-time for more than two years and had a hand in it for more than seven. It was always supposed to be temporary, but things were shaping up much differently than I'd planned. I worried that maybe they were looking exactly as he'd hoped, and that was why he and Martha were dragging their heels on listing the place. He'd seemed amenable when I'd suggested we sell it this summer. We were doing everything we could to make it show-ready and saleable. Meanwhile, I recently found out he'd spent all his time applying for grants and who knew what else to assist since it was a sustainable project and somehow qualified. I'd stayed out of all of that with one focus: sell the farm, free them up to be fully retired, and free myself up to live my own damn life.

The only problem? I had a feeling they didn't have the same thing in mind.

Dahlia pulled up next to me and rolled her window down. "Oh, hey, did I mention I got a few new recruits for planting this weekend?"

With all the legal and support logistics in place after this meeting, this weekend, we'd begin some of the initial planting for the show. We'd gussied up the beds, brought new displays in, and then the day of, Dahlia would bring in her arrangements. We'd decided we needed a lot more help this year than we'd had last year, so we'd both been tasked with bringing in ten volunteers. Something about the glint in her eye told me I wouldn't need to ask, but I did anyway. "Who'd you get?"

She grinned. "All the girls, of course. And my new friend, Maddie Reynolds."

CHAPTER EIGHTEEN

Maddie

I should probably feel embarrassed by how long the week had felt without Aidan here the last few days. I'd seen him on Tuesday. We'd agreed to be friends. Then... nothing. His crew had showed up every day with two new men I hadn't met—they must've been the ones he'd stepped in to replace.

Could I have texted? Called? Sure. But was I going to? No. Absolutely not. Because as much as I'd declared we were going to banish our weirdness and be friends, I didn't know how to get there.

"What if you ask him to dinner? Invite him and Luca so it's clearly not a date, and see how that goes?"

Juliet's suggestion kept swimming around in my head. She'd left two days ago, which contributed to the way the week stretched out and dragged.

In my normal life, weeks flew by. I'd settle in on a

Monday and what felt like hours later, my Friday agenda would be getting checked off and Anthony would be listing what he had booked for the weekend. At one point, I'd relished it.

I hadn't missed that pace—much of me had dreaded returning to it and knew I needed this break to circle back around to being able to tolerate it. And yet this week? I'd take it.

It was weird to be here without plans or obligations. I'd done every bit of work I could on the two projects I'd promised to wrap up. Now I was just pacing the house, making odd desserts that didn't taste as good as they looked on the box I'd bought from the market. No-bake Oreo cake batter pops? Not actually very good at all. Far inferior to a plain and simple Oreo.

A text came in as though Juliet knew I was thinking about her. *"Just text him. Invite him to dinner. Dazzle him with your planting abilities tomorrow and all will be well."*

I missed her. I always did—we only saw each other in person a few times a year these days. But right now, I missed her so fiercely it made my head ache. It had to be thanks to knowing it'd likely be a solid six months before I'd see her again. Maybe I could fly out and track her down in the fall, but who knew what I'd be doing then?

My stomach sank because actually, I did know. I'd be back in New York, back to my regularly scheduled programming. Because I had to be. Because that was the plan.

I groaned aloud, glad that Anthony was taking some well-deserved vacation and wasn't there to hear me. Security was off-duty, too, thanks to the surveillance of the property Wilder had set up and the surprisingly quick quelling of the hysteria over the stalker incident. Instead of finding me here, people had swarmed Saint Security and had been flatly and entirely shut down by Wilder and his partner, Bruce.

Good men.

"Fine, woman. I'll do it," I said aloud to Juliet's text, then followed it with sending that very response. And then I did the weirdest thing—I called Aidan instead of texting because I didn't think I could handle a slow back-and-forth and potentially getting ghosted. This way, I could leave a message, get it all out there, and I'd see him tomorrow at the planting and he could decide whether he wanted to pretend he'd never heard the message or not, like all normal people did.

But instead of ringing through to voicemail, he answered. "Hello?"

Wait. That couldn't be Aidan. "Luca?"

"Yeah?"

"This is Maddie Reynolds. Is your dad around?"

"Oh! Hi, Maddie. Let me get him. He just got out of the shower. Hold on a sec." The line went completely silent—he must've muted himself—and after a beat said, "Okay, he's getting some pants on, but he'll be here in a sec."

I covered my mouth so he couldn't hear me laugh, even as I banished the rather tempting mental image of a shirtless Aidan wrestling on his pants from my head. Only a child would tell me all those details. He was even a little old to be giving me that level of information, but somehow, it fit. I wondered if he was a bit like my friend Julian—a little too smart to set people at ease and a little less socially capable than most. I had a bit of that going, too. I'd learned how to mask it over the years, but I'd never had the social graces my brother Nate had. My parents still bemoaned the fact that he wouldn't leave the military and do something that would capitalize on all that charisma.

"Maddie, hi. Sorry about that." Aidan sounded out of breath.

"Hi. Sorry to interrupt."

"No problem. What can I do for you?"

My heart sank a bit. That was a very familiar response. In fact, it was fairly unfriendly and much more businessy. I didn't want Aidan my landscaper. I wanted Aidan my friend.

"I'm hoping it's something I can do for you. I'd love it if you, and Luca would save me from a Saturday night alone and join me for dinner tomorrow night." I rolled my eyes at myself. Why did I have to highlight the *aloneness* of it all?

"Uh, sure. Of course. Do you have a time in mind?"

We talked details, and right when we'd hang up and I could wallow in the questions running through my head about why I was so willing to throw myself under the bus with this guy, he kept the conversation going.

"Why would you be alone?"

I swallowed a little thrill of excitement that he'd kept it going and embarrassment that I'd made my loneliness so blatant. "Hmm? Oh, Juliet left on Wednesday. And Anthony is on vacation—much needed after the last few months."

"Ah, I see. What about you? Will you get to take vacation?"

I paced the kitchen, adrenaline making me restless. "This time in Silverton *is* my vacation."

"Oh, right. Of course."

"Well, I'm going to run and get some work done, but I'll see you tomorrow?"

"Yes. See you tomorrow, Maddie."

"Bye, Aidan."

I arrived three minutes early. Dahlia waved me over and gave me instructions—how to space the plants, a quick review of how to actually plant something, and finally, where to find her after I finished. I hadn't realized how big this would be, but it was a fairly large park with a central meeting area that had natural shade thanks to towering pines and aspens. She disappeared with a roll of her eyes when someone called her away. I was curious enough what made sweet, friendly Dahlia react that way that I tried to see who'd elicited that response from her but sadly missed it.

The bed I'd been tasked with planting was part of the edible section. Apparently, several local chefs had worked together to design this section that would later act as a community garden. I loved the idea and wanted to talk to Aidan about including something like this in my own yard—I didn't cook much, but I could use basil, oregano, and chives without too much angst.

I couldn't recall the last time I'd dug around in the dirt or planted something. Anytime I had one of these thoughts, it made me realize how little I'd been living. I loved nature and trees. My brother was an avid hiker, skier, outdoorsy type of guy in his own way, and I used to join him a few times a year. But in the last handful or more, those trips had dwindled, and my exposure to the natural beauty of this world, the feel of a bulb or roots in my hands, the tang of moisture-darkened soil, had been all but erased.

This realization gave my work a new level of pleasure as I layered in dirt around my current little plant and relished the heat and the give of the soil as I pressed it gently into place.

"Nice work here."

The masculine voice startled me but sent a pleasing little thrill in its wake. Or maybe that was the scent of the lemongrass I'd been enjoying for the last hour as I lined the bed with it.

"Thank you. I can follow instructions with the best of them," I said, glancing over my shoulder to give him a smile. The quick look showed me Aidan in utility pants, a T-shirt, same familiar hat, and opaque sunglasses staring down at me where I kneeled on a soft mat next to the dirt.

He dropped into a squat. "Let me help you wrap these up. We're going to double our efforts to finish the front beds before lunch today. Some of the bushes will need some time to root, so I want those in first."

He smelled like mint and dirt, and he was melting my brain by being so close. He was masculine and rugged in the way he'd been at my house, but this morning, after not seeing him for a few days, he turned my insides to mush. He was so much *more* than simply a man in that moment. What a silly thought, but here he was being all sexy and capable and down to earth in a way I wasn't sure I knew how to resist. *What is happening to me?*

Yet again, I had the thought that I hadn't been this drawn to someone physically in... ever. But the same could be said for the man, not just his face and body, and I didn't know where that left me except tripping over my, "Okay. Sure."

He dug and I unpotted, pinched the roots like Dahlia had shown me, then set it in the hole. We both patted around and moved to the next one. A few minutes later, we had finished. He stood, then held out a gloved hand to me. I took it with my bare one, and he pulled me to standing.

"We've got to get you some gloves."

I looked at my soil-stained fingers still resting in his glove. "They'll wash."

His brows jumped enough I could see them over his glasses. "Maybe. But they'll wash easier if you wear gloves. Plus, we've got some roses going in later, and you don't want to snag on a thorn."

I couldn't even see his eyes, but I felt a bit mesmerized by his holding onto my hand, concerned for their welfare. Thankfully, that thought shook me from the daze of his proximity, and I removed my hand. Was I *that* desperate for attention that his basic concern for me sent me into a brain fog?

It went on like that, though. Not just for me, but for everyone. Aidan was the dad to the entire volunteer crew of more than twenty people. He made sure everyone had gloves. He forced water breaks on those planting in the direct sun beds. He walked around with sprayable sunscreen as the sun rose high in the sky. They brought in sandwiches donated by the diner, and he handed out napkins, then collected trash. Luca was right there with him, emulating the paragon of care.

I shouldn't have been surprised. From the minute I met him, he'd given me this feeling like I was surrounded. Not in an intimidating way or like he wanted to impress me. More like he had everything covered. It was that capability. Even before I'd known he was a dad or just how much he was capable of, I'd sensed that.

And when I left hours later to get cleaned up before our dinner, he was still working. He'd thanked every single person, sending them home with thanks and a smile. He'd patted my shoulder and thanked me, too.

And I'd left relishing that I'd see him again tonight. That craving for more of his time and attention might've signaled just how lonely I'd been, but I didn't care. I never shied away from admitting weaknesses in my professional life, so why did I resist that so aggressively in my personal arena? Clearly, my methods the last few years had failed on that front, no question. So that stopped now.

I couldn't wait to see him for dinner, and if that made me weak? Well, no one could be strong all the time.

CHAPTER NINETEEN

Aidan

I hadn't been nervous for a date in a long time. Maybe my track record set me up to anticipate failure, or maybe I'd always mentally prepared for the pity that came. Whatever the case, even though this *wasn't* a date, as evidenced by my son fidgeting next to me at the front door, I was still nervous.

Maybe because I'd spent all day trying not to just stare at her. Madeline Reynolds, with her grass-stained knees and shorts revealing long, tanned, gorgeous legs... *yeah*. Not exactly friendly feelings.

A few seconds after we rang the bell, she pulled the door open. I hadn't expected her to be the one to answer, nor did I expect the sight of her smiling at me like she was genuinely glad I'd showed up to hit me right in the ribs.

"Welcome! Please come in." She stepped back, a short white dress swishing around her knees, and waved us in, greeting Luca with enthusiasm that seemed surprisingly genuine.

Though why surprising? What had I experienced of her that hadn't been like that? So far, she'd been real with me—direct, even. Maybe it came from the lingering twinge of regret over the reality that both of us had omitted large parts of ourselves the first time we met?

"Thank you for inviting us, Ms. Reynolds." Luca handed her a paper plate with cookies covered with plastic wrap that didn't stick to the bottom.

Perhaps that was the source of my anxious thoughts tonight—we were the paper plate in her multi-million-dollar home.

"Please call me Maddie. You did earlier, right? We're friends, aren't we?" She smiled at my son.

Luca grinned. "I guess we are since we know we're both Tolkien nerds. It's just... my dad said we should be polite, and—"

"If she says to call her Maddie, then you do that," I interrupted, before he could throw me under the bus and reveal all my secrets.

Her lips pressed together like she found that humorous but wouldn't reveal it. I found myself riveted on the hope of her smile, but she simply nodded, and Luca shrugged.

He'd told me all about his conversation with her earlier this week—about how rare it was to find a girl who liked the books as much as he did. I gently suggested there were probably lots of girls who liked *Lord of the Rings* but that maybe he hadn't met them yet, at which he scowled but seemed to reluctantly agree.

Maddie nodded decisively. "Exactly. We're agreed. You'll call me Maddie."

She glanced up and gave me a secret smile like it was

just between us. This adult moment shared, our amusement over blatant, honest Luca, had me feeling like I wanted her on my team indefinitely.

My insides dipped. *Pathetic.*

"I'm about done with everything—just need to drain the pasta in another two minutes. I hope that's okay?"

She said this as she bustled into the kitchen, and I made the heroic effort to not admire the slim line of her neck or the way the dress hugged her torso and flared out at her hips.

"I love pasta. We have it at least once a week because it's cheap and filling." Luca slipped onto a barstool and opened his book.

"I love it, too. Like Gollum loves the precious. And you're not wrong about the cheap and filling part," she said, clearly still charmed by him and not annoyed he'd already dived back into the world of orcs and hobbits.

A timer beeped and Maddie whirled and pressed a button on the stove. I set down the bottle of wine I'd brought and moved to the sink to wash my hands. She pulled a pan from the stovetop, and I stepped in and grabbed the handles of the giant stainless steel pasta pot.

"Oh, thank you."

"I'm more comfortable put to use." I glanced at her before turning toward the sink. The reward? A pleased little grin she tucked away before she spoke again.

"I appreciate that. You do realize I'm perfectly capable of dumping that, right?"

I poured the pasta into a waiting strainer sitting in the deep stainless sink. "I imagine you're perfectly capable of just about anything. My doing this is no reflection of whether I think you have the ability and more to do with the fact that I feel fundamentally uncomfortable standing by and watching people do things I could be helping with."

I set the steaming pot aside and turned to find her squinting at me, lips tucked in.

"Bad answer?"

She shook her head once. "Nope. Perfect answer."

Luca's eyes flicked to me, then away, then back again.

I didn't hide my amusement. "Need something?"

"Can I be excused?" he asked.

"You got big plans?"

I could feel Maddie watching the exchange. She sat back in the comfortable dining chair like she had nowhere to be, cradling a cup of tea.

An exaggerated smile covered Luca's face. He'd entered that in-between stage, where he didn't have a baby face anymore, but he wasn't quite a teen, and times like these I couldn't help but think his eyes and teeth were endearingly too big for his head.

"Thought you could carry on some adult conversation, and I could read quietly in the corner?"

Maddie's chuckle made me look at her in time to see her grinning at him. She raised her brows at me like she couldn't wait to see my response.

"Sure, bud. You can hang out wherever Maddie says is okay."

Luca's big eyes swung to our host, who smiled brightly back at him.

"I was just going to see if your dad wanted to step out onto the deck and enjoy the view now that the sun is setting. You're welcome to join us and sit in a chair out there, but anywhere in the kitchen or living room is fine, too."

Luca nodded and excused himself to the living room. Maddie rose, so I followed, collecting the last of the silverware and glasses so she wouldn't have to clear the table later.

"Oh, thank you. You—" She shook her head. "Thanks."

I nodded, pleased she seemed to accept the help without insisting she didn't need it. For a woman who had hired help in several different capacities, the fact that she'd cooked and served the meal herself came as its own surprise. But her ease and casual way of doing things—family style served from the stove, tea and the cookies we'd brought for dessert—it all felt so normal.

Nothing like I'd assumed. I'd thought at the very least she'd have a personal chef, who I'd been certain existed, cook for us. During the meal, we talked about everything from cooking tomato sauce to the finer merits of Mithril as a defense against orcs. We really covered the full gamut, and the fact that Maddie held her own in everything from tomato selection to the most trivial details of my son's *Lord of the Rings* obsession had my mind racing.

"Thank you for coming tonight. I'm glad we could do this," she said as I closed the door to the deck behind me.

"Me, too."

She leaned on the banister and looked out at the sunset. Predictably for this property, it was astounding. The sky's pinks and oranges bursting above us cast her in a warm glow as I approached.

"I made sure not to plant anything that'll grow tall enough to disturb the view. It's all shrubs out that way other than what you've already got coming up here." I pointed to the copse of aspen trees on the south side. "Those boys will get tall on you, but they'll frame the view like the curtains of a stage."

She didn't turn toward me when she said, "That's a nice image. I like the way you put things."

Warmth suffused me. I wasn't an eloquent man—at least, I didn't think of myself that way. Someone as highly educated and sophisticated as Maddie probably knew all kinds of intellectually brilliant people. Heck, she was one of those people, based on the handful of interactions we'd had. So her thinking I said things she liked? It pleased me.

We watched the sunset a while longer before I gathered up the courage to ask her what I'd wanted to for days now. I hoped it wouldn't ruin everything we'd slowly rebuilt.

"Can I ask about what happened? The stalker?"

She sighed, her shoulders deflating before she stood tall. The furrow at her brow shot me right back to the last time I'd asked her about it. "Please, just tell me to shove it if you don't want to talk about it."

She tilted her head to the side. "Why do *you* want to talk about it?"

I exhaled and gazed out at the desert sunset, wondering how I could put this that didn't sound like a come-on. "I realize that a few hours together months ago doesn't mean I knew you or know you now, but something feels different."

Her brows jumped. "Could it be that you know who I am now?"

I was shaking my head before she'd even finished. "No. I mean, yes, I do, and that gives some insights, I guess." I ran a hand over my too-long beard. "I just keep thinking how scary it must've been. Wondering if you knew about it for long. Wondering if you were hurt. If you're still dealing with any of it."

Her eyes were on mine, studying me. I couldn't tell what she was gauging or what she expected, but she sighed again. "I was in a pretty bad place coming here a few weeks ago. It'd been months with this guy leaving me notes, sending me things. There was an issue with my security team, and I'd wanted an extended break, but I stopped sleeping. I couldn't remember basic things because I was so stressed and exhausted, and I worried I'd make a mistake I couldn't fix if I didn't remove myself. I couched it in the shell of a sabbatical, which isn't all that typical, but it's more acceptable than 'I have to take time off because this stalker is freaking me out so much I can't sleep or think.'"

She forced a laugh but my heart twisted, wretched with the thought of her so stressed and scared she couldn't do what she loved—work. I heard the fear and pain and regret, and I guessed there were many other thoughts and feelings underneath.

"I'm so sorry."

"I'm just glad it's over. The day we ran into each other, I was finally starting to wrap my head around life without that cloud hanging over me, and seeing you..."

I didn't know if this would cross a line, but I couldn't stop myself from reaching for her. "Come here, please."

She looked at me askance but stepped closer. I kept her gaze as I slowly wrapped my arms around her and held her close.

CHAPTER TWENTY

Maddie

Aidan's arms were as strong and appealing and safe as I remembered. Granted, the night we met, the kiss, and brief embrace we'd shared, hadn't been on the heels of the most traumatic experience of my life. I hadn't worried about *safe*, then.

But he had been like that the first time, too. There was no other explanation for why I'd been willing to talk with him—to even stay at that bar without security nearby—if I hadn't felt he was safe on some level. Maybe we could blame a bit of that on his ridiculously appealing looks, too, but I saw plenty of beautiful men, and I certainly didn't talk to them all.

Granted, they didn't have that *thing* that Aidan possessed—that rough, capable handsomeness. Add to that the whole loving father and devoted son-in-law, and he was catnip of the highest order.

I wrapped my arms around him so he'd know this wasn't a transgression. If only he knew how welcome it was. Juliet hugged me. She was a naturally physical person—she touched shoulders, held hands, hugged, kissed cheeks. The woman starved for affection at times, but she'd admit it. I felt it the same, but only she knew that about me.

Breathing in the warm scent of him sent champagne bubbles bursting in my belly. He had this clean, warm scent that was part soap, part clean detergent, part spicy, manly deodorant or something. All completely appealing to me.

He tucked his head in close and spoke in that low, sturdy voice I'd dreamed of hearing. "I'm so glad you're okay. I'm sorry you had to go through that. And I'm glad you came back here."

On reflex, I turned my face toward his and the sides of our heads grazed each other, my temple to the curve of his jaw. It was intimate. This was close. Our bodies were just shy of fully touching—just whispers of breaths apart.

He couldn't know how much the possibility of seeing him had driven me to return. I wouldn't admit that to Juliet when she'd prodded, or even myself, but I'd known it was true. I hadn't wanted to take the crap storm of a stalker to my brother's doorstep. My parents weren't an option because we would've argued nonstop. But coming back to Silverton, where I'd had this tiny glimpse of a fantasy life? It'd seemed like the answer to a question I'd been asking ever since I'd left all those months ago.

His muscles tensed with one last squeeze. I thought about resting my head down on his shoulder or sliding my hands up his back and over what were definitely beautifully defined muscles. But before any of that could happen, he released me, stepping back and far enough away I couldn't easily touch him.

"Sorry. I don't know if that's legal in our friendship or not. I hope you'll forgive me if it wasn't." He looked back out at the sky, hands gripping the banister.

"Don't be silly. Of course it's fine." *In fact, I'd like another, please. And another after that.*

The slight flush to his cheeks made me wonder if he really had no idea how much I wanted to have him close. Maybe my suggestion of friendship had confused things, but it certainly seemed preferable to the tundra that stretched between us before. I attempted to lighten things. "I've realized a lot is lacking in my life. That might sound insane to say, but one of the things I've been missing is high quality hugs."

Surprise flitted across his handsome face. "A truth no more."

I grinned. "Well, there's one thing down."

He inched toward me, his eyes instantly so full of fire, I could hardly stand to return his gaze.

"What else is lacking?"

Heat sizzled through me. Goodness, the man had a way of making normal words sound suggestive. Paired with this intense stare, my heart rate had tripled.

"Simple joys. Rest. Deep relationships." *Love.* But I couldn't say that now. It'd be too obvious, and I didn't like how obvious I'd already been. He'd been the one to reject me, after all.

He nodded but stepped back to the edge of the porch. "I can relate to that feeling—the sense that something is missing."

I took up position next to him, our elbows brushing when he shifted. He'd given me facts about his life, but I felt farther from him now than I had months ago when all I had to go on was the fantasy of our singular evening together. "What is it for you?"

He squinted out at the sky, though it wasn't bright anymore. "Similar as you, I think. I'd probably add freedom."

I straightened, my brows high on my forehead. He saw it and continued without my having to ask.

"I've been stuck a long time. Everything I told you that night about the obligations to family is true. The tree farm is my wife's family business. But what her parents don't know is that she was going to suggest they sell. She'd made up a packet of information, had a sales plan and even a few potential buyers identified."

My throat tightened, guessing what came next.

"She died a few weeks before she planned to present them with the information. And in the wake of their loss, I've stepped in. Even more so since my father-in-law had some health issues a few years back. It's taken over, and I can't leave, but more every day, I feel like I can't stay."

While I didn't have parents-in-law, I knew the sense of obligation well. "I'm sorry. Is there any chance you can convince them to sell it?"

He shrugged. "I've been working on that. We're supposed to be showing it in July, actually. I have a sales agent and everything worked up, but my father-in-law is dragging his feet. I don't know..." He ran a hand over his beard again.

The desire to touch his face gripped me in a tight, unrelenting fist. I shoved the impulse out of my mind. "Hopefully, he'll rally. Maybe he'll get excited when the time comes—that flexibility of true retirement?"

His face betrayed his doubt. "Maybe."

"And you'd work more on your own business if you didn't need to do so much for them?"

He nodded. "I've missed it. Your place is the first larger project I've had in almost a year. I know it's selfish. I owe them. It's not hurting me to manage things for them. They deserve—"

I set a hand on his where it rested on the blond wood of the deck railing. "How do you owe them?"

His eyes focused on where we touched. "I can't explain it, but I do. They lost so much."

"And you?"

His serious gaze shifted to meet mine. "I did, too. She was..." He trailed off but shook his head.

My heart clutched. We weren't romantically involved, but a desperate little voice shouted, *What was she!?* Was she the love of his life and that's why he wasn't interested?

He shifted gears after a beat. "But it's not the same. I've got my whole life ahead of me." He shook his head again, even as he said it. "And at the same time, I feel like I've been losing time. I hate that I feel this way, but I'm starting to resent the obligation. I'm not that man—I shouldn't feel that way."

"You can feel however you need to," I said, parroting something my therapist had said to me just last week.

A soft laugh emerged. "John says the same thing to me."

"Your cousin?"

He gave me a half-smile. "Yes. I'm sure you'll meet him. I'm surprised he didn't track you down today to introduce himself because he's about the most outgoing person you'll meet, but I'm assuming he's going to wait for me to do it."

Something fluttered in my chest. They'd talked about me. Such a silly thought considering how many people had talked about me in a hundred different contexts, and yet knowing this man had discussed me with his cousin and best friend? *Sigh.* "I'd like to meet him. Maybe you can both come to the little garden party next week when the yard's done?"

He made an uncertain face. "I don't normally attend things with clients."

"You wouldn't be here as Aidan Wallace, landscape architect. You'd be here as my friend. The first person I really met in Silverton."

His gaze hooked into mine. "Guess I better make sure we meet that deadline, then."

I grinned. "Guess you better."

CHAPTER TWENTY-ONE

Aidan

I gripped the wheel, then relaxed my hands. Any further sign of nerves and I'd never hear the end of it from John. "Saw that."

Okay. Hearing the end of it was a pipe dream. He'd been dissecting my every move since he entered the car. Apparently, not greeting him had been a sign of nerves. My shoulders were bunched up. My eyes were crazy. Reportedly, I was driving a little slower than normal...

"You saw nothing."

He shifted around in his seat, but I kept my eyes glued to the road ahead.

"I know a nervous Aidan when I see one, so don't go thinking you're fooling me. My question is, why am I your date? Why are you not gonna be there as Madeline Reynolds' date since she clearly has a thing for you?"

I shot him a glare and ignored the little flip in my gut.

"She does not, and it wouldn't be appropriate. I'm not even sure me going in the first place is okay."

"Uh, pretty sure if the hostess invited you, that means it's okay."

We arrived at the neighborhood and rolled through the impressive entrance. The gates stood open tonight, and the security guards waved as we entered. They knew me, and Maddie had likely submitted a list of vehicles to make the process smooth for attendees.

My stomach twisted yet again. The guests tonight would be Silverton's finest and likely then some. I'd heard she had friends coming in from Salt Lake and farther reaches. I had no problem with Julian Grenier or anyone else I guessed would be attending from the local crowd, but hobnobbing with a bunch of rich people and inevitably being introduced as the gardener just didn't sound like my ideal evening.

And yet, here we were.

We pulled up to the house, and I parked a half block away behind another car. John wouldn't stop staring at me as he exited the truck, so I finally gave in to him as we walked toward the house.

"What's going on here, Aid? I don't like seeing you all tense like this." He reached over and shook my shoulder as though to loosen me up.

I shook out my hands. "Yeah. I know. I'm nervous to see her. Nervous to be at this party even though I've seen or talked to her every few days. We're doing well with our friendship, and I don't know why but showing up tonight makes me feel stupid. Like my head's too big for my body and everyone can see."

"You do have an unnaturally large head, but your dark hair and beard hide it well, so no worries."

He jumped away before I could shove him, his gleeful cackle helping to loosen some of the tension that'd wound around my chest in the last hour. It wasn't that I didn't want to be here for Maddie—I did. I hadn't actually seen her in three days, and it'd mostly been from afar. I had the full crew working long shifts, but they'd finished everything yesterday around noon.

We'd texted back and forth a bit. Simple things like how Luca was doing and if she had any friends coming into town for the party. I hadn't really wanted a list or anything, but I could admit I wanted to know if Chadwick what's-his-face would be there. Happily, the answer was that she had a few girlfriends coming, but no mention of Chadwick.

As a rule, I wasn't a big party-goer. I didn't know what to do with my hands at these things. Did we really all stand around and talk? How much could I possibly have in common with these people? If they ran in Maddie's circles, they would undoubtedly be wealthy, brilliant, and transient. Ultimately, not people I'd be likely to see again.

So my nerves tonight were two-fold. First, I was anxious to see how things went with Maddie. Would she be aloof? Friendly? Would she introduce me to anyone and if so, how would she refer to me? All of that was exhausting enough in itself since I didn't remember the last time I'd overthought so many things.

And second was the more general anxiety over small-talking with strangers. Thankfully, my wingman was the king of small talk, so he'd make up the difference for me.

"It'll be great. I can't wait to meet her and get a feel for you two together in a room."

I grunted, clearly displaying my highest levels of sophistication for the night. He chuckled and may have even skipped a little.

"Seriously. I have a feeling it's going to be really easy to tell that there's more than friendship between you, but obviously I have to see for myself."

"We're friends. That's all."

"Mm. Mm-hmm. A friend you had a hot fling with a year and a half ago and that you haven't stopped thinking about since? Yeah. *Friendly*."

"It wasn't a fling. It was a few hours of talking and a kiss." A *great* kiss. But still.

He snapped and pointed at me. "Precisely my point. It was a blip that should've gone down in the history of your life as an interesting evening but instead, you got hung up on it. So now I get to see where things stand."

We reached the door, and I knocked twice in lieu of ringing the bell. "Well, you can shut it for now and—"

"Welcome! Oh. Come in." Anthony grinned and waved us in, shouting, "Maddie! He's here!"

John gave me a wide-eyed look with one of those ridiculous, impressed smiles.

"She's been greeting people in the living room but made me promise to let her know when you arrived." Anthony winked, gesturing for us to move ahead.

It was all a little more casual than I'd anticipated, if Anthony's holler to Maddie, or even referring to her as Maddie versus Madeline, indicated the level of decorum.

We rounded the corner to the kitchen and living area. My heart kicked at the sight of her in a light purple dress that hit just above her knees. Her hair fell in spirals over her shoulders, and she listened intently to what someone was saying to her until something made her look up.

Right at me.

Those eyes hit mine, and I exhaled from the direct hit.

"Hey, there you are! Thank you for coming." She spoke

to me and as she did, set her hand on the arm of the person who'd been speaking to her and moved toward us. In seconds, she'd not only reached us but thrown her arms around me.

She pulled back before I could even respond in kind. Her beaming smile was poison to my anxiety, and at least half of my worry shriveled up in an instant.

"Glad to be here. This is my cousin, John Wallace." Because I'd planned that as my intro, that's what came out. I should've thought more creatively. Something like, *I like your dress* or *you look beautiful* or *let's find somewhere to be alone together*.

Okay, maybe not that last one, though I wished for that with an intensity I hadn't anticipated. I wished I had the boldness to say it and mean it, damn the consequences.

"Nice to meet you, John. Thanks for coming this evening." She let go of me entirely and extended a hand to John, who was absolutely beaming.

"It is a pleasure, Ms. Reynolds. I—"

"Please, just Maddie."

He nodded. "So glad to meet you. Aidan's really enjoyed the project here."

Her eyes glittered. "He does amazing work. I think you'll love it."

John grinned. "I have no doubt I will."

"Well, follow me inside. We're slowly filtering people outside since it's finally starting to cool down. We've got some appetizers ready to come out soon, and I think the music's starting now, too."

Her hand on my back guided me forward, the light contact drawing all my mental and physical attention. The small group she'd been chatting with had made it outside, so John and I continued toward the back deck. I wondered at her warm greeting—did she greet everyone that way? It wasn't that she didn't typically seem friendly or open, but something about being ushered through the door just like the last people had been made it seem suddenly very... planned.

John opened the door, and I moved to follow him out until her hand slipped into mine. Surprise and no small amount of thrill fizzed through me.

"Can I grab you for just a minute?" she asked when I looked back at her.

"Uh, sure. John, I'll—"

"Yep. I'm good. Just come find me." He didn't look back, and I knew he wouldn't have any issues talking with people. I shut the door and turned to her right as she started walking, pulling me along after her through the kitchen and into... the pantry?

She flipped on the light as we entered, guiding me past her, then shutting the door. The small room was probably three by six and held all manner of food.

"Everything okay?" I asked, more than a little off-balance at this detour.

She bit her lip and crossed her arms. "I need to ask you a favor."

"Okay."

"Only for tonight, I promise."

"Uh, okay..."

She shook her head once, frustration so clearly broadcasted in the gesture. "My mother is here. She wasn't supposed to come for another few weeks."

"And you don't get along?"

She exhaled slowly and her eyes shut like she was praying for patience. "It varies. But the bigger issue is that she's renewed her quest to set me up after everything that's happened. She's the reason Chad showed up out of nowhere, and she only backed off because I told her she needed to stop because I was seeing someone."

Surprise and unease hit at the same time. "I see."

She chuckled and looked at her feet before reaching for my hand. "You can't see because I haven't shown you."

I studied her face, working to suss out what this was. Would she say she couldn't be friends now that she was dating someone else? Or... now that she was *saying* she was dating someone else? Would I have to watch her cozy up to another Chadwick what's-his-name and resist eye-rolling all evening?

But before my mind could elaborate on any of those thoughts, she derailed everything.

"I told her I'm dating a nice man named Aidan Wallace. That we've been seeing each other on and off since my first visit here, which is why I haven't seriously dated anyone else. And now, she's bound and determined to meet you for herself."

CHAPTER TWENTY-TWO

Maddie

Aidan blinked back at me like I'd truly stunned him. I probably had.

"I don't understand."

"I'm sorry. I shouldn't have said it, but she kept pushing me and—" I exhaled, beyond frustrated and supremely embarrassed to have to admit this but determined not to deal with any more of my mother's antics. "It seemed like a good idea at the time."

He just stood there, taking it in. His handsome dark brows knit together, and he searched my face like looking *harder* or *longer* might somehow solve this ridiculous puzzle I'd created.

I forced my feet to stay in place and my hands to remain clasped in front of me rather than twist and squirm under his gaze. "I'm sorry, Aidan. I don't want to make you uncomfortable. I know you said you wanted to keep things professional, and I know this is not it. Agreeing to friendship happened after this, and honestly, it was after we'd talked and things were so weird between us. I assumed you and she would never be in the same place so it wouldn't be a problem."

Crap, this was so not ideal. Somehow, I'd genuinely fooled myself into thinking this wouldn't ever affect him, and yet here we were. I was asking him for a favor, and though I'd long since given up the concept of refusing to ask for help, this was particularly humiliating. My lungs felt tight, and I couldn't take a full breath. I huffed, pushing out air.

"Are you okay?"

Aidan reached for me right as I pulled in another long breath. "Yes. I'm just... slightly freaking out. Sorry. This is so stupid."

I paced a small circle in the tight space, wondering why I'd dragged him in here instead of, say, a normal-sized room. Why had I created this problem for myself? And why was something like *this* making me feel so upset, so anxious, so *off*?

We'd barely crossed the bridge from awkward disappointment to friendship. Now this?

"This is fine. We can do this." His hands on my shoulders sent a jolt of energy through me and brought my focus back to him. "I don't mind. I can pretend to be dating you, if that's what you want."

If that's what you want. If I had a desk, I'd let my head drop face down on it with a solid *thunk*. Could he be any nicer, and yet any clearer about how much he didn't want this?

The whining needed to come to an end, though. I'd dug

this hole and now he was going to help me fill it. So... on with it. "You can?"

He nodded. "Of course. We're friends and it's not like..." He trailed off and I got the distinct sense he was censoring himself. "It's fine. I don't know who else is here that might know me, but I can give John a heads-up just in case and we'll handle it. After I do that, you can introduce me to her, and, what? You tell me."

"You seriously don't mind?" Maybe that wasn't quite the right phrasing, but he seemed so certain. And Aidan wasn't a waffler. So far, he'd been certain about everything. Coffee, check. Sustainable plants, check. Not dating, check. Friendship, check.

Fake dating? Apparently also check.

"Maddie, no. I'm fine. It's one night."

And because I didn't want to scare him away from the current plan, I didn't mention it might not be that simple. My mom wasn't flying home until Sunday, which meant I had at least forty-eight hours before I could officially end the ruse. That said, I thought I could avoid going out with her. I could. So it could, hopefully, just be this one night. But if he was up for pretending, I'd take him up on it.

And yet again, Aidan Wallace proves he really is that good of a guy.

He asked to know the details of what I'd told my mother—that we'd met months ago and kept in touch. That when I'd come into town, he'd been eager to see me and we started dating. That he'd been there after the stalker and had been so supportive. That we'd continued dating and it'd gotten serious quickly.

My cheeks had reddened, but I hoped in the dimmish light of the pantry maybe he couldn't tell. Or maybe they were already burning, so he wouldn't see how my little fairytale mimicked actual thoughts and wishes I'd had. *He's amazing, but he can't read minds,* I reminded myself.

And just like that, he slipped out, vowing to find John and let him in on it while I composed myself, then left a few minutes later. If anyone had been watching, they'd assume we'd stolen a moment for ourselves and not that I'd dragged him in there and we'd hatched a plan to deceive my mother.

But this approach was far better than admitting it was casual or that we were just friends. Otherwise, Chad would be back here in days, or another one of her socialite friends' sons would, anyway. I didn't need that. I didn't want it at all.

And it just happened that I was more excited to pretend Aidan was mine than I'd been about anything else in a long time, even if it was couched in mild embarrassment at putting us in this position in the first place. The giddy feeling welling in my throat and the desperate need to keep eyes on him at all times wouldn't let me lie to myself: I wanted this.

Aidan found me talking to a small group about ten minutes later and sent fizz into my veins just by coming near me. Though I'd planned to keep the party small, it'd ballooned to nearly forty people, all of whom stood near high-top bistro tables planted in clusters around the beautiful yard. A bar with a very busy bartender had been erected on the deck, and waiters passed trays of hors d'oeuvres.

In seconds, my mother approached. "Is this him, Madeline?"

Aidan's eyes flicked to me and my breath caught, his

attention on me sending awareness through me like I was surprised by it. I'd arranged this, hadn't I? And yet here he was, clearly playing the part. *I should introduce him.*

But he didn't wait for me to find words. "Aidan Wallace. Nice to meet you, Mrs. Reynolds."

She shook his hand, those shrewd eyes of hers taking in every detail. He'd cleaned up nicely for the evening—dark jeans and a plaid button-up. Not fancy, but we were in the mountains here. People didn't get all dolled up for things like a garden party, nor should they. He looked heart-flutteringly handsome. In fact, I preferred all of Aidan's attire to yet another suit. Seeing him here, like this, made me wonder if I'd ever truly enjoyed dating men in suits. They were the uniform to my other life, the life before, and this was... *now.*

But my mother could price the clothes on his back in seconds the same way I could. The difference? She cared and I couldn't care less.

"You've known my Madeline for how long now?" She withdrew her hand and surveyed him again.

My stomach pitched, the sensation threatening to dim the gauzy glow of Aidan's role as my date—my *man.* Not a surprise that she'd adopted this aloof tone, but I'd hoped for better. It took me right back to when Nate had brought Ariel to Rome and my mother had treated her like a peasant who shouldn't deign to want him. Fortunately, neither one of them had been too fazed by the abrasive lecture we'd all received at dinner about dating "beneath" ourselves, and Nate and Ariel were now married with one child and one on the way.

"Just over eighteen months I believe, right?" Aidan turned his milk chocolate eyes to me.

Oh my. Even standing here next to the firebrand that

was my mother, he made something in me wake up and another more anxious part melt away.

"That's right. We met when I came before the wedding." She'd know which wedding, as we'd only had the one in the family—a fact she never failed to remind me of when I wasn't willingly dating one of her chosen suitors.

"Well, that's quite a courtship, especially considering I just now heard about it." Those brows raised and so many episodes of this exact expression aimed at me over the years flashed through my mind. It made me feel young and naïve, maybe even a little silly, like my not telling her about it meant it couldn't be real. And yes, technically it was fake, but Aidan Wallace had been living rent-free in my head for that long, and that had been very real.

So her comment also sent a flair of frustration zipping through me, needing to counter it.

"We were friends for most of that time, Mother. We only recently started dating." I tipped my head to the side to smile at Aidan. He put an arm around my shoulders in the closest contact we'd had since he'd hugged me. My whole body lit up at his touch, at his soliciting it. Of course, it was for my mother's benefit, but I didn't mind being on the receiving end of contact with him.

"I'm certainly glad we did," he said, a fond smile beaming down at me.

Dang, this guy's good. Aidan didn't really strike me as someone who could pretend. I mean, I'd hoped he could be at least mildly convincing tonight, but as a towering, serious man, I didn't need him to charm my mother. I just needed him not to deny or look horrified when she asked him if we were dating.

I smiled back at him, fully aware it might seem a little dreamy. But who could blame me? He had his arm around me and was gazing down at me with an expression I wished was genuine. *Crap*, I liked him. Even with the pressure of lying to my mother in a crowd of people, I liked him.

And I especially liked the feeling of his arm around me, his hand resting perfectly in the bend of my waist like it'd sat there, belonged there, countless times before. But *oh*, it hadn't. We had barely touched. In the history of our relationship, this contact was precious ground. I wanted to hoard it, memorize it, crawl into a corner and stroke the memory like *the precious*, but regrettably, there was no time for such things.

"And you're in the lawn maintenance business?"

"He's a landscape architect," I practically snapped, yanked from the exultations over his touch. I nearly rolled my eyes at myself for letting her get to me so quickly and wished Nate were here to distract from me. His adorable baby would woo her into sweetness in ways her adult children couldn't. Sadly, I wasn't surprised by my mother's supercilious tone at the mention of his business. More like disappointed. She really wasn't like this all the time, but something about me dating someone not "of our ilk"—shudder. The idea that we were dating beneath ourselves, and once we stopped we'd find happiness, seemed to be her operating thesis these last few years.

I didn't think of humans like that—stacked up on a ladder or whatever it was she envisioned. She saw Aidan as a man I had nothing in common with who lived in a place where I'd purchased a vacation home. And on the surface, it could seem that way.

Underneath it, and what I couldn't tell my mother, was a connection I'd never felt before. He understood the desire for freedom. The feeling that I was a little trapped, a little overwhelmed, and a little lost. He laughed at my jokes and seemed to enjoy who I was regardless of the number on my paycheck or the location of my apartment in New York. He understood *me* in a way I'd only found with Juliet.

Too bad this was one-sided. Or if not one-sided, then certainly dead-ended. Or however you'd describe the fact that he'd clearly said he didn't want to date me once he knew who *me* really was.

Except... here we were. Standing close, shoulders brushing, his fingers splaying along my side with a kind of possessive spread I wouldn't have imagined when I'd hauled him into the pantry minutes ago. The soft smile he gave me, the patience with my mom... it didn't feel fake.

It felt like more. Another fantasy. Another chance to spin a reality where Aidan was mine, and everything was right with the world.

"And you designed Madeline's back yard? It's certainly lovely."

She glanced out over the porch at the stone patio, the beds of drought-hardy bushes and sustainably sourced *everything*. He'd worked with the land in a way that felt kind of magical and made the whole outside of the house feel the same. I'd spent no small amount of time exploring the details of the space long after his guys had given me the tour yesterday afternoon. I'd been excited about seeing the finished product, but the more time I spent outside in my yard, breathing in the mountain air and relishing the determination of the things that grew here, the more I loved it.

Another version of myself might laugh at how cliché the thought was, but it rang true. Allowing myself to stop and smell the actual roses, to feel the velvet of a sage leaf on the pad of my finger, to stand under the shade of the towering aspens with their bleachy trunks and quaking leaves, had awakened me.

Or at least, it'd shaken me from what could easily be called a nightmare and shifted life, especially tonight, into a dream world.

"Thank you. Yes. It's a beautiful piece of land." His humble nod made my stomach flip.

He was adorable. And so sturdy. He didn't shift or try to edge away from the questions, the thinly-veiled criticism in almost every word out of my mother's mouth.

"And your family? How long have they been settled in Silverton?"

"Several generations. My great-grandparents were one of the founding families here."

She nodded. "So your roots run deep."

"Yes, ma'am."

"So you're unlikely to move away from Silverton, I imagine." She stated it rather than posing a question. No hinting for Annette Reynolds, especially not when it came to someone associated with the Reynolds name.

Heat burned in my cheeks, but I pasted on a smile and pressed closer to him, hoping he'd sense my appreciation. I didn't want Aidan offended by her, and he'd done his time. "That's enough of an inquisition, Mother. I think Aidan needs to check in on his cousin."

She waved a hand like it was all the same to her. "I'm only observing the reality, darling. He's a man tethered here in this town, and you're a woman devoted to her work, which happens to be based in New York and LA. I'm not sure how you envision things moving forward, but I hate to see you fooling yourselves—assuming this is even something to consider."

She turned and left, a punctuation mark on the moment in her signature direct-and-slightly-painful style.

It took a few seconds, both of us watching her go, before

I peeled myself away from his warmth. But her parting shot had hit its mark, so I reluctantly let a few inches come between us.

"A woman devoted to her work." I might've stood taller at that description in the past. The idea of devotion to my work had always seemed kind of romantic. Right up until it felt like practically all I had was that devotion, and it was something that would never love me back.

CHAPTER TWENTY-THREE

Aidan

Maddie's mother was, as they say, a piece of work.

I didn't tend to dislike people based on a single interaction because I understood that sometimes, people aren't at their best. This came from several years after losing Viv when all I could do was function. It took everything I had to just get up and take care of Luca, so being friendly? Accommodating? Welcoming? Thoughtful? These were thrown to the wolves of grief. They were qualities I had mined and worked to refine more aggressively in the last four years or so, and I still had a long way to go.

Annette Reynolds clearly had the ability to charm. She fluttered from group to group around the garden and overtly delighted the people she spoke with. Even Quinn Darling and Julian Grenier, both of whom I viewed as generally undelightable, had been ensnared. They were not easily impressed or charmed, and yet she'd had them chuckling cheerily into their champagne glasses while she told them a story.

As the yokel whom she no doubt viewed as the man who wanted to steal away her daughter and ruin all her hopes and dreams, I very clearly didn't rate on the need-to-be-charmed scale. I already had the lingering feeling that I was silly for having thought of her so often, and even dreamed of what it might be like to have something real and long-term with her, before realizing she was... her. But seeing her mother so thoroughly unimpressed with my existence drilled it home.

I was nowhere near good enough for Madeline Reynolds. Maddie and I hit it off. We had great chemistry, and I got a little weak when I talked to her or looked at her too long, but Madeline and I?

What could we possibly even have?

Maddie's hand on me drew my eyes away from her departing mother. Pleasure at the feeling of her fingers on my skin shivered up from my wrist, over my shoulder, to the base of my neck. I'd just had my arm around her, and it'd felt right, but her touching me now, with no one around to see, made my pulse jump anew.

"I'm so sorry." She crushed her eyes closed for a second and sighed. "She can be so rude."

"She's very direct, that's for sure."

She chuckled humorlessly. "Yeah. I'd like to defend her and say she can be really great, but lately, this is what I get. It's something about me and dating and who I'll eventually marry. My brother already ruined her hopes for marrying up, so now it's on me, I guess."

I nodded, pushing away the twinge of regret that news

caused in me. "Well, I think it's safe to say I'm not going to make her list of eligible bachelors."

She stepped closer and surprised me by putting her hand on my jaw, cradling my face. "You're amazing. I'd be lucky to be with someone like you. Don't mistake her opinions for mine."

Her hazel eyes shone with a fierceness I wouldn't have expected except maybe in a boardroom negotiation or... whatever it was she did that made her so formidable in the land of business.

"Thank you." I wanted to say more, to prolong this nearness between us, but John tapped my shoulder. Maddie's hand dropped to her side and she stepped back.

"Sorry to interrupt you two lovebirds, but I wanted to introduce you to some friends, Aidan. They're looking to do some similar work and wanted to speak with you for a bit, if you don't mind."

"Please. I'll see you in a few," Maddie said, then stepped away.

I watched her move across the room, feeling shaken and off-balance yet again.

"Aidan?"

John's voice shook me from whatever daze had come over me, and when I looked up at him, he was smirking wildly.

"Glad you've returned to us. Now, let's talk landscaping."

The next hour and a half moved quickly, primarily thanks to John smoothing the way between conversations with strangers, though he also gave me no small amount of crap for the way I couldn't take my eyes off Maddie. I couldn't deny they sought her out wherever I found myself, but I shoved that off on the whole fake date thing.

"Sure, sure. You just hate to look at her and are only doing it as a sacrifice for the sake of your friendship, is that it?" He crossed his arms and waited, leaning against the kitchen counter, like he had all day.

"Don't be an idiot," I grumbled. He didn't need to know how my body reacted every time I saw her. How I'd hoped she'd come near so I'd have an excuse to put my arm around her again. If this was only for tonight, the clock was ticking toward the end, and soon, I'd be out of excuses. Back to before.

"Me? Oh, between the two of us, the idiot is definitely not me."

"Is this weirdo bothering you, Aidan?" Dahlia Price came up and gave me a side-hug while eying John.

"Now, now, kids. No fighting. We're guests in this home," I reminded them, only partly joking.

John's entire demeanor had hardened. "Don't worry about me. I can keep my mouth shut."

Dahlia's sunny expression dropped. "Is that so? Is that why every time I look at you, I see your giant jaw yapping away, not letting anyone get a word in edgewise?"

"You watching me, Price? Just can't keep your eyes off me, huh? Listen, whenever—"

"Don't even start with me, Wallace. You are a ridiculous human being, you know that?" She turned to me. "I'm heading out. I'll catch Maddie outside, and I'll see you tomorrow, right?"

"Yes, see you tomorrow."

John grumped something under his breath, and I shoved his shoulder. "What is it with you two?"

"What? She started it."

"Come on, man. One minute you fight like siblings, the next you're flirting, and then you're back to fighting." It was truly insane, and since I worked with Dahlia a lot and John backed me up whenever he could, I had a front row seat to their interactions.

If I hadn't witnessed some of their squabbles, I'd think they liked each other. But then they'd have one of these fights and... it just didn't compute for me.

Most people had filtered out by now. The kitchen staff had cleaned up and left only trays of desserts lining the kitchen countertops. I hadn't spotted Maddie's mother in a while, so I figured she must've left. Maddie had walked out with a few friends who'd driven up just for this event. They all seemed like surprisingly nice people. In fact, the worst of the bunch was definitely Annette.

"Guess we should probably head out, yeah? I think you've stayed long enough as the dutiful boyfriend." John's effort to shift away from him and Dahlia worked well.

We wandered up to the front door right as Maddie opened it.

"Hey, sorry. You really didn't need to stay this long, but thank you. You were awesome."

She said this to me, a pleased smile on her lovely mouth.

"My pleasure." Heat shimmered behind my words, in my chest, at my fingertips, where little magnets were drawing me toward her.

"I'm going to wait in the truck. I need to, uh, make a quick call. Take your time, Aidan. And nice to meet you officially and everything, Maddie." John gave a little salute and then practically jogged down the front steps.

"Okay, sure," I said, cheeks heating a little at the obvious exit.

"I really appreciate you playing along tonight. She's only here through the weekend, so it's not a huge deal." Her smile didn't quite touch her eyes this time.

Whether it was the sense that she regretted having introduced me in the first place, or that the night was now over, my heart squeezed and I needed to reassure her. "You're an impressive person, Maddie. And I don't say that because I know your last name now or because I've been in your house. Watching you navigate respecting your mom but figuring out how to give yourself space drilled that home."

She huffed. "If I had any backbone at all, I'd tell her the truth and just deal with it. But right now, this is easier."

"You've been through hell lately. Give yourself a little grace."

She tilted her head like the words didn't quite compute. And then she did it. She rose on her toes and pressed a kiss to my lips—soft, sweet, and far too quickly.

"Thank you, Aidan."

A thrill raced through me, but my words locked up in my throat. I nodded, glancing toward the house, reveling in the odd sense of victory her kiss, her touch, had given me. "I should probably go."

"Of course. You're up early for planting, right?"

"Yep. Bright and early so we get it all done. We're cutting it close this year, but we did the same last year. One of these days, we'll get an earlier start." I babbled like an idiot as though she cared, heat and longing still rushing through me.

I didn't want to leave, but I didn't want to kiss her the way I'd thought about for months with her mother just inside and John likely watching from the truck. And maybe more than that, it'd only leave me with that crushing longing, a feeling I knew so well by now and also couldn't stand. No use kissing her like that again because after that? It'd surely all come crashing down.

CHAPTER TWENTY-FOUR

Maddie

Sunglasses in place because the June sun blazed bright, I did my level best to avoid screeching away from the house. I'd left under the guise of running errands before dinner, but my mother's long look before she went upstairs told me very clearly that she knew I was escaping.

So what if I was? I could admit that I'd met my capacity for her lectures. I needed to recommit to my life in all its facets when I got back. I should consider cutting my time shorter since the stalker situation had "resolved itself." I must remember that Aidan Wallace wasn't the kind of man who could make me happy.

She left no stone of my life unturned to her criticism and suggestion. My hair? It needed to go back to a caramel or blond—the darker color with fading to blond made me look like I was trying too hard. Like an influencer rather than a mature professional. My garden was nice, but without a perimeter gate on this property, I could never expect to be truly safe. This little break was an *interesting sojourn*, but really, it was high time I returned to work and stopped hiding out in the mountains.

And on. And on. And on.

Something was up with her because while she could be critical, I'd always felt like at her heart, she really did root for us. We might make different choices than she would, and she would make her opposition to those choices very clear, but once made, she'd get behind us and she'd bulldog anyone who didn't do the same into a corner.

The woman I'd been dealing with the last few weeks and who now occupied my house like a little troll determined to steal any sense of peace I'd cultivated was someone different.

But for now? Freedom. Fresh mountain air and a destination I felt no shame in pursuing: the community park. The morning was burning off faster than I'd realized, and by the time I pulled into a spot, it was just shy of noon. Based on the last time I'd helped, they would be breaking for lunch.

"Maddie, hey!" John waved a hand and flashed a broad smile at me.

"Hi," I said, nerves ticking up as I followed the paved path toward him.

"You here to get your hands dirty, or just looking for my cousin?" He slipped his gloves off and shoved them into the back of his jeans pocket.

"I—well, either way, I guess." I laughed at how unprepared I was for that question. I'd had no real plan other than *get out of the house* and obviously I'd wanted to be near Aidan. What I'd actually do or say? No idea.

His smile quirked up on one side. "Great answer. And speaking of, has he asked you yet?"

I gave him a questioning look as we walked slowly into the depths of the garden. "What question?"

A spark of mischief flitted across his face before he shook his head and forced a cough. "Oh, no, never mind."

"Why do I feel like you weren't supposed to ask me that?"

He grinned. "I have no idea what you're talking about. Anyway, I've got to run and help with lunch before Dahlia Price forces everyone into tears over sandwiches, but check in the archways. He's just giving them a last once-over."

And like that, John shuffled away in the opposite direction, and I finally took in the space where I stood. I'd ended up on one of the winding pathways, and flowers absolutely burst from the beds around me. These had been nothing but weeds the last time I'd been here. The beds I'd worked on were farther along, metal archways located at most intersections of the paths that wound through these gardens. The main party would take place in a more open space, but I could just imagine couples wandering along these lanes and stealing a romantic moment.

My heart flipped when I caught sight of a familiar work boot and denim at the base of an arch. After an entirely futile attempt to slow my pulse, I approached to find Aidan completely ensconced in the task at hand, which appeared to be weaving a branch through the lattice of the arch.

"Need any help?" I asked, relieved I could offer rather than just wander up and moon at him.

He ducked his head under a section of the vine and simply said, "Of course."

Warmth spread through me at his response, and I had to stop myself from sighing. I liked him so much it was stupid.

His answer shouldn't be something to make me gooey, and yet here I stood, rapidly melting at the way he just said yes. Not, "Are you sure you want to get your hands dirty?" or "No, not from you, Maddie," or "I'm about done but you can have a seat and talk with me."

He didn't put me off or set me aside. He drew me in. And while on one hand, it didn't make sense that this proved so alluring to me, on the other, it did. People catered to me so much it got silly. They also always had ideas about what I should or shouldn't be doing with my time, my hands, my body, my face, my business.

But Aidan? Other than that initial rough patch after discovering who I was, he took me as I came. He'd done a remarkable job of treating me like... me. Like someone he was getting to know and not someone who was a foregone conclusion based on the media portrayal or network.

Wasn't that what I liked so much about our first meeting? To him, I'd simply been Maddie, a woman on a work trip who'd only lifted her head for a few hours before she'd left. I didn't need anyone to tell me I'd burnt out on work and overextended myself. Whether that would've happened at the same time without the stalker, I couldn't say, but it would've at some point. Because when I met Aidan, I'd already been feeling the strain. Meeting him, then Nate's wedding, and all mixed with the gauntlet of book press... each day that the stalker element came to a close allowed me to see just how quickly I'd been hurtling toward burnout even without the added specter of someone following me.

Here with Aidan, that seemed to melt away. I wasn't on a pedestal, and I wasn't excluded. I was in the dirt, so to speak, and it felt better than I could've imagined.

"Just hold here. That's actually—perfect."

His fingers grazed over mine as he twisted and tucked and did things I couldn't see while I held a formerly droopy part up. I tried not to let that fleeting contact affect me, but I was only human and I'd kissed him last night. Some insane flurry of boldness in me had given me the guts to press a quick, soft kiss to him after all those nice things he'd said.

I wasn't someone who needed flattery, but again, he'd seen *me*. It was, frankly, irresistible.

"You okay there for a second?"

"Yep. All good." My arms would get tired held up like this but not just yet. He moved around, his boots barely audible as he shuffled to a work bag that I'd noticed on the ground. And sure enough, another few seconds later, he returned, his nearness ushering in a wave of awareness so strong, it necessitated I brace my feet a little wider.

"There. We. Go. I think we're good. You can let go."

He stepped back and touched my elbow in signal. That quick contact sent my stomach cartwheeling around my body as I took a large step away and clasped my hands together.

"Good work," I said, pleased to see the vines all cooperating. He'd woven them together and pinned them so they looked incredibly ornate. They were honestly stunning, and amazingly, also alive, rooted in place at the base of the metal archway. "These look incredible."

"Thank you. It's a pet project that is more time consuming than I should tolerate, but I can't seem to shake it." He tossed a small bag of what looked like twist ties into his larger work bag and crouched to gather it up.

"Will they bloom again next year?" I asked, taking in the fact that he'd replicated this same style at every intersection and archway.

"They should. Most of these were planted last year, and

I'm—" He abruptly cut off and dropped his head to focus on something in his bag.

"And you're... what?"

He glanced up just enough to reveal his pinched brow. "Oh, never mind. It's not important."

Oh my goodness, he was killing me. He looked like *that* and he was shy? How many times had I sat through unending diatribes on a given man's business, investments, real estate opportunities—you name it, I'd feigned as much interest as I could in the name of social graces. And the one person I actually wanted to hear more from held himself so close I had to pry his words out of him.

And pry, I would.

Likely thanks to the general fed-upness hounding me out of my house this morning, I set a hand on his. My heart flip-flopped around when his eyes met mine, and I didn't let go or back away.

"Tell me. I want to know."

His gaze slipped over my face, those dark eyes tracking from my own down to my lips. "It's not all that interesting."

I huffed a breath. "I want to know."

His attention seemed to intensify, as though the sun had spotlighted us where we stood and everyone else had left the stage. But we'd already been alone in this little corner of the garden, and now it felt like we were somehow *more* alone. Like the air had charged with energy.

I lifted my chin and stood tall, suddenly possessed of the need to push him a little. To insist that he tell me, or better yet, touch me again.

Or better than that, kiss me again.

What did he do? He blushed. Just a little, but I could see the bright tinge creeping up over the line of his dark beard, and all I could think of was running a finger along his jaw.

He gave a little shake of his head. "I've been happy with how they're growing. I wasn't sure if I'd lose some of them and—"

"If you weren't secretly a bridge troll on holiday, I'd be more likely to ask you." Dahlia's words whipped through the air, and we both turned toward the sound.

"Bridge troll? Yeah? What bridge is mine? And how do you know about my secret profession?"

John's voice came through clearly enough that I'd bet they were standing on the other side of hedge a few feet away.

"Probably a little irrigation ditch," Dahlia said, irritation lacing her words.

John laughed, a sharp shot through the space. "What did I do to deserve your ire, Price? Seriously, how have I wronged you so thoroughly?"

Aidan heaved a silent sigh, but the movement drew my eye. He gave me a look that fell somewhere between frustrated and disappointed before saying, "John, can I have your help with something?"

In seconds, John and Dahlia came wandering out from wherever they'd been, and John shot Aidan an exasperated look that had me stifling a chuckle.

"You rang?" John said, all evidence of disgruntlement gone.

Aidan handed him his bag of tools and other stuff. "Can you run this to the truck?"

"You got it." He turned to me with a nod. "Maddie, good to see you again." Then he tossed over his shoulder as he walked away. "Price."

Dahlia watched him go with a hard expression before turning to me. "Hi. How are you? Is your mom here?"

"No. Thankfully. I escaped, and we're T-minus twenty-four hours until she's heading back to the city." Gratitude and relief swelled in me at the reminder that I'd have my space back and wouldn't need to keep avoiding her for much longer.

Dahlia grinned. "Let's get lunch this week. I'll be fairly busy, but I always need to eat. And I'll see you Saturday night for sure, right?"

"Wouldn't miss it."

She nodded decisively and shuffled off with a farewell to both of us. I needed to ask her what the deal was with John and why they fought so much—maybe she'd tell me why since I hadn't heard John willingly explain it.

"I told you. It's weird between them," Aidan said as we turned to walk the path on the way to the parking lot.

"I'm going to ask her about it when I see her this week. I'm too curious."

"Well, if you find out anything good, let me know," he said, a small smile on his face that sent my stomach to my toes.

"Sure will."

We'd stopped walking again, and his eyes had hooked into mine, all serious and encompassing. "Any chance you'd be my date next weekend?"

My heart thudded. "To the Night in Bloom?"

He nodded.

"Um... sure. Yeah. Okay. I can do that."

He loosed a small chuckle. "You don't have to. I didn't mean to put you on the spot. I just thought it'd be fun for us to go together."

Hope and disappointment twisted in me, but as though

he could see straight through me, he added, "If you're still interested, I'd like it to be a real date. I mean, if you want. Not if you've—"

"That sounds good. Yes. Please."

He grinned, and I beamed right back at him because *yes*, the man's smile was too gorgeous and *yes*, I wanted to date him.

He held out a hand, and automatically, I placed mine in it. He raised it to his lips and pressed a kiss to the back of my hand, sending butterflies fluttering wildly in my chest.

"I'll see you Saturday, if not before."

"See you then."

CHAPTER TWENTY-FIVE

Aidan

I breathed out slowly, willing myself to stay calm even though I didn't feel it. "Rich, I know Viv loved this place. And I know you and Martha do, too. I want to do right by you all and make sure we get what this place is worth."

My father-in-law had this way of frowning that made it look like his whole head was sad, and it shot me in the heart every time.

"I just don't know about letting it go, Aid. I know we've talked and talked about this, but—"

"We have. The reasons we're listing it are still the reasons we discussed, but these reasons have grown. I don't want you toiling anymore. And frankly, I don't want your future hanging on how bad the drought is. It's only getting worse for the next ten years, and I can't stand the thought of losing crop and you and Martha taking the hit. I won't do it." And my gut told me if we could just get past this, everyone's lives would improve.

Somehow, his frown intensified, and another arrow notched, ready to fire and shatter my control. I blew out another breath. "Let's just see what kind of offers we get. You don't have to accept them. But I think we need to do this."

He nodded, admitting temporary defeat for now. "All right. All right. There's sense in seeing what comes in."

"There is. Night, Rich."

"Night, Aidan."

And with that, he exited the small office building where I'd been buried for the last seven hours and would shuffle his way the half block to the home he'd lived in for forty-odd years. The house he'd raised Viv in and the place where he'd originally run the farm. They'd put in the small office and employee room a few decades ago, long before I'd joined the family, and I thanked God for that degree of separation. They could keep their home, and we could still sell the place.

If they'd actually accept an offer. Which I'd begun to doubt would really happen. Maybe that was the source of this dread creeping in from the edges.

Why don't you try being honest? The voice, as usual, sounded like my brat of a cousin, John.

Why wasn't I honest with my in-laws? I scrubbed a hand over my face and closed the laptop in front of me. Nothing else productive would get done tonight, especially not now that I'd let my mind wander off track.

As I gathered up my things and locked the building, I reminded myself: the reason I couldn't tell them I had no interest in the business and wanted to live my own life was because I knew it would gut them. It would feel like yet another loss—no. It would actually *be* a loss. Selling the farm was loss enough, and though part of me feared they were still holding out hope I'd "come to my senses" and want to take it over and have that be my whole life, I didn't have the heart to outright destroy that for them.

Speak of the devil, John texted right as I got in the car. *"You need to come home. It's eleven at night and I want to go home. Your son is asleep and my guess is you're not about to tell them the truth, so hang it up and get back here."*

I shot back saying I was on the way and drove carefully, window down, because sleep pawed at me and had been for hours. My day had started at five a.m. and while it'd been a good day, running into the farm issues and having yet another late-night heart-to-heart with Rich about its future hadn't been on my list. It would be an insane week between a site visit for a new design project, managing the last pieces of Night in Bloom wrapping up, and making sure I actually saw my son while he was awake... I didn't need farm drama, too.

But hell, could I blame them for being unsure? For dragging their heels? No. That was the brutality of it. I couldn't blame them for not wanting to sell their life-long business even if it would give them—and me—freedom.

At some point, they'd see that. Hopefully when we had a handful of solid offers coming in and they got a glimpse of what was possible.

For now? I'd get home, get cleaned up, and let myself relive the few minutes I'd had with Maddie.

Just thinking her name sent a rush of warmth and anticipation through me. Her jeans and T-shirt had surprised me, but the second I'd seen her, I'd wanted to touch her. I'd had that privilege at her party in the alternate universe of our pretending to be together and now, bereft of that access,

I wanted it all the more. I'd never had that compulsion to be near and touch someone until her. Even before, with Viv, we'd been friends first. Our love story was best friends who'd loved each other and started a family. We'd had a great marriage for the most part.

But I'd never felt this overwhelming *need*. Not like with Maddie. And the short drive back to my house had me almost on edge just remembering her smile, her curiosity about John and Dahlia, and how much I wanted to kiss her again.

Why had I resisted something with her so resolutely? Someone I had so much connection with, and who'd already proven to be better than I'd imagined? That was why I'd asked—John's pushing had been the perfect excuse, as had the event itself. But more than anything, I'd asked because I wanted to.

Probably due to general exhaustion, or maybe it was a leftover bit of the fantasy that we'd spun together months ago and had revisited in a small way the other night playing out in my head. It seemed so possible, and in this moment, I wanted it. Whatever *it* was, after parking in the garage, I sent a message to Maddie before stopping myself. *"Any chance you're free for breakfast tomorrow?"*

"Crap," I said aloud in the empty, quiet cab of my truck. Too late. I shouldn't be asking her out *again*, even though she'd said yes today. Too much, too soon, and coming on way too strong. And late.

I shoved out of the vehicle and made it inside without stomping up the stairs like I sometimes did. It wouldn't wake Luca, but I still felt like a jerk doing it. Inside, John sat snuggled into the corner of the couch, reading glasses perched on his nose, book balanced on the armrest.

"Finally. Dude. You're lucky I get to sleep in tomorrow."

"I know. I'm sorry."

He launched off the couch, book and glasses in hand. "You should be. You said ten at the latest. He was trying to stay up for you."

The painful ache of knowing I'd disappointed Luca twisted through me. "I know. Rich was at it again, and we've had some other issues. It should be fine until after next weekend."

John's mouth slid up into a sly smile. "That's right. Next weekend when you take Madeline Reynolds on a date."

My stomach flipped. "Yep."

He grinned full-out at me. "Proud of you. Seriously. Wasn't sure you'd go for it, but it'll be great." He patted me on the shoulder as he walked past, breezing toward the front door. "I'm out. Talk to you tomorrow."

My "Yep" fell into a silent room. He was probably already into his car and would text me when he got home. It was an unspoken habit, and a small way he took care of me. It'd been long enough since the accident, I probably didn't need it anymore, but I always appreciated it.

A few minutes later, I'd showered and taken care of the necessities after checking in on a sleeping Luca. My phone lit up with a text from John saying he'd made it home, but my eye snagged on the message just below. A response from Maddie.

"I'd love breakfast. Just got back from dropping my mom at the airport."

I tapped out a response, my pulse spiking at the thought of her on the roads so late. *"That's such a long drive this time of night. Glad you made it back safe."*

In seconds, her reply popped up. *"The Silverton Airport, don't worry."*

I laughed soundlessly. Of course, her wealthy, upper-crust mother had flown from the Silverton airport. Only chartered and private flights came and went from the small airfield here, but it got enough traffic thanks to all the high-profile people that Julian Grenier's investment had been a sound one—no surprise. I pushed away the embarrassment over my ignorance and shoved on.

"So, what time works?"

CHAPTER TWENTY-SIX

Maddie

Quinn held out her hand, sparkling with her engagement ring *and* a wedding band, chuckling as I took it.

"Well, aren't you two sneaky!" I gawped at the gorgeous set, pulling her into a quick hug and shaking my head. She was absolutely beaming. Just literally glowing with happiness.

Apparently, she and Julian had ambushed all their friends on Saturday afternoon and flown them to Vegas for their wedding. They'd worked out all the details, and the only people who'd had any idea were Quinn's family, Jamie Morris and his wife, and Dahlia, who'd coordinated flowers.

Everyone laughed and recounted the dramatic reveal. They'd all been told to meet at the Silverton Airport, and Julian had *two* jets to take everyone. He'd hauled them all to

Vegas, put them up at one of the hotels, and brought them back late in the day on Sunday.

"I'm sorry we didn't pull you into our evil scheme. I wasn't sure your mom would appreciate you being kidnapped after recent events." She flared her eyes and made a face that had me laughing.

"She wouldn't have, for sure. She was already upset I'd left during the day. Plus, I wouldn't have expected an invite to such an intimate, special event."

No part of me felt bad or left out. I loved that Julian had done something so adventuresome and free. It had to be Quinn's influence, because when we'd interacted in the past, I'd never gotten the "fly my friends to Vegas and marry my fiancée" vibe from him.

Quinn nodded. "Fair enough, though I hope you know you would've been very welcome. We wanted it full of people who support us. Dear friends and family. We're new friends, sure, but you're already a part of us."

Sarah squeezed my shoulders from behind in a little hug, and Dahlia toasted her wine from her seat by the fire pit in my back yard. The summer evening had turned cool, and I couldn't resist the luxury of a small fire on a cooling night with the sweet smell of pine and sage surrounding us.

Calla hadn't been able to come since the travel had worn her out, and she wasn't feeling well, though she'd assured everyone she was just fine. And Sadie sat next to Dahlia and cradled her wine, smiling at me like she agreed with everyone else.

My heart lurched. How had they accepted me so quickly? We were new friends, baby friends, and here they were opening their arms to me. I'd shared a lot of myself that first girls' night, and they'd clearly sensed my need to connect, to share. Or maybe more accurately, to unload. But this openness and welcoming, this willingness to accept me as part of them even though I was here as a transient guest? It nearly gutted me. And it absolutely drew a line under any doubts about coming tonight.

I'd waffled. Wavered. Wondered if I'd feel out of place after hearing about the wedding fun and if they might want it to be just their original group. Sarah and Dahlia had both individually assured me they wanted me to come. I'd had a chat with Dahlia yesterday, and she'd given me a quick update, but we'd had to cancel our lunch. Instead, she'd set up this evening and insisted I come. Then I'd insisted that at least I take a turn hosting, and they'd all agreed.

My eyes were verging on wet, and I cleared my throat. "Well, that's truly an honor. Thank you," I finally said, hoping it hadn't come unnaturally late.

"Don't thank us. Tell us about you! How was your mom? How's Aidan? Have you fallen in love with Luca yet?" Sarah asked in rapid succession like she'd been holding back.

I chuckled and accepted a glass of wine Quinn shoved in my hand, ever the bartender even at someone else's house, before taking a seat on a cushion next to Sadie and Dahlia.

"My mom is gone, bless her. She apologized when she left, actually."

Quinn's brows raised as she folded herself into a cushioned chair in the circle around the fire. "I didn't take her for a woman who did that kind of thing."

I chuckled. "You're not wrong. But I think some of her criticism was coming out as a weird version of grief. I know it doesn't totally make sense, but between her apology and my check-in with my therapist this week, I think that was it. She hates to be out of control and what could make a woman like that feel less out of control than nearly losing her daughter to a crazed stalker?"

They all shifted or took sips of their wine, some nodding, some just looking at me with compassion.

Sadie was the first to speak. "That's a generous perspective, Maddie. You should be proud. It took me a long time to see my parents clearly but not just be angry at them once I did."

I swallowed hard but summoned a wry smile. "Oh, don't you worry, I work through the parental anger issues every few years."

On cue, they all laughed lightly, and Sarah and Dahlia both agreed they'd been challenged to do the same.

"And Aidan?" Dahlia prompted.

My smile gave me away and everyone reacted with grins, claps, and of course Quinn's "Oh thank goodness."

"We're going to Night in Bloom. And I think it's an actual date, not a fake date. Plus, we had breakfast the other day, and it was basically perfect. So I think it's not just friendly." I'd debated that for a bit but decided there was no reason for it to be fake. I hoped like crazy it would lead to more, and yet if it didn't, at least I'd have this one night to remember.

"Wait. Fake?" Quinn's eyes narrowed.

Busted. Yeah, somehow, I'd been hoping to slip that one in. Granted, she and Dahlia had been there, so they could've seen us. A memory of Aidan's strong arm around me visited like a corporeal touch and sent my stomach dipping.

I cleared my throat. "Uh, yeah. Pathetic as it may be, I told my mom Aidan and I have been dating to keep her from flying Chad or anyone else back out to become my next date."

Sadie ducked her head and Sarah grimaced. Dahlia snapped and pointed, like something finally made sense. "I was wondering why you two seemed so cozy but had hoped it was actually happening."

That familiar pinch of longing hit until I remembered it *was* happening. That just maybe, the dream could continue. "Yeah, well, it kind of was, but it seemed to thaw him to the idea because then he asked me to go with him this weekend. Not as friends."

"Yes! I knew it! I knew he'd get his head out of his butt." Quinn clapped and seemed genuinely overjoyed, as did everyone else. They shared in the excitement, but eventually the questions about my dress and other plans died down enough that I could address the last thing.

"And Luca is adorable. He's at such a sweet age where he's kind of a man but not quite in that teenager way? I haven't spent a lot of time with older kids his age, but he's really special." And I'd known from the minute I saw his *Lord of the Rings* paperback that he'd be my kind of kid. The fact that he'd started grilling me on my company's stock value had drilled it home.

"I love that. I mean, he's adorable, so I'm not surprised. I swear he's in the bookstore every time I go in there. So polite but not shy... It's a cute combination."

Sarah's familiarity with Luca reminded me how precious the small-town life was. In any other life, the odds of a friend of mine knowing another friend's child were essentially zero. Maybe if they worked in the same building or company, *maybe*, but ultimately the tight-knit community here in Silverton brought with it so many elements that improved quality of life.

Feeling *known* was so valuable. I loved that Luca had lots of people in his life to give him that, especially after losing one of his most important people. That thought sent a split of sadness through me for the boy, and for my friend, or... whatever he was, Aidan.

"Well, I need to request everyone's help. I'd hoped to find a dress in Vegas but no dice." Dahlia sighed, shoulders drooping. "I know it's silly, and I don't even have a date because honestly what's the point? But I want to look good. I want to look... *great*."

Quinn's eyes narrowed. "You could totally get a date if you wanted one."

She snorted. "Yeah, but the key there is, you have to want one."

She appeared honest enough, but there was a glint in her yet that struck me as off. She seemed naturally quite romantic, so it hit me as unusual that she wouldn't want her own date to an event she was hosting.

It hovered on the tip of my tongue to ask about John when Sarah beat me to it.

"You wouldn't want to go with John Wallace? You two seem to have some crazy chemistry."

Her expression dropped, but she burst out laughing, startling all of us. She leaned forward, her eyes shut like it almost hurt to laugh that hard, but she managed to sober quickly. "Yeah, no. Not going to happen."

As though I could see inside their minds, I could've sworn each of them was thinking the same thing I was. *The lady doth protest too much.* And yet, who wanted to push her on it? That twinge of haunting in her eyes made me hold any further commentary on him—at least for now.

"Okay, so you need an amazing dress. Any ideas?" I asked, hoping maybe this was something I could do for her. A small thing to repay her kindness in being my friend, and in turn, a small gesture for the group too, in a way.

"Is it dumb to say something floral but not horrible?" she asked, a half-smile and wide eyes blinking at me.

We all chuckled, but in an instant, it hit me. I knew exactly what she should wear. It was a friend of a friend of a friend situation, but I thought maybe I had the perfect dress for her. "If you'll trust me with this, I'll have something for you by Friday night. I don't know if I can get it here sooner, but if I can, I will. Find a backup you can live with, but... I think you're going to love this."

Excitement lit her eyes, and I had that feeling again.

How lucky I was, how blessed, to be sitting here with these women, receiving their trust.

How would I ever leave them?

CHAPTER TWENTY-SEVEN

Aidan

Rich frowned. I hated that I'd hardly seen anything but that expression on his face lately.

"I think you and Luca should eat with us more. We're here to support you."

I exhaled through a wave of impatience, more than ready to get out of the office. Night in Bloom was tomorrow. I'd promised Luca I'd be home by seven so we could spend some time together tonight, and that was already two hours later than I should've been, but thankfully, John had stepped in to bridge the gap after Luca's day camp ended at five.

"We appreciate it. You support us so well. But Luca and I haven't had much time together lately, so we're having a guys' night. Maybe we could join you Sunday?" I'd have to make excuses with my aunt and uncle, but they'd understand. They knew taking care of Rich and Martha was important.

He nodded. "All right. And we'll have Luca tomorrow, won't we?"

I gathered my notebook, computer, and a few loose papers I might need Sunday. Ideally, I'd avoid coming back here until Monday. I could dream it, anyway. "Yes. I think he's at a friend's until three, and they're dropping him over with you and Martha after that. I'll be late, so he'll probably sleep at your place and I'll get him first thing."

Rich waved that away. "You know he'll want Mar's pancakes so no rush. I'm sure you'll be exhausted." He eyed me a beat. "You taking a date?"

I managed not to flinch, but discomfort still twisted through me. "I am."

He nodded. No frown this time, just something slightly north of neutral. Damn, that was the closest thing to a smile I ever got lately. "Good. Have fun. Good luck. See ya Sunday."

And with that, he was out. He'd be back at his house and slipping into his chair next to Martha's in T-minus four minutes if I timed it.

I scraped a hand over my face, relieved to have acknowledged I had a date. I'd had a bunch of them in the past, all terrible or mediocre at best, and he'd never once asked me. I figured he knew I was out there, dating, but I'd been unwilling to mention it because it hadn't meant anything. I knew I didn't need his and Martha's permission, but I also hadn't felt there was any need for them to know. No one I'd seen had any potential for being in our lives.

Until Maddie.

And maybe that was why satisfaction slipped in as I locked

the office door and made my way to my truck. He'd done the work for me of broaching the subject, and he'd approved. I mean, we couldn't go anywhere, and this was just one date, but it'd been so... easy. I'd have to tell John about that almost-smile.

After running to pick up our food, I fumbled my way out of the car, praying none of the containers had busted open in the process of rushing so I wouldn't be late. Inadvertently, I slammed the door against the interior wall as I burst through from the garage. "I'm here! I'm here. I made it."

In a moment of a flashback and déjà vu colliding, John ran toward me yelling, his face covered with some kind of mask and holding a sword. Luca was close on his heels, also masked and weapon ready, also trailing an *ahhhhhh* down the hallway. They both skidded to a stop, sword tips at my chest.

"What's the password?" Luca demanded.

My eyes flicked to John, who was grinning back at me behind his silvery disguise. I didn't know how long it'd been since Luca had played dress up, but this had to be the first time in at least a year. It sent a pang of nostalgia through me for those days when all he wanted to do was dress up like Daniel Tiger, then an Ewok, then Luke Skywalker, and finally, Kylo Ren. We'd had a definite Star Wars theme for a while.

"Movie night?" I said, hoping that might do. I actually really needed to set my bag down and change out of my work clothes before I could relax, but I wouldn't spoil the moment by insisting they drop this.

"Wrong. One more chance or you're doomed," he said, a little grit in his voice to provide menace.

I widened my eyes and dropped my bag—well, my work bag. I held up the other one. "What about the password, *I have Guac and if you want any, you'll have to let me through.* Could that be it?"

Luca's eyes narrowed and he squinted through his mask. He growled but nodded.

"That's it!" He whipped off his mask, tossed his sword and shield, and held out his arms wide. "Welcome home, Dad!"

I laughed, love, satisfaction, and that purely parental kind of joy filtering through me at his large smile and silly gesture. Foolishly, I thought he might give me a hug, but instead, he spun on his heel and slid away without touching his discarded toys. I'd deal with that later because we'd all need food before we addressed the messy house.

John removed his costume and took the food bag from me. "He's had a good day today, as you may have gathered."

"Dress up?" I asked, keeping my voice low. I wouldn't want to scare away the return of his imagination.

We'd had a bit of a crisis when he'd turned ten. Something about the day had struck him as horribly sad. He'd termed it the end of his childhood and even sobbed that he didn't know how to use his imagination anymore.

At the time, I'd been at a total loss. It'd been John who'd come to the rescue and pulled him aside. He'd explained that sometimes it was make-believe and dress-up and setting up Lego guy battles in your room, and sometimes it was letting your mind escape to other worlds through a book. No surprise, that idea had clicked in a big way, and the crisis had been averted.

But it'd been that long or more since he'd actually donned a costume outside of Halloween.

John nodded. "I was surprised when he accepted the suggestion, but I wasn't about to say anything."

I chuckled. "Oh, so it was your suggestion to attack me

upon entry?"

He shrugged. "Of course. We had the element of surprise."

I nodded. "Fair enough. Lucky for me I had the element of dinner."

"Lucky is right," Luca said, sliding back toward us, his socks gliding over the wood floor in a practiced movement.

"Well, if you'll get it all set up, I'll go get changed. I got a ton—you want to stay?" I asked John as he set the large bag onto the kitchen table.

Luca immediately started rooting around as John said, "Nah. I've got to go... You guys enjoy your night."

Something stretched in that breath after *I've got to go*, but he grinned and ruffled Luca's hair, patted my shoulder as he passed, and made his way out the front door to his car. *Huh.* I'd been so wrapped up in all this Maddie stuff and the farm and managing in-laws, I'd been totally self-absorbed. It was the first real glimpse I'd gotten, but based on that moment, my gut told me something was up with John.

After quickly changing into comfy clothes while Luca unpacked the meal, we sat down to our feast. Total silence settled in as we ate for the first few minutes before he came up for air.

"So did Uncle John have a date?"

"Don't think so, but he might just not want to say." He'd been hurt before and hadn't seemed to put a real emphasis on dating, but he'd also been in the thick of starting the brewery, and frankly, supporting me. Again, the selfishness of that hit me in the sternum.

"Is dating something people don't talk about?" Luca followed this with a giant bite of shredded beef taco, the crunch sounding sharp and crisp between us.

I smiled at the question, so innocent of the baggage that easily builds up as a person accrues dating experience. "Not usually. But sometimes, a person might like someone a whole lot, but they aren't sure it'll work out. Sometimes, it feels easier for other people to not know just in case it doesn't."

He nodded as he chewed. "That makes sense. Is that why you haven't told anyone about dating Maddie?"

That had me choking on the bite I was chewing. When I swallowed, I shook my head.

"No. I mean, I haven't been dating Maddie." But this felt disingenuous in light of my plan for tomorrow, and I wanted to be honest with him—as much as I could, anyway. "But we are going to Night in Bloom together tomorrow."

He smiled with his mouth full, and I cringed away.

"I'm glad, Dad. She's nice and super smart."

I chuckled. "True." And beautiful. And kind. And kissable. And funny. And...

"Are you gonna kiss her?"

Had I said that aloud? No. I hadn't. *Phew.*

"Uh, I hope so," I said, stifling the laugh. We'd done the basics of reproduction and a bit about other stuff, but he'd been flatly disinterested in romantic feelings of his own thus far.

He made a face but then shrugged.

I grappled with whether to give him the "no one will ever replace your mom" speech I'd cued up long ago but had never given, but he cut in with a story about camp and we moved on. He saved me from any more turmoil, though something heavy sat in my gut at the reality I couldn't ignore. It didn't make sense to take it deeper anyway, especially since whatever we might have would only last so long before she moved on.

CHAPTER TWENTY-EIGHT

Maddie

I hadn't seen him since our breakfast six days ago. That beautiful hour had flown, and before I was ready, he'd been kissing my cheek, sending butterflies exploding in my chest, and telling me he looked forward to our date. *Sigh*.

Well, no, actually I'd *glimpsed* him but hadn't gotten to talk to him in person. We'd texted back and forth a few times a day, and each time I got anything from him, I felt like high school Maddie with a crush who'd just noticed her.

I'd said as much to Juliet on a quick video call two days ago, and she'd giggled and clapped her hands with glee. "Finally! I'm so happy for you I could cry."

I'd spent the rest of the call and the rest of the night, for that matter, shaking my head and smiling into the empty spaces of my house. It was stupid to feel so giddy about this date, and yet I couldn't tamp down my excitement or hopes.

His resistance to me and the idea of us being involved romantically hadn't dissipated entirely.

Or so I hoped.

There was the outside chance he'd invited me to Night in Bloom because I'd helped. But a ton of other people had, too. And I wasn't going to demur and pretend like I didn't think he liked me. I knew he did. He always had. But he hadn't been up for all that was Madeline Reynolds after finding out. That'd changed, thank God, and now I hoped it would stay that way.

I also hoped tonight would be as good as I'd imagined. That we'd click like we did when he rescued me from more blinds dates courtesy of Annette Reynolds or more simply, when we were just chatting over tea while Luca read next to us. I wasn't going to hope it'd be like that first night, that first meeting, because our inhibitions weren't down. We weren't living in that fantasyland anymore. But I hadn't been able to shake the sense of calm and groundedness he created in me, and I hoped the pressure of a date at a big public event wouldn't spoil that.

As I stepped out of the car and thanked the driver, my hopes reached sky freaking high. I'd had no luck taming them, so might as well embrace it. I'd arrived a few minutes after the start time to avoid showing up in a crush of people. I didn't want attention on me though there'd be far more famous than me. Still, I wanted a quiet entrance. Aidan had been there almost all day, side by side with Dahlia and a few other volunteers. I'd asked if they needed help, but they'd shooed my offer away. When I'd delivered Dahlia's dress last night, she'd promised me they had preparations in hand. She'd sent me a selfie earlier and she looked stunning.

I wasn't so bad myself. I wore a deep rose-colored gown that swooped across my shoulders and left my décolletage on full display. Along with ornate diamond earrings and no necklace, my hair artfully pinned so the sides had been pulled away from my face and it all fell down my back. The bodice was fitted to the waist and the skirt fell straight, though the silky material moved generously.

Anthony had grinned and told me I would be arrested for murder tonight. I'd told him he was crazy, but I did feel *great* in it. More than anything, I felt ready.

"Oh, now there she is," John said, drawing my attention to him as I walked through one of Aidan's archways.

"Hey, it's good to see you. I—*wow*. This is incredible."

Flowers burst from everywhere. I'd seen many of them last weekend, but I hadn't been around to see Dahlia's additions. Along with the planted items, arrangements had been placed on every tall bistro table and practically everywhere I could see. Apparently, all of Dahlia's were portable and would be auctioned for the benefit or given away to volunteers so none of them would go to waste. They'd strung fairy lights across the open areas, and tucked into several alcoves were bars with servers. The space wasn't packed, but the general hum of talking and laughter made it feel lively. A feeling of expectation hung in the place that I related to completely.

"It's impressive. Even seeing it as they did it, I'm always amazed at the final product." John glanced around.

I took him in. He'd cleaned up well. Nice suit, shiny smile as always, and hair styled rather than tucked under a hat like I usually saw him.

"You look nice, John," I said, biting my tongue before I asked him if he'd seen his cousin.

He smiled. "Thanks. I clean up okay. I'd say you do, too, but I'm guessing Aidan is about to make that very clear." He nodded to someone behind me.

My stomach flipped and dipped as I turned, knowing who it'd be. Bracing myself, I looked at the vision of Aidan approaching in a tux. *Wow.*

There was nothing special about a tux. I'd been to a thousand events with men in tuxes, and the suit itself never particularly thrilled me. But Aidan Wallace in a tux? Aidan with a trimmed beard and hair styled? Aidan with his purposeful gait and that look on his face like he'd been waiting all day to see me?

Deadly.

"Hi, wow." And yes. That's what I said, because despite all my social skills, the man had struck me senseless.

Aidan didn't waver on his course to greet me. He kept coming, right up until he set a hand on my upper arm and leaned down. I couldn't tell whether his movements slowed or if it was a kind of hallucination, but it felt like he moved at half speed, his face dropping slow, slow to mine and his lips pressing gently into my cheek.

"You're beautiful," he said, those eyes on mine making my heart pound.

"You are, too." Because it was true.

He grinned, furthering the stunning effect of the encounter. "Thank you. I'm glad you're here."

"Me, too."

"And I, too, am glad we're all here." John's voice pierced through the hazy, thick feeling.

"You just had to bust into their moment, didn't you?" Dahlia patted my hand, appearing out of nowhere.

"Of course I did. I—I, uh..."

His words faltered so suddenly, I looked up, then immediately ducked my head to hide my grin.

He appeared to be utterly winded as he gazed at Dahlia. She did look stunning. The dress was a cream-colored princess style that cinched in at her tiny waist. As though growing from the dress itself, little stalks of embroidered lavender twisted up the bodice and the tiny purple hand-stitched flowers edged the delicate swooping neckline which did gorgeous things for her. A friend of a friend had hosted a party for her designer friend—the woman who'd made the dress. With a call, some begging, and Anthony working his magic, the dress had arrived just in time and, miraculously, in just her size.

Dahlia clearly loved it, and she'd gone all out to coordinate and accentuate her own beauty along with the dress's. Her dark hair was in spirals, her makeup perfect, and I honestly thought John might've swallowed his tongue.

"What my cousin is trying to say is that you look beautiful, Dahlia. And everything is perfect." Aidan gestured to the flowers surrounding us.

"It is gorgeous. I had no idea what to expect and I'm just amazed. I hope there's a fair amount of press here tonight?" I asked.

Dahlia nodded. "Of course. Quite a few people came earlier to photograph in the daylight, but we've got all the local channels here and the committee funded hiring someone for future publicity shots, too."

"That was smart," John put in, like he'd suddenly remembered how to speak.

Dahlia glanced at him sideways. "Yeah. Thanks." Turning to me, she gave me a small hug and whispered, "I love this dress. Thank you."

"It's perfect."

She turned without another word, certainly nothing to John, and left. The second she stepped away, Aidan glared at his cousin.

"You need to get it together, man."

John just scowled and stomped away.

And then, it was just us. Nerves fizzed awake again, but Aidan spoke before I could overthink it.

"Do you want to get a drink? I'll have to circulate a bit later on, but for now I'm all yours."

I inched closer. "That sounds good."

"I agree."

"Thank you for agreeing to come tonight. I know it's not a very conventional first date," he said, reaching for my hand.

His warm, calloused hand in mine made my heart flutter wildly. "*First* date? You think we'll do this again?"

One side of his mouth slid up in what I was quickly learning was a Wallace man trait. "I certainly hope so."

Little cheerleaders in my head mentally threw pom-poms and did tumbling passes at that. But since I didn't want to seem as relieved as I did considering I'd pushed for more with him from the very beginning, I shrugged. "You don't even know how the night will go. It could be awful."

And then he squinted like he needed to in order to see me better and bit his lip, studying me. I'd never seen something so aggressively sexy from him, but there was nothing rehearsed about it. The man was smoldering at point-blank range, and I had zero defenses against it. Especially not when he said, "It's already a better night than any I've had since the night I met you. Anything else is gravy."

CHAPTER TWENTY-NINE

Aidan

The miscalculation I'd made when I invited Maddie to be my date tonight could not be overstated. While the bulk of my obligations had been fulfilled before the official event ever started, I still had a few things to do. And doing anything other than look at, touch, and ideally taste Maddie was akin to torture.

But of course, I hadn't anticipated how distracting she'd be. I'd never felt like this. I'd never had this animal-level attraction that was multiplied by my genuine like of someone. And every minute I spent talking to her or texting only reeled me in more. I was firmly on her hook, and in truth, I always had been. Whatever meager effort I'd made to stay away from her in the beginning had failed so handily, I was now praying I hadn't missed the window with her.

She'd come here tonight. She'd been at my side, charming people, handling their surprise when they realized she was with me, and generally being blindingly beautiful and appealing. After recognizing the volunteers with Dahlia before the auction began, I slipped off to the side of the garden, where I'd seen her chatting with Callaway Rice-Saint, Sadie Miller, and Sarah James.

"There he is now. Great job with everything tonight," Calla said, smiling broadly. She was somewhere around six months pregnant, and I'd never seen Wyatt more elated. They made a beautiful couple, and it was good to see him so happy.

"Thanks for all of your help. And Sadie, I hear congratulations are in order."

The tiny, quiet woman beamed. "Thank you," she said, glancing down at the diamond on her left ring finger. Her boyfriend Warrick's proposal had come early in the night, and the celebratory feeling had permeated the entire event.

Last year—the event's first—had been surreal and the culmination of planning and collaboration for months. Tonight felt surreal for different reasons, and part of that was because the woman I'd been wishing to see last year was here. Standing next to me. Slipping her hand into mine and sending little bursts of heat through me whenever we made eye contact.

"You and Dahlia outdid yourselves this year. I can't imagine what you'll do next year." Sarah smiled and leaned to the side when Wilder approached and set a hand on her hip.

The simple action made standing in the group suddenly intolerable. Something about the possession—the freedom to touch another person like that. It had been so long since I'd had that. I wouldn't have thought I missed it—not such a simple gesture, and yet here I was aching for it. Here I stood holding Maddie's hand, but only because she'd taken mine.

I had no *right* to her. And the desire to have that—her permission, her trust, her adoring gaze as she leaned into me like my nearness made everything right—gripped me by the collar.

"Thank you all for coming, and for all of your help. Maddie, could I have a moment?" If I was speaking too fast, so be it. These people wouldn't judge me too harshly.

"Of course. I'll see you all later," she said diplomatically, hustling after me where I pulled her.

We slipped down a lane, under an archway, past another, until we'd distanced ourselves from any other voices or bodies. Every step ratcheted up the anticipation and need that cranked through my veins.

The sun had set, and just the faintest hint of purples and pinks hung on to the west, where it sank. The only light we had now was that of the moon filtering in overhead through the slim branches of a Japanese maple.

"Is everything okay?" Maddie said, turning to face me.

And though I'd intended to ask her, to explain what I wanted, the build of that longing, bracing desire for her had overtaken me. Her hand pressed against the lapel of my jacket, and I dropped her other hand I'd held to lead her away. I threaded my fingers into the hair at the back of her head, eyes flickering from her concerned ones to her lips, and I took.

God forgive me, I kissed her like I'd wanted to for so long. For so, so long. And the existence of mercy meant that she didn't startle and push me away, or stay frozen in surprise. The beauty of the night, the magic of this garden, meant she kissed me back with every bit as much enthusiasm and need as I did her.

Her lips were soft and responsive. Just like I'd remembered a hundred times, but better. They were no longer a memory, nor was the slide of her tongue against mine, her fingers clutching my shoulders, the soft skin of her neck and silken strands of her hair. They were here. They were mine, for the moment anyway.

She shifted closer, pressing against me and fully wrapping her arms around me. It was only the sound of a distant cheer and round of applause that brought me back to awareness of anyone but her and the reality that though we were tucked away, we were still in public. Anyone could wander these paths and end up interrupting us.

I pulled back with extreme reluctance, promising myself that if she showed any desire, it wouldn't be long before we did that again. Her glittering eyes and the slight flush on her cheeks paired with that *thoroughly kissed* look made my stomach clutch low.

"I was going to say something along the lines of, 'I really want to kiss you, is that all right?' but I didn't get there."

She cracked a pleased smile. "It worked out okay."

I raised a brow. "Just okay?"

She grinned, biting her lush bottom lip. "How about *quite well?*"

I narrowed my eyes. "That's a little unenthusiastic for my taste, but I'll take it."

She smoothed down the sides of my suit jacket where I realized belatedly she'd been holding on at some point, then rose on her toes. She was still shorter by a small space, but she tilted her chin up and, compelled, I leaned down.

"Yes, you can kiss me," she whispered, right before pressing a short, soft, mind-numbing kiss to my ready lips.

"Good. Thank you. I will." I pulled her close, one hand on her lower back, and made to lean in and steal another kiss, but the crowd cheered again and I came to my senses. "But maybe not right now."

She huffed but smiled. "That might be smart."

"Thank you. I have my moments," I said, that same loose, free quality I'd felt at our first meeting permeating the air between us. I never talked like this. Never spoke intimately with someone, held them close. And yet maybe that was because I hadn't felt like this before—not since Viv, and that had been different. Wonderful, but different.

I stepped back, forcing a little distance between us. The small smile on her lips sent a new sizzle of longing through me, so I stuffed my hands in my pockets to keep from reaching for her again.

"We should go," she said, glancing around like someone might be lurking. Maybe she'd grown used to that—between the threat of her stalker and the general publicity in the last few years, it made sense.

But the idea of losing this time with her, of missing the chance to say what'd been hounding me all night, made my neck itch. I reached up and tugged at my collar, well aware that my time dressed up in a tux was about to expire and I'd turn back into a pumpkin like I belonged. I reached for her hand and she gave it to me—the small gesture sent a wave of relief through me.

"I hope this isn't too much, but I want to say that I've enjoyed tonight. I'm sorry it took me so long. And I want to do it again. And again. And again after that. If you're—"

"I'm interested."

We both grinned at each other and inched closer.

"Good. I know you aren't here forever, I know that. But maybe that's... right. For us. I want to..." I trailed off, a sudden horror that I'd messed up everything filling me instantly.

"I get it. And I agree. I'm leaving at the end of the summer. I don't know when I'll be able to get back here. But in the simplest, most facile terms, I like you. And I hate the thought of keeping my distance just because we know it can't..."

She stopped short of saying what we both knew. This couldn't go anywhere. I was a single dad with two small businesses and family here. She was the CEO of an international company with a demanding schedule and responsibilities to boards and organizations and who knew what else. This thing between us had a ticking clock, and yet it sounded like we agreed.

"It's worth it to me," I said, hoping she understood. Whatever pain we'd face in the end, it'd be worth the time we had. I'd learned well that life was fragile, and nothing was guaranteed. And if I wanted this with her, even for the fleeting time we had, I had to make it happen instead of just standing by and wishing.

Her face lit with what could only be described as joy. "Me, too."

I exhaled a small laugh, relief coursing through me. "Thank God," I said, and hugged her to me. She held me close for a minute before stepping back.

"Okay, but now that we've decided that, I need you to stay away from me."

Alarm shot through me. "Oh?"

She bit her lip as her eyes slipped over me like a sheet pulling down, down. "Yes. Because I cannot be trusted near you in that suit."

CHAPTER THIRTY

Maddie

The next two weeks were something out of a dream. Aidan was working like a maniac, but he was so attentive and engaging, it didn't feel lonely. Every moment was filled with anticipation and fun. We'd managed one quick date the next weekend, but his babysitter had called just as we were finishing dinner and said she was sick. Other than that evening out in town, we'd had coffee at Rise and Shine and managed two other outings with Luca.

I wasn't exactly qualified to evaluate such things, but the younger Wallace was definitely gifted. The obvious element of being moved up a grade and taking advanced math obviously proved that, but I saw glimpses of a truly shrewd mind. Between his love of reading and his grilling me on different aspects of my business like he was a new applicant to our internship program, he was an average eleven-year-old with moods and the desire for attention. He also gave his dad a run for his money, which was adorable and dangerous.

Adorable, because I loved seeing Aidan respond to him. Dangerous because... he was such a good dad. The man was patient and kind, and even when I could tell he was exhausted, he still put his child first. I couldn't be mad when he wasn't available because he was busy helping Luca with this or that because I loved that he was like that. My dad hadn't helped me with anything. Truly, I couldn't think of a single thing my father had ever done to aid my development one way or another.

But finally, *finally*, three weeks after Night in Bloom and just days from what I was fast learning was a favorite local holiday, I had Aidan to myself. I'd woken with a headache and felt a little off, but nothing was going to keep me from enjoying this day together. The calendar was slipping by and what used to be months was now only weeks. Weeks left to enjoy the man I'd been dreaming about for actual years.

Weeks until I had to wake up.

I wouldn't think about *that*.

"Have you done this one?" Aidan asked as we pulled up to a familiar trailhead.

"I think I've done the Pine Ridge trail, but just the shorter loop. Which one were you thinking?" I asked, breathing in the scent of wildflowers and pines as I exited his truck.

"I think we'll do the Sego Lily Bypass Trail, if you're up for it? It's got a great little waterfall and some nice views." He pulled his cap down low on his head and swung his backpack over one shoulder.

"Sure. I'm up for anything." I meant it, even if I didn't quite *feel* it. A headache hovered stage left of my brain, and I hadn't been able to eat much this morning, but I was queen of pushing through. I didn't get sick, and all this fresh air would set me to rights.

I followed him to the trail and he turned to look at me. "Nice boots."

"Thanks. My effort at embracing my time here."

Anthony had ordered me top-of-the-line hiking boots when I mentioned wanting to hike. Dahlia and Sarah had started going on hikes with a local group and had dragged me with them once. That was all it took to hook me, and I was convinced one of Anthony's favorite things was buying niche equipment that was extremely useful, like a champagne pressurized stopper or the perfect mini speaker for workouts or, as was the most recent case, hiking boots.

Aidan must've liked this answer, because he reached up and ran his thumb over my cheek. An odd, sweet gesture that I liked way too much. I wished he'd lean down and kiss me since we hadn't had anything more than a quick peck in greeting or farewell since Night in Bloom.

"All right. Let's go," he said, those dark eyes staring into mine under the brim of his hat.

"Let's do it," I agreed and grinned at the way he just stayed there, gazing at me for a moment. His hand slipped down my neck with a soft, fleeting caress, and then he turned.

"Anytime you want to go first, let me know, but I'll get us going since the trail diverges a few times in the first half mile."

And with that, we were off. I kept pace with him fairly effectively the first mile. We'd gained crazy elevation and my legs burned like I'd done squats and lunges as a full-time job before starting the hike, which didn't make any sense. I tried to focus on the scenery and even let myself indulge in appreciating Aidan's long legs and yes, sue me, his butt. But half an hour in, I was desperate for the break when it came.

I slumped onto a nearby rock and dumped my small pack down next to me.

"It's warming up quickly. Not sure we'll want to do the full trail if it keeps getting hotter like this," he said, stance wide and then head tipped back to take a long drink from his water bottle.

I fumbled with my bag, pulling my own water from its spot and taking a sip. My stomach rolled and a wave of heat made my skin prickle. I'd worn summer-weight running tights since Leo, one of the women who led the summer hikes, suggested pants were preferable to shorts despite the heat. On top, I'd worn a linen button-up and a white tank and sports bra underneath. I'd figured the loose, light top would keep me warm if it got chilly—hilarious—and keep the sun and bugs off my skin.

But just now? That shirt felt like a punishment for some crime I'd committed in a past life. I ripped it off so fast I nearly tore the sleeve, then blotted my forehead where tiny speckles of sweat had sprung up in the last few minutes. I didn't mind getting sweaty or working out, but this was unusual for me.

"You okay over there?" Aidan said, crossing to me with concern notching his brow.

"Yeah, just overheated. I'll be good in a minute." I smiled, hoping it'd convince him. As much as part of me wanted to call it and just go back, I also wanted to do this hike and have lunch with him after. I wanted this day with him since odds were I wouldn't get another big chunk of time until we went out for his birthday later this week. And the reality of my like for Aidan meant I wanted every minute I could get.

He studied me for a moment before nodding. "Okay. Just let me know when you're ready."

A few minutes later, I rallied and shoved my water bottle in its spot. Aidan's hand appeared in front of my face before I could haul myself up, and I gratefully took it. He pulled me up and gave me a soft smile. "You sure you're okay?"

"Yes. Just needed a rest."

But oh, what lies. What horrid, monstrous lies I told. Another half hour and I felt shaky and weak. We arrived at a small waterfall and all I could think about was walking straight into the little pool of water, or covering myself in the icy mountain runoff and curling up on a cool rock.

I considered telling Aidan how bad I was feeling, but at this point, we were more than an hour into the hike. I was fairly certain we'd be coming up on the halfway point any minute now, so going forward made more sense anyway. Instead of tipping him off to my currently climbing internal temperature and the way my eyes felt a little too big for their sockets, I convincingly *oohed* and *aahed* over the little spot, and we pressed on.

Another twenty minutes and I'd gone inside myself. I'd managed only a few grunts and mumbled "Mm-hmm" and Aidan had been glancing back at me more often.

"Let's stop right here and have a snack," he said, pulling his pack from his shoulders and reaching for me as I neared. "Maddie, you feel warm."

I swayed where I stood and he helped me ease onto the

wooden bench set to the side of the trail. If one were to sit on this bench, one would see a glorious view of the mountainside, then farther out to the mountains beyond, and all the way to the horizon. But if one were currently burning up from the inside out, one would hardly be able to see beyond her hands.

He sat next to me and removed my backpack, forcing my water into my hand. "You need to drink this."

I did as instructed, taking a drink and finding my throat soothed by the cool water. I hadn't even fully registered it hurt, but sure enough, when the cold liquid was gone, it hurt. His hand came up to my forehead, and he swore under his breath.

"You're burning up," he said, concern painting his features. "How long have you felt bad?"

Guess the question of whether I did wasn't worth asking. If I looked anything like I felt, the answer would be clear. "Been off since I woke up, but it's gotten worse as we've climbed."

His frown deepened and he smoothed some hair off my forehead. I'd long since ditched my hat. His cool fingertips felt so good, I nearly groaned.

"I've got some pain reliever in my bag. Do you want to take it? We'll eat something and get going. We're actually over the halfway mark and should be hitting the downhill soon."

"Okay." I had no other comments other than the fleeting thought that maybe he could tie a little rope around me and lead me down so I could keep my eyes closed. They felt so heavy.

"Take this."

He dropped two small pills into my palm and waited while I took them. If I ever needed a test to gauge my trust in him, blindly taking pills without a thought would be one of them.

Wincing as I swallowed, my shoulders sagged. Aidan's large, cool hand cupped the back of my neck. His touch felt so good and I leaned into it, my head falling back enough that he now cradled it.

"Maddie, what hurts?"

The tenderness and concern in his voice made my heart twist. Good grief, he was too good. "Um, everything? My throat. My bones? My head. My eyeballs."

He huffed. I cracked an eye open to see amusement laced with frustration. "Okay, eat this and then we're leaving. We need to get you down this mountain and to the doctor."

My stomach rolled at the thought of eating anything, but I saw the logic. I forced down a few bites of the banana but couldn't take much more. All the while, he kept a hand on me—my neck, my shoulder, patting my leg and saying things like, "That's good. Great job. Can you do one more bite?"

Sometime between minutes and a small eternity later, he packed up our stuff, shouldered my bag, too, and helped me stand. My legs were wobbly, and I immediately wanted to cry.

Crap. "I think I'm really sick," I said, sounding pathetic even to my own ears.

"I think you are, too. Let's get you home."

Soon, we were off. His arm locked around me and held me close. I trudged along, eyes fighting to stay open, until he said, "I think I'm going to need to carry you."

Thankfully, he did. First, on his back, until all I could do was drape myself over him, and eventually in a full-on bridal carry the last fifteen minutes because whatever this was, humiliatingly, meant I had no energy to even hold on while he did all the work.

And every step of the way, despite how exhaustion pulled at me and everything hurt, I knew he'd get me down safely. I hated that he had to do this. With Aidan, I knew I was in good hands.

CHAPTER THIRTY-ONE

Aidan

Doc Lindsay scribbled something on a sheet, tore it off, and handed it to me. "I'll call this in when I get the results, but in case they need a hard copy..."

"Thank you. And you'll have the results when?" I didn't mean to sound impatient, but I wanted to get medicine in her and get her well. Seeing someone as indomitable as Maddie laid up in bed and delirious with a fever was disturbing on a cellular level.

Or maybe that was just the part of me that found her being sick and in pain intolerable. It was akin to when Luca was sick and all I wanted, all I *needed*, was for him to get better. This felt different than that, but also just the same.

"Three to five minutes," he said, checking his watch.

"Oh, I thought you had to take them to the lab or something."

The doctor smiled and shook his head. "Fortunately, no.

These rapid tests are very accurate, and I also happen to know it's going around. We see things like this roll through the clinic fairly predictably."

I nodded, familiar with how different illnesses swept through the small town in waves. In fact, Luca had had strep about a month ago, so it'd been making the rounds for a while. "And the meds will take how long to kick in? Help her feel better?"

"This time tomorrow, she should feel significantly better. Two days, all the more. My guess is the next twelve hours will be very uncomfortable and waking up first thing tomorrow might be rough, but keep treating symptoms along with the antibiotics. Keep the fever down—the medicines, a tepid shower if it spikes. She'll hate you for it, but she may need it as the afternoon sets in. Fevers always seem to climb."

I stared at Maddie, who'd fallen asleep, completely dead to the world, about three minutes after the doctor had swabbed her throat. My heart literally throbbed at the sight of her passed out and so miserable. "It's weird how that happens."

"It is. I—" His phone alarm chirped. "Ah, let's see." He moved to the side table where he'd set up his bag and the test equipment. "Yep. Positive for strep A. Give me a few minutes to get this called in and then you can go pick it up. They'll have it on hand for sure."

A few minutes later, I'd roused Maddie enough to tell her I'd be back with medicine. Her eyes were glassy and she seemed disoriented, but she said a soft, "Okay, thank you" and then slumped back over on the couch.

By the time I got back a half hour later, she hadn't moved. Nice as her couch was, I wanted her in bed and resting more comfortably as soon as I could get the medicine in her.

"Maddie, I'm back. Let's get these antibiotics going so you can feel better." I set a hand on her shoulder and tried to wake her, but she stayed asleep. "Maddie, wake up. Let's take your medicine."

The increased volume roused her just slightly, but it took another minute or two to get her eyes open. She looked miserable and when all she could do was let out a pathetic little groan, I brushed her hair away from her face. *Crap.* She was absolutely burning up.

"I'm going to sit you up," I said, sliding a hand behind her back and slowly tilting her to the upright position.

She made another sound of protest.

"I'm sorry. Have to get these meds in you. Do you think you can eat something?" I patted her hand, and she blinked up at me.

"Guess I should, but everything sounds awful."

After a little more coaxing, I got her to eat a slice of very lightly toasted bread and drink some orange juice. Not exactly the ideal diet for cushioning her stomach against the medicine, but when I suggested yogurt, her glare answered for her. At least she ate something.

I'd also hoped sitting at the bar, where I made her sit while I got her food, would help her cool down. She'd been buried under a blanket and I'd hoped that was the reason she'd been so warm. But when we took her temperature, it blinked an angry 104.

"Ohhh, that's bad," she said, looking at the thermometer's bright red read-out screen with one eye.

Anxiety spiked in my chest, but I smiled at her, all my dad expertise at staying calm coming into play. "It'll be okay. We know why it's high, and you just took some medicine to help. But we do need to get you cooled down."

"I'll change clothes," she said, moving from the barstool with a lurch toward the stairs.

"That's a good start. You may need to take a tepid shower or bath. It's the worst, but it usually does the trick." I steadied her at the elbow and walked alongside her as she gripped the railing and took the steps one at a time. She was moving like every inch hurt her, so I took over.

"Wait, wait. Wait, Aidan."

Her words were full of anxious surprise when I lifted her into my arms. I'd already carried her down part of the hike, and I wasn't about to have her fall down the stairs and break her neck on my watch.

"You're all right. We need to get you cooled down, so I'm going to help."

She rested her head against my chest and shoulder but spoke softly. "You don't need to do this. I can do it myself."

I suspected that if she felt normal, she wouldn't be so relaxed while protesting, but right now, she was practically dead weight. My heart squeezed at the reality that she felt so horrible, but at least we'd gotten meds. We'd addressed the larger issue, and it was a matter of waiting out the antibiotics and letting them do their thing.

"Which one's your room?" I asked at the top of the stairs.

"End of the hallway."

I moved as quickly as I could without jostling her too much and nudged the door open. As curious as I might've been about her bedroom, this was not the time to enjoy the details. I spotted the bathroom and took her in, setting her down by the giant tub.

"You'll need to get undressed and get in there. I'll start

the water and get out of here, but you've got to stick with it and don't turn the heat up."

She frowned like I'd said something truly awful, but asked, "You're not coming with me?"

I coughed, taken off-guard. "Uh, no. Not today—er, no. No. If you want me to come back and help you wash your hair or anything, I can, but..." I glanced at the giant shower with glass panes boxing it in. Rain shower heads in two places and enough room in there for two people, but that was not happening. There would be no way to keep her covered and help her, and I—

"It's fine. I can do it. I'll do it."

Every word sounded exhausted and pained. I wanted to hold her, to help her, but this was one of those times when I couldn't help her. Not without crossing a line I wasn't sure she'd be okay with in the light of day without a raging fever and headache.

"Okay. Yell if you need anything, and if you're not out in fifteen minutes, I'm coming in."

A little smile perked up at one corner of her mouth. "That a promise?" She wiggled her brows.

Little feverish beast was taunting me. I chuckled, letting some of the tension and worry for her leak out with my breath. "Sure, Maddie. That's a promise. Now go cool off."

And in the meantime, I'd make sure everything else was ready so she could get to bed and sleep this off. I'd call John and see if he could stay with Luca, and I'd let Anthony know she was sick just in case I was missing something on her schedule.

CHAPTER THIRTY-TWO

Maddie

Six hours after the shower of doom, as I'd lovingly come to think of it, I woke feeling less horrid than I had since we'd gotten back from the hike. This meant I still felt run over by a truck, but I could tell my fever had broken fully. The sleep had been a drug of its own, and while I still felt like someone had smashed my brain in a book and my throat hurt, I wasn't practically delirious, which I took as solid progress.

On the bedside table sat a tall glass of water, my phone, and a note from Aidan that said, "Let me know when you're up. I'll be downstairs."

My cheeks heated at the memory of him coming to find me in the shower. I'd heard him crack the door and ask if I was okay, but I couldn't make myself speak. I'd huddled into the far corner of the shower after hurriedly scrubbing my body and washing my hair. I'd been shivering so violently, I couldn't stand, so I curled into myself and let the spray of the water rain down until Aidan appeared and turned it off. He had his back to the shower. "I have a towel here. Can you stand?"

I couldn't remember the last time I'd felt so bad, and just now, I couldn't summon words. He couldn't see anything but my bare shoulders and knees and wet hair matting down my back. Fortunately, I'd wedged myself into the corner next to the wall so he hadn't seen my butt pancaked against the glass—at least I'd spared myself that indignity.

"Do you want me to get you?" he'd asked after my silence.

"Yes," I'd whispered, trying to spare my throat from any unnecessary pain.

He'd held up the towel and approached before draping it around me and tucking his hands in so he pulled me up and against him. In some other scenario, me being sopping wet and separated from Aidan by only a towel would be quite an event, but all I felt in that moment was relief to be off the cold shower floor and into his arms.

"Well, you definitely cooled off. Let's get you into some dry clothes and you can sleep it off."

And then he did, preserving my modesty at every turn. He'd found the clean clothes, not blanching at bringing me underwear and socks along with them. He seemed impervious to the intimate elements of taking care of me, and I was miserable enough not to allow myself to think about them.

But now? Hours later and a little less battered by fever and an aching everything? Embarrassment and no small amount of dread sluiced through me, sudden and violent. This was not the way I'd wanted this to go, and while I couldn't do anything to change what'd happened, I needed to apologize. No doubt he'd felt obligated to take care of me. I was here, alone, with no family and friends who were all busy with their lives. Aidan wasn't the kind of person who would just abandon a friend, or whatever I was, in their time of need.

But this couldn't go on. He'd done more than enough, and I didn't think my heart could take much more of his kindness. I already liked him too much. This all felt so much like the kinds of fantasies I used to spin. Not just kissing and closeness, but caring and sharing mundane things like getting sick and running errands. Hard to pretend I wanted any other version of life.

I took the stairs slowly enough that when I padded into the living room on shaky legs, Aidan didn't notice me. He sat on one end of my overstuffed couch with a lamp on. My heart tripped at the sight of him in glasses with thin wire frames as he tapped away on a laptop that rested on the arm of the couch. He looked so focused, I hated to interrupt him. But when my slippers hit the hardwood of the kitchen right next to the living room, he startled and bolted off the couch.

"I didn't hear you moving around, I'm sorry. How are you?" He pressed his hand to my forehead, searching my face and surveying my body like looking me over would tell him my pain level or speak of any new ailments.

"I'm okay. A lot better than earlier, for sure. I think the fever's gone, and I might actually be a little hungry." Amazing, considering how horrible food had sounded for the last twelve hours, but I'd take it. I rarely lost my appetite, even when sick, so that alone told me how bad I'd been.

"That's good. I made soup and it's ready whenever you are. I got some bread as well, if that sounds okay. You can take more medicine since the doctor wanted you to get a second dose in today, or you can wait a bit." His hand on my back steered me toward the bar.

"That sounds amazing. Thank you."

He helped me into the seat, which wasn't necessary, but I could appreciate that I'd been a basket case earlier, so he expected me to need his help. When he dished up chicken noodle soup from a pot on the stove, it clicked that he had made soup. Not like, opened a can and dumped it in to heat it, but this was actual homemade soup.

And based on what I knew about Aidan, he'd made it. A pang of longing and affection for that part of him—that *can do, take control, and make it happen* piece—made my ribs ache. He'd taken such good care of me, and if I hadn't been sitting, it would've taken me to my knees to think about just how thoroughly he'd managed things.

"Did you make this?" I asked after taking a spoonful and finding it soothed rather than excoriated my throat. *Wait, he just said he did.* Ugh, my brain was still fogged.

"I did. Well, I had some frozen from when Luca was sick a few weeks ago, so I warmed it up. It's just so much better when it's homemade." He gave me a soft smile and set a thick slice of bread slathered with butter on a plate next to my bowl.

I continued taking small bites of the soup while he delivered ice water, a small glass of orange juice, and a little bowl of pills. Each delivery he made cinched my throat tighter, and by the time he came to check my temperature, I had tears in my eyes.

"Oh, hey, if you need to go back to bed, I'll help you. You're almost through the worst, I'm sure of it."

He ran a hand over my hair in a gesture so familiar and affectionate, it made the tears track down my face when I shut my eyes to savor the touch.

"It's not that. You're just..." How did I explain it? How could he know how seldomly people treated me this way? They deferred to me, yes. Catered. Made sure my needs were met. But it was done because of the name, the status, the wealth, and not because they genuinely cared. Even Anthony, who was an amazing assistant and friend, couldn't be like this. Frankly, it wouldn't be appropriate. Aidan's tenderness nearly gutted me. "You're being so sweet."

He chuckled quietly, and I opened my eyes just in time to see his soft smile. My heart swooned at the flash of teeth against his dark beard. Goodness, he was handsome. And if I wasn't disgusting and ill, I'd kiss him.

"I'm glad I can help. Eat up and you can get back to bed." He squeezed my shoulder gently and went to putter around the kitchen.

After a few more bites, I took the pills and started feeling a little better mentally but a bit worse physically. "I think I need to lie down again."

He abandoned whatever he was doing at the sink and came directly to me, hooking his arm around my back as I stood. "I'll help you back upstairs. Need anything?"

"You really don't have to. I should be fine—"

"I'm here, and I'm helping you."

I grabbed the railing, and he guided me from the other side. "This is overkill. I'm sure you have to get back to Luca, and I—"

"I know you can out-stubborn me ten days a week, but you're not getting rid of me tonight, Maddie. Luca's with his grandparents and I'm here with you. I've got you."

We reached the top of the stairs, and the need to cry hit me again. I didn't want to feel so emotional, like I'd never been cared for in my life. I had. But it'd been a long time since I'd been sick and felt so pathetic physically that it gave me this puny feeling emotionally. I'd only just recovered from the stalker nonsense, and for some reason, Aidan's insistence on being here for me made me want to curl up and sob.

After I slid back under the covers and he sat on the edge of the bed and felt my forehead, I tried again. "You really don't have to stay. I appreciate it, but you don't have to."

He pinned me with those dark eyes and nodded. "I know I don't have to. I nearly had to kick Anthony out earlier when he stopped by after I texted. Juliet offered to fly herself here."

"From South Africa?" I'd texted her yesterday that I felt terrible. I hadn't realized she knew how to get ahold of Aidan, but it didn't surprise me that she had. She was like that when she wanted to be.

He dipped his head. "Yep. And I'm sure if I'd given your mother even a hint that you were sick, she could've made it out here in minutes by the sheer force of her will."

A scratchy laugh escaped me.

"But I'm here. I want to be here. I've honed my skills of taking care of sick patients in the last eleven years of parenting, and I'm not going anywhere."

I slumped back against the pillow to show my defeat, which only made his smile widen. *Ugh.* Too handsome for his own good, or maybe more accurately, for *my* own good. I wanted to say something meaningful, something that would convey how much this meant to me without it seeming like a love confession.

But more than anything, I wanted that last statement to be true. I wanted him to stay with me, to not leave. And the desperate grasping for that reality I felt deep in my chest told me just how much.

CHAPTER THIRTY-THREE

Aidan

A few days later, John eyed me with that squinty, suspicious gaze I knew all too well. How many times had I seen it over the years? Countless.

"You're good? Really?"

I nodded. "You know I am. I'm just doing my usual. I appreciate you taking Luca and letting him have a fun night."

My cousin's small smile showed his understanding. He knew I wasn't a wreck over the day, but I think, as much as he could, he understood I needed the space. I never asked my in-laws because I didn't want to draw attention to the day for them. Maybe that was stupid, but we had other benchmarks we made a big deal of—birthdays, special events she would've loved.

"Does that mean you're free tonight?"

Maddie's voice hit me in the chest in the best way. I turned to see her looking healthy and vibrant. *Thank goodness.* It'd been four days since I'd left her house, promising her I'd let her know if I felt sick and waving off her repeating thank-yous. She'd improved so much overnight, I hadn't been scared to leave her. At the same time, I hated leaving and wished I could pause the rest of life and stay with her.

She assured me Anthony would help if she needed it, but that didn't sit right with me. I knew the man was a close friend *and* employee, but I hated the idea of her paying someone to do the most basic things for her, things that a partner would do.

But I didn't know where that line was. I'd stayed while she was nearly delirious and insisted on staying the night, but I sensed staying any longer than that would be too much. The space we now occupied was unknown territory to me. I'd married Viv young and hadn't dated anyone seriously since she'd passed. I didn't know how to manage this in between, especially when my feelings were far too strong this early in the game *and* she was leaving. No doubt, no equivocation, she would leave.

One part of me felt a gut reaction to end it now before I fell any further. I'd had the thought too many times over the weekend. And yet, if the years since losing my wife had taught me anything, it was that I didn't want to live half a life. I didn't want to cage myself in and keep myself safe, because who knew what lay ahead. Too often, we have no idea what's coming. I wanted to live with a full heart. I'd done enough bracing against the possible futures for a lifetime, and I'd promised myself and the legacy of my marriage to Viv that I wouldn't limp along in fear forever.

"Luca and I are having a guys' night. Pizza. Video games. Books. All the craziest party games." John grinned and wiggled his brows like he'd mentioned a list of frat party plans instead of hanging out with his eleven-year-old sort-of nephew.

"And you?" Maddie's gorgeous hazel eyes shifted to me.

"Uh, I'm—"

"Hey, I'm going to stock up on snacks. I'll be by in an hour or so," John said, giving me a look.

A meaningful look that said something like *you should just tell her* or maybe *you shouldn't tell her, that's too much.* I hesitated, but I wanted Maddie to know. Much like our first encounter, I wanted her to see me as I was. Ironically, at that point, I'd specifically left out the whole widowed father thing, but we'd still had such an honest exchange. Such a real evening. And every interaction since had felt the same.

So I wouldn't lie to her now. I just... went for it. "It's my anniversary."

"Your... *oh.*" Her eyes grew wide and her brow furrowed. Not pity, though—concern laced her features.

"Before you worry or ask, I'm okay. I just always feel like I owe it to her, or maybe at this point more to myself, to take some time and... remember her."

She set a hand on my wrist. "I don't know what that's like, but it makes sense. And please know, if you ever want to tell me about her, I'd love to hear."

Something gripped me, deep in my chest. Emotion clocked me in the skull and I swallowed hard. "Thank you."

Her eyes searched mine before she let her hand drop. "Can I hug you?"

A breathy laugh escaped. "Of course."

And she did. She leaned in and hugged me close, one hand on my back, the other soft but strong on my neck. Not trying to distract me from the memory or convince me to spend time with her. Not attempting to act like she knew what this felt like, or could guess. No begging to ignore the calendar and live a little. No suggestion that maybe spending time with someone new would make it easier, better. All the things other people had tried? She didn't do that.

She just hugged me, offering a moment of compassion and human connection, then she stepped away. "I'll be around, but if you're busy until then, I'll see you on the twenty-fourth."

I grabbed her hand. "I won't be busy until then, Maddie. Just tonight."

She smiled, and with a small nod, she slipped away into the crowd milling along Silver Street.

Hours later, I found myself calling her. I'd gone through the traditions I'd made over the last eight years, letting emotion overwhelm me. Revisiting the sense of loss. Allowing myself to remember all the beauty Vivienne Templeton-Wallace brought with her, and that she took away. I could get pretty dark on days like these, but this year, I didn't feel that pull to drown my sorrows late into the night. And I knew why.

It wasn't that Maddie took away the pain or loss. At some point, I'd lose her, too. And I could circle that date on the calendar, or at least the general time frame. It was a known loss, and I'd decided it was worth it.

But what had improved this year, a little more than it had last year, was the hope. I now had the genuine belief that I could find someone to love again. Hell, I was more than halfway there already. And while I didn't fool myself into thinking a man would be lucky enough to love more than one amazing woman like I had Viv, somehow, I'd tricked Maddie into spending time with me. And maybe that meant I could find something meaningful and long-term with someone else. Eventually.

Once I recovered from this glimpse at a second chance.

So the fact that I physically relaxed when she answered didn't surprise me. I'd spent the day thinking of and remembering Viv, but Maddie had been on the fringes, and it felt good to come back around. I wanted her to understand, and I'd decided to just call her and tell her. To ignore all the social awkwardness surrounding talking about someone you've lost and simply tell Maddie about my first love.

"Hey, I didn't expect to hear from you."

She sounded tired, but I'd learned she liked to stay up late sometimes and lucked out with her answering now.

"I wanted to tell you about today. About her. If you're not too tired." The second the words were out of my mouth, a sharp bolt of second-guessing shot through me. Was this a huge mistake? Was I reading way, *way* too much into things between us? So I'd taken care of her while she was sick. So we'd gone out a few times. That didn't mean—

"Of course. I'd love to hear anything you want to share."

Relief gusted out in a sigh. "Okay. Good. First, I guess I should tell you how we met..."

And I did. I told her about loving Viv as a friend first and then falling more and more for her as we moved through college up at Utah State. By the end, we knew we were both coming back here, and we knew we didn't want to be apart. We were married for years before we had Luca, our miracle baby she called him, and then had three years together.

That's when my life changed in ways I'd never imagined. A nightmare come to life, I lost her and lost myself for a long time, too. When I choked up telling Maddie about the days Luca wouldn't stop crying for her, she'd gone silent, too. I composed myself after a few seconds. "Sorry. Remembering that time still gets me."

I heard her sniffle on the other end of the line. "I'm so sorry. I'm so sorry you went through that, and I'm so sorry Luca lost his mom. She sounds wonderful."

I nodded, eyes glassy again. "She was. She was my best friend, and I miss her every day. But I'm not half a person anymore." I breathed through the ache for a moment before continuing. "I remember thinking I'd never feel whole again —that I'd be this version of me walking around with a gaping flesh wound, my chest torn open and my heart mangled."

"I can't imagine."

"I hope you don't ever have to. But I'm not there anymore. It wasn't one lightning bolt of clarity or some real- ization that I'd love again or whatever. It was more the inevitable passage of time and dulling of that constant agony. And I can say that we are well-loved. John, his brother, his parents, even many of the locals who were here when she died... they try to smother us."

She chuckled like I'd hoped she would. "And your parents?"

What used to hurt only released a dull ache now. "They retired to Florida. They were here for us the first year and a half, but they'd been planning to leave before the accident. They're good people, but they're older and were ready to start their new life as retirees in a warmer place. I don't blame them, though I wish Luca had more of a relationship with them."

"And her parents?"

I smiled even as I sighed. "I love them. I do. But as I've mentioned, I feel this... obligation to them. To make up for what they lost. To make up for how they had to help with Luca when I couldn't get out of bed. I know I can't ever repay them or make up for losing their only child, and yet there's this gut-level feeling that it's up to me."

She was quiet again for a moment, then hummed. "I can see why, I guess. But I hope you'll let yourself off the hook. And I hope they'll agree to one of the offers."

That had me exhaling roughly. We'd received two very solid offers on the farm and they were dragging their heels even more than they had been—or, Rich was, anyway. "Me, too. I think we'd all be a lot happier, especially if we found someone who'd really love the place. I think that friend of Wilder Saint's could be a great option. He seems like he's ready to put down roots here. I like the idea of it going to someone who's going to make a life from it, and who's also seen a lot of hardship. I get the sense that he needs the space and the trees for himself as much as he wants them for the business."

"That does sound like a good match. Rich doesn't see it?"

I sighed again, which tipped me off to the fact that I needed to move on from this topic. Too much sighing was always a bad sign. "I don't know. But... never mind him. It's getting late. I appreciate you letting me talk about her. It's kind of an odd thing to tell the woman you're dating about your wife, but I hope..."

What did I hope? I couldn't put that into words.

She saved me from having to. "I'm honored to hear about her. I'm so glad to be here with you, and I'm grateful you've given me this glimpse into your past, and your present. And I'm honestly so glad you got to love someone as amazing as she was. I guess that probably sounds like a line, but I mean it."

I swallowed past a lump in my throat and worked to keep us in lighter territory. "You're not really one to use lines, are you?"

She laughed softly. "No. I don't suppose I am."

"Lunch tomorrow?" I asked, knowing for sure I wouldn't last until the weekend without seeing her.

"I'd love it. Just text me."

"Will do. Night, Maddie."

"Night, Aidan."

The line went quiet, and I let my head fall back on my pillow. Last year, I'd spent the day feeling the loss, but honestly, I'd thought about Maddie. We'd met nine months before for a matter of hours and it was the first time I'd thought I might actually find someone again. My first encounter with a woman who I was both attracted to and interested in. And yes, the reprieve from her knowing my history helped, but it wasn't just that, as our time together lately proved.

The fake date that rolled into the Night in Bloom real date... those, too, had given me a glimpse of what could be. What was... for now.

Tonight, I was closing out the day feeling the familiar ache of missing Viv, but also like she was with me in a new way. Maybe just telling Maddie about her had done that. Maybe remembering how devoted John and my aunt and uncle had been to us helped.

Or maybe it was sharing this huge piece of myself with a woman I wanted, for whom I could easily care deeply, and not have her want to save me or heal me or do anything but accept me. To accept my past and a life I'd loved, but lost.

I wouldn't dare put my growing feelings on her, but tonight, Maddie had cared for me well. Maybe even loved me by letting me share with her.

Whenever this was all over, I'd remain grateful for this night.

CHAPTER THIRTY-FOUR

Maddie

It had to be last night's conversation. That had to be the reason everything Aidan said, everything he did, every scoop of guacamole or bite of taco he took, appealed to me. Like, really? Why was his chewing sexy?

The emotional discussion last night had left me reeling. Not so much over Aidan sharing about the love of his life dying when Luca was only three, but the fact that he'd shared those things with me at all. We'd been honest and had some good heart-to-hearts, but that was beyond anything I expected. Maybe because I'd only dated "computer-loving vampires" as Nate would say, who never seemed to be able to access their emotional circuit boards.

Aidan was so... mature. And he'd mentioned it'd taken years and therapy and support, but it was just all kind of stunning. He'd had to work to heal and he'd needed time, but he had. He'd made it clear he'd never stop missing her, but he wasn't closed off to the world. He hadn't sworn off love or relationships, and it struck me as nothing short of heroic. And it had the very strange effect of making me want that kind of love. I didn't want to lose it, of course, but I wanted to experience it. When I'd said I thought he was lucky to have loved someone like he loved Vivienne, I meant it.

I'd wanted that kind of love for a long time, and especially since I'd witnessed it between Ariel and Nate. Seeing my brother that happy was incredible, but it left me wanting. And there was no coincidence that at their wedding, I'd been thinking of Aidan. I'd been remembering our connection that night at the lounge at Silver Ridge Resort and wondering.

I'd known it for weeks, but after last night, I couldn't deny it. I was in danger of wrecking myself with Aidan, and even with that awareness, I had no intention of cutting our time short.

Aidan laughed as he crumpled his napkin and tossed it onto his plate. Brodie came by and cleared our plates immediately, and we both slid out of our booths to free up the space for the next party.

Aidan grabbed my hand and laced our fingers together. He wasn't shy about being affectionate now that we'd made our relationship official at the Night in Bloom, but we'd only been out in town together like this a handful of times. It made my stomach flip, especially when he pulled me around the corner and tucked us under the awning of Wallace and Sons law firm.

"Thanks for getting lunch with me."

I grinned. "I should be saying that. You're the one with a job. I'm just lazing around doing nothing."

And honestly, I barely missed work. It was something I

was still grappling with because I'd never taken a sabbatical. I'd always assumed I'd be miserable. Survey says? Not so much.

"You've earned some downtime. But hey, I wanted to say thank you. For last night. Thanks for listening."

I bit my lip because he was cupping my cheek and looking at me with those eyes that made me weak. "Thank you for sharing with me."

He nodded just slightly, then leaned in and pressed a kiss to my lips. I hadn't kissed him in a week, which was an absolute crying shame. I squeezed his hand where we still touched because if I didn't, I'd throw my arms around his neck and forget about the fact that we were standing on the street and I'd be meeting John and Luca any minute now.

When he pulled back, he gave me a devastating smile. "You sure you're up for Luca?"

I chuckled, knowing my cheeks were hot just like the rest of me after the kiss. "Absolutely. I think we can get through his interview questions first and get that out of the way. Then we're going to the bookstore and probably Scoop. After, I'll take him to your place and we'll be ready for the movie when you get off."

Luca had requested some time to interview me for an upcoming project for school and I'd happily agreed. We'd decided to schedule it this afternoon so I could bridge the gap for Aidan and, if I was being honest, I looked forward to spending time with Luca. The fact that this project gave us a good excuse was enough for me.

"Ah, so it's all bribery after he gets the goods, huh?"

I grinned. "Obviously."

He chuckled and shook his head, bringing my hand to his lips. "Thank you again for last night."

"Stop thanking me for being a woman greedy for every

bit of you. Now shoo!" I literally shooed him away and enjoyed the sight of him jogging in the direction of his car.

"Oh, oh, oh, hello! *Thank you for last night?* What have we been up to, Ms. Reynolds?" Dahlia sidled up next to me and nudged my shoulder with hers.

Shaking my head, I let out a little chuckle even though my cheeks flamed again. "Nothing like that. We talked. *On the phone.*"

She wiggled her brows. "Must have been *quite* the conversation."

I laughed more freely at that. "You're incorrigible. And yes, it was, but not in that way, you weirdo. We talked about his wife."

"Oh." She sobered instantly. "Well, not nearly as sexy as I'd hoped, but I'm thinking that was pretty important."

"Your thinking is correct."

She glanced at the sign above us. "And now you're just hanging out next to the law firm to be close to some other Wallaces?"

I crossed my arms and leaned against the brick of the building. "Of course. I'm desperate for any Wallace energy I can get."

She made a face like she wasn't satisfied.

"I'm actually meeting John. He's handing off Luca after they had a guys' night."

Her face instantly changed. From interested to irritated in a snap. "Ugh, that man. If he's coming, I'm going."

She started walking as though leaving our conversation that suddenly was normal because I'd mentioned John.

"Uh, okay, wait. It's time to talk about this."

She glanced over her shoulder but kept speeding down Elk Street toward her shop. She'd have to stop before she crossed the road and if nothing else, I'd catch her then.

"Seriously, Dahlia. What is with you and John?"

She huffed and spun on me. "I don't know."

It wasn't an evasion. Based on the unending frustration on her face, she really didn't.

"How is that possible? You guys catfight constantly. Just the mention of his name sent you practically sprinting away from me. I don't know you all that well, but I know enough to know that is not... typical."

Her lips firmed and her eyes skated away from me, across the street and back toward her shop. "I honestly don't really know. I moved here a few years ago, and he was one of the first people I met at a meeting for small businesses in town. It was just... like that. Immediately. And while I am normally not a walking jerkface, he brings it out of me."

"So you actually dislike him?" This just seemed so crazy. They were both genuinely nice, likeable people. The fact that they butted heads so completely felt like a mystery to be solved.

She sighed and ran a hand down the strap of her purse. "I know it's insane, but I don't know. I can't separate the fact that I know he dislikes me. And it may be pathetic, but I hate that he's so nice to literally everyone else, and then he's this weird, critical jerk to me. So, as much as I try to talk myself into being the bigger person, I have yet to succeed. Maybe that'll be my new year's resolution."

I blinked. "It's July."

She smirked. "Well, I don't really think it's happening anytime soon, so I'm giving myself time to work up to it."

I laughed and waved as she blew me a kiss and shuffled across the street. Elk Street had such a quaint feel to it, and I loved spending time here. By the time I turned back toward Wallace and Sons, John and Luca were high-fiving.

"Hey, Maddie. You ready?" Luca asked, waving at John without another word to the man.

"Uh, yes. Is your uncle ready for me to take you?"

John pressed a hand over his heart. "I may suffer from our separation, but I think the time has come. Enjoy the bookstore, you two."

"Will do," I said, turning to Luca, who was facing the bookstore like it had him in a tractor beam. "You have a list?"

He quirked a brow. "I *always* have a list."

And so off we went, our first time hanging out totally by ourselves and I wasn't even nervous. Books and ice cream would smooth the way, but something told me I didn't need the bribery with Luca anyway. Still, I was glad to have it and happy to know that in a few hours, Aidan would be joining us. If anything made me nervous, it was what questions he'd have for the interview. He might rival some of the press I'd met on my book tour, if past conversations were anything to go by.

I'd never imagined looking forward to spending time with an eleven-year-old, and yet here I was.

CHAPTER THIRTY-FIVE

Aidan

I hadn't worried about Maddie and Luca's time together, but I'd been curious enough to be distracted all afternoon. It didn't matter if it hadn't gone perfectly, and yet I wanted it to go well. Some primal part of me needed Luca to connect with another woman who wasn't a grandmother or aunt, even though that was never the purpose of their time together. I needed him to have that attention, and Maddie was frankly excellent at making the person she was talking to feel important.

Her willingness to engage with him, to let him interview her and pester her with questions about stuff I had no idea he was interested in, only made me value her more. Steal my heart by seeing me, but keep it by seeing my kid.

And even though I resisted admitting it, I wanted her to like Luca. Not just like him, but want to be around him. I didn't expect her to grow motherly feelings or something insane. We'd been dating for a few weeks. She'd met him just over a month ago. That was crazy.

But honestly, I'd felt a little crazy the last few hours. And even though there was an end to this, having them enjoy each other made it stretch a little farther into the future somehow.

"You're home!" Maddie yelled, and my heart traded places with my stomach, all my organs swapping around and leaving me rattled.

Luca smiled from his spot on the couch. "We made Rice Krispie treats."

A little tray sat on the bar of our kitchen, stacked with misshapen squares. "These look... good."

Luca and Maddie eyed each other, then cracked up. Luca hadn't laughed that hard in I don't know how long, and I wasn't sure I'd seen Maddie laugh like that either.

She recovered first, though, and wiped an invisible tear of hilarity from her eye. "Um, yeah. We had some challenges with cutting them."

Luca cracked up again as I eyed their busted treats. They were misshapen and messy, but I lifted the plastic wrap and snatched one off the plate. I took a bite, dramatically flaring my eyes before swallowing. "Well, they look terrible, but they taste delicious. Good job, you two."

I wasn't prepared for their high five or for the warmth that spread through me like ink in water. It saturated every bit of me, making my heart feel like it might start glowing. They were getting along so well. I had to work not to choke up.

I wouldn't do that. But *this* was what I wanted. This was why I'd gone on date after crappy blind date. To find someone else to be on Luca's team.

And here was Maddie, on his team *and* on mine. If I could keep her, it—

But no. I couldn't think like that. All this did was confirm that I was glad we were doing this—dating, and soaking up the time we had. And it would spur me on later. Once I'd recovered from her leaving. I'd be able to remember these moments and how valuable they were to me, and more importantly, to my son.

I could find someone for him. Even if everyone paled in comparison to her, I could do that for him. It'd always been something I'd wanted and felt a kind of fatherly obligation for, but it hadn't worked. After meeting Maddie, my standard changed, and I knew with the clarity I'd never felt before that my standards would have to change yet again if I planned to go back to blind dates and the RuralMatch app to help me.

But for now? I'd enjoy these ridiculous two and savor their silliness and the fact that Luca was laughing and high-fiving instead of withdrawn into a book.

"All right, crazies. Should we have pizza or did you fill up on dessert first?"

They both grinned but promised they wanted pizza. I asked them to get the oven going and the ingredients out while I hopped into the shower. I hadn't gotten too filthy at work—not like some days, but I'd jumped in to help guide some larger trees in place, and I didn't feel like getting close to Maddie and having her horrified by the layer of dirt that coated my forearms.

I blew through the shower quickly, anticipation for a night spent with two of my favorite people driving me to wrap it up despite the sore muscles in my back and neck. I pulled on jeans and was running a towel through my hair when someone knocked lightly.

Probably Luca wondering about which pan to use since I'd cracked our pizza stone in half the last time we'd done homemade pizza—not my best move. I grabbed the door and pulled it open. "Hey, bud, just use—"

My words dropped off at the sight of Maddie, who was smiling until her eyes tracked down my body. She shifted and opened her mouth, then snapped it shut as her gaze jumped back to mine.

The moment hung between us. I felt frozen in place, one hand stilled atop my head with the towel, the other on the door. She blinked rapidly, turning to the side.

"Uh, sorry—"

"Sorry. I'll grab a shirt. I thought you were Luca," I said, leaving the door open but retreating to my dresser to grab something and work to ignore the rather blatant appreciation I'd just seen on her face.

Did I like it? Absolutely, yes. Could I do anything about that just now while my son waited for us in the kitchen? Sadly, no.

"It's fine. I apologize for, uh, for—"

Call me a jerk, but I couldn't help the grin that pulled at my lips. Hearing Maddie a little tongue-tied over *me*? I wished I could've savored the moment.

Alas, Luca hollered from the kitchen, "Oven's ready!"

I tossed the towel on the nearby bed and pulled the T-shirt over my head. It was thin and a little ratty—probably not what I would've chosen if I'd been alone to make the choice and hadn't rushed it.

"Ready?"

She huffed a small laugh. "You mean have I recovered from seeing..." She waved her hand like the sight of my chest had disturbed her.

"Yes."

She cracked half a smile. "I'm not sure I'll ever recover from that."

I chuckled at her ridiculousness. Yes, I was in shape. I had a frequently physically demanding job—whether we were talking about the tree farm or my own business—and I used exercise to help me decompress and cope with the realities of single-dad life more often than not. I wasn't sporting the usual dad-bod look, though no shade for anyone who did.

I wouldn't pretend I didn't enjoy her reaction to me. I so often felt out of my league with her, no matter how I tried to tamp that down.

"I'm sure you'll be fine," I said, daring to sling an arm around her shoulder.

She leaned against me, making my heart trip. We hadn't actually gotten to touch all that much. We'd kissed a handful of times. I wanted to take some liberty and hold her at her waist, slide down to the curve of her hip, but no. *No.*

Pizza. Movie. Child in the other room.

But the impulse drove me to dip my head and whisper into her ear. "If we were alone, I would kiss you."

She inhaled and bit her lip as I looked down at her. "I would kiss you back."

And then we were in the kitchen watching Luca spoon jarred pizza sauce over a misshapen circle of dough and loading our individual pizzas with cheese and toppings. We were laughing over our meal, arguing over the best kind of cookie and whether it was legal to put ketchup on pizza.

I didn't remember the last time I'd laughed like this. John kept me guessing and often made me chuckle, but something about Luca feeling so free and comfortable with Maddie loosened a tightness in me I hadn't realized was there. It unwound me, unspooled this string of contentment and pleasure I wanted to follow.

We watched the movie from the couch, sides smashed together and one of my arms around Maddie's shoulder. Luca sprawled in the chair and occasionally looked over at us and rolled his eyes, but after, he'd tuck his chin and grin to himself like he thought I couldn't see.

By the end of the night, I felt like it was all a dream. Right up until she said goodnight to a sleepy Luca as he stumbled into his room with a mumbled "See you soon." When his door shut, and we'd nearly reached the front door, she pressed against me until my back hit the wall, and I lost my breath.

Our lips met in a kiss that'd been building for what felt like days or years, not just hours since this afternoon. We chased each other, devoured, then lost ourselves for some span of time I didn't calculate until my hands were in her hair and pressed against the skin of her lower back and hers had slipped under my shirt to grip my sides.

It was glorious. It was painful. And I would never have enough of her. So when she pulled away looking mussed and hungry, eyes flicking to my lips and back to meet mine, desire and affection twined together and wrapped tightly around me.

"So... I'll see you Friday."

My brain was still working to come back online, but I nodded. "Uh, yes. Friday."

"The twenty-fourth?"

Ah. "Yes. Yes. But we could do coffee or something tomorrow? Thursday?"

She grinned. "I'm in Salt Lake tomorrow, and you've got a crazy schedule Thursday if I'm remembering right?"

I made a face, mind fully back to reality. "Sorry. I think my brain stopped functioning a few minutes ago."

She chuckled and it sounded about as delighted as I felt. I cupped her face and kissed her again, loving having her so close.

Loving everything about this night.

Oh. Crap.

Loving her.

"Talk to you tomorrow," she said, saving me from finding words in the midst of the realization.

"Yes. Text me when you get home."

She tilted her head and gave me a look I couldn't decipher, but nodded. "Of course." After one more kiss to my cheek, my jaw, my neck, she slipped away and took part of me with her.

I hadn't intended to give it to her, but in truth, I'd felt it coming. And now, I'd just have to make peace with that bit missing once she left for good.

CHAPTER THIRTY-SIX

Maddie

Anticipation twisted through me for the evening's events. Not only was it July twenty-fourth, a Utah holiday celebrating pioneers and a local favorite excuse to throw parties and shoot off fireworks, it was also Aidan's fortieth birthday.

And he hadn't told me. Not a word of mention. Fortunately, John had. He'd planned an entire surprise party under the guise of the holiday and assured me Aidan would love it. I couldn't see him being mad, but I worried. His day yesterday had been meetings back-to-back, one of which was with Rich and his realtor. He'd been too talked out to explain everything last night when I'd called, but it was clear Rich was resisting taking an incredible offer, the one Aidan was recommending he accept, and Aidan felt boxed in.

I didn't fully understand why he couldn't just tell his in-laws that he didn't want the business. After some of Aidan's comments, I'd started to suspect that Rich was waiting for Aidan to say he wanted to buy it or do something with it himself. If he was holding out that hope, I didn't think Rich would ever sell, and that would only create more problems for Aidan.

I ached for him, and yet, I didn't fully understand. On one hand, yes, I did, because of course he didn't want to hurt or offend his in-laws after they'd lost their daughter. On the other hand, this was Aidan's life and his Vivienne had died eight years ago. Obviously, I could switch into callous businesswoman mode on a dime, but I didn't think suggesting he needed to be upfront with them was unfeeling.

Based on my suggestion last night? *Yeah.* Bad timing, at least. He hadn't been able to hear it, and I should've known better. But things between us felt close—they felt good. And I was used to sharing my opinion. Heck, I was paid for it, begged for it. It'd seemed natural for me to help, maybe try to fix things for him.

But that was where I went wrong, and I'd only realized it after the words were out of my mouth. *"Maybe you should just be honest?"*

He'd been quiet a moment before saying, "Yeah, maybe I'll try that." Then he'd begged off, claiming he was exhausted. That hadn't been a ruse. I could tell he was absolutely running on empty, but everything hurt once he'd hung up.

We'd texted short good mornings today. A few notes about logistics for tonight—he'd pick me up. We'd arrive at the brewery together. Timing.

I hoped we could clear the air in the next few minutes

because if not, it'd make the whole evening disappointing, and I'd have no one to blame but my know-it-all self.

When Aidan rang the doorbell, I answered with nerves in my throat. He had his hands crammed in his jeans pockets and glanced up through thick, dark lashes with enough feeling in his eyes to make my heart flip flop.

"Hey. You look beautiful."

I glanced down at my white dress, momentarily forgetting that I'd gone all out for the night. Despite the weirdness between us, I wanted to look good for him. I wore a white sleeveless dress with a skirt that flared and ended above the knees, along with nude sandals with a healthy heel since he had plenty of height on me. I'd done my hair in waves with just one side pinned back behind my ear.

"You look very handsome." He did, too. A navy button-up rolled at the wrists and jeans with his perpetually handsome face had my heart fluttering despite the feeling that I wasn't sure where we stood.

He reached for my hand. "I'm sorry I was short last night. I was exhausted, and it was a little hard to hear, but—"

"I'm sorry I said anything. I knew you were exhausted, and it wasn't the right time. I stand by what I said, but I am truly sorry for *when* I said it."

A soft smile pulled at his cheeks. "You were right to say something. And I agree. As much as I hate to admit it, I do need to just tell them. It's a long time coming and I'd hoped to avoid it, but I don't think I can put it off unless I want to lose this offer."

"I know it'll be difficult, but I'm hoping that in the end, everyone will be relieved to have the truth out there."

He nodded, pulling me in for a hug and I gladly accepted it, giving the embrace every bit of me and tucking my face into his neck. We breathed together for a minute, and then he pulled away just enough to look at me so closely, it made my heart twist. The expression was raw and open. It was a gift. And in that moment, his vulnerability and willingness to share these difficult things with me hammered home what I'd suspected for days now.

I loved Aidan Wallace. I loved him with a breathless, heart-wrenching kind of love that felt impossible and yet more significant than anything I'd ever experienced. It hadn't even snuck up on me. It was as though, in hindsight, I'd seen it coming since the first time we met. Maybe my heart had been chasing after him all this time, trying to catch up and fit itself back together.

I didn't believe in love at first sight, but we certainly had connected.

"Thank you," he said softly, further cementing his place in my heart.

As though *he* needed to thank *me*. Ugh, this man.

I shook my head, a kind of doom circling my mind in the wake of my realization. I loved him and knew on a gut level I'd never love anyone like this again, but he would never leave here and I couldn't stay. What kind of idiocy was that? "You know you're ruining me, right?"

His brow furrowed and he dipped his head to touch mine. "I don't want to do that."

I huffed and pressed a kiss to his cheek before pulling away entirely. "Yeah. That's just another way you end up being so good at it."

CHAPTER THIRTY-SEVEN

Aidan

The "Surprise!" rang out loudly enough it made my ears ring for a few seconds afterward. My heart had seized up as well, and now it sprinted in my chest, cranked up with adrenaline and genuine surprise. A giant *Happy 40ᵗʰ Birthday Aidan!* banner hung along the back wall of the Silver Ridge Brewing Company's event space.

"I take it by the blush and the surprised face that you were, in fact, surprised?" John said, beaming at me and looking incredibly pleased with himself.

"Yes. You got me."

A whole string of people smiled at me, grinning at my winded, blown-away expression, no doubt. I could hardly absorb how many people had come. Jonas Bauer and Leo Morrison, Jamie and Bel Morris, Dahlia, all the Saint brothers and their partners, my uncle and aunt, my cousin and his wife, my crew and several of the guys from the farm... who *hadn't* come was probably the better question.

He turned to Maddie. "You didn't tell him? I'm impressed. I thought for sure you'd do the old insider girl-friend spoiler."

Maddie frowned at him. "Who hurt you?"

He chuckled, but I knew well enough the question was valid. Granted, he'd been joking, but John didn't talk about women in the romantic sense much, and when he did, it was very rarely in a positive light. He wasn't angry or conde-scending, but he had a skepticism or wariness about him that made his walls thick.

"I just figured you might give him the heads-up." He shrugged, grinning to cover whatever else lay under his words. "But hey, welcome to your fortieth and shame on you for thinking we were going to let it just skate by."

I shook my head. "I wasn't really thinking anything about it."

Strange though it may have sounded, since seeing Maddie in town weeks ago, I hadn't thought about much other than her save a few key dates. My birthday had never rated as a big event, especially in light of sharing the day with the ever-popular Pioneer, or here at Silver Ridge Brew-ery, Pie n' Beer day.

Maddie chuckled and kissed my cheek. "I'll go grab us some beers. Be right back."

I watched her go, appreciating the fit of her dress and the way her hair trailed down her back. I loved that she felt comfortable enough in the space and with these people to go off on her own. And of course she did. She'd negotiated million-dollar deals. She was probably far more capable at just about everything than I was, and frankly, I relished it. As someone who made his way in social situations out of necessity, I liked being with a woman who wasn't afraid to take charge and make things happen.

"You are busted, man," John said, patting my back as he watched Maddie line up at the bar and begin chatting with Julian Grenier and Quinn Darling, who stood in front of her.

"Busted?" I asked, mind only half on his comment as Maddie smiled and laughed at something Quinn said. Julian's face even showed a flicker of amusement.

"You're making my point for me, frankly," he said, waiting until I turned to eye him. "Yeah. You with the hearts in your eyes, looking at a woman who is frankly untouchable."

Not exactly, the jerk in my mind said. I'd touched her. Kissed her. Wanted a lot more of that. I would never say such a thing out loud, but apparently, I was getting surly in my old age. "Weren't you encouraging me to go for it with her just weeks ago?"

He nodded. "Yes. Go for *it*. Or just go out and have fun with her. Make a few memories, have a few laughs, enjoy having a sugar mama—whatever. But not fall so hard you're flattened on the runway as she drives by in her private jet on the way out of here."

"Well, that's not dramatic at all."

He shrugged again. "I mean, I get that it's too late. I'm just wondering what your exit strategy is. How are you going to get out of this?"

I eyed him, wondering where this was coming from. Maybe it was obvious to him that I had feelings for Maddie. He knew me well enough and spent a lot of time wading through things with me, but why would he be so worried? I'd actually thought he might be happy for me, but he seemed genuinely concerned.

"Why are you so worried? If I get my heart broken when she leaves, I'll deal with it." I didn't like the idea, but I also had no other choice. I couldn't rewind and remove myself from all contact with her to avoid developing this feeling, nor would I want to.

He sighed and crossed his arms. "I'm just saying it's going to be messy."

Turning back to see Maddie grabbing two beers and pivoting toward us, I closed the discussion right down. "Then it's messy. But I'm taking it while I can. And if that makes me an idiot, I'll deal with that later. I know what this is and where it ends. And that's all we're going to say about that tonight, okay?"

He scowled, but nodded, then flipped the switch and smiled to greet Maddie. "Now that you're back, I'm going to circulate. Don't want to be a rude host."

Maddie handed me a beer and held hers slightly aloft toward me. I did the same.

"To your fortieth year. May it be your best ever."

"And to you, for being willing to celebrate it with me," I said lamely, wanting to say it already was the best year because here in the first minute of it, she was with me.

That thought had me admitting John was right. This wasn't just a crush or even puppy love. This was big love, and it had the possibility of crushing me.

But I'd been crushed. Absolutely, brutally destroyed. And I'd made it out of that. And the lesson I'd learned and had no desire to repeat was that life is short. I'd never closed myself off to the possibility of love again because to be on the receiving end of it would be the utmost privilege. To feel it again was a revelation and a blessing I would never regret, even if I had to lose her in a matter of weeks.

We touched glasses, took a sip, and as though that was

the signal for people to come talk with us, a kind of line formed. Liam and Wells Morrison came and hugged me, then eagerly met Maddie. I'd known Liam all my life and since he was John's business partner, we'd become good friends over the years despite not seeing each other all that much. He and Wells had kids and were in that young-child phase of life.

All through the evening, I kept thinking how odd it was, turning forty. I hadn't meant to keep it from Maddie. She didn't seem upset, though she didn't seem to be the kind of person who got upset about things like that. I honestly hadn't been thinking about it that much.

Now that I was here, chatting with friends and seeing John's brewery packed to the gills with well-wishers, the unwieldy reality of my life hit in a new way. I couldn't hold all this love and friendship inside me. I didn't deserve it, either, but I'd learned a long time ago that that didn't necessarily stop people from being generous and kind.

Had I ever imagined a moment like this? The last time I'd been in a room with most of these people, it'd been at Viv's funeral. It'd been in the darkest days of my life. But they'd stuck with me, insisting on believing in me, hoping for me, feeding me, loving my child. They'd demanded I come back into the light after darkness had shrouded everything. Some did this more directly than others—my family, Liam Morrison, more recently, Julian Grenier, Dahlia, and even Wilder Saint.

It was an evening I would never forget, both because of the woman at my side and the friends and family surrounding me. I'd never bemoan getting older, or going gray, or finding my crow's feet deepening by the year. These were rites not everyone got to experience, and it was a vow I'd made to myself long ago.

But tonight, I made another vow. I promised myself not to dissolve into misery when Maddie left. I would mourn her leaving, but I would remember this night. I'd think of Julian and Quinn grinning like crazy people in their newly-wedded bliss as they chatted with us. I'd think of Liam keeping my pint glass full all night. I'd feel gratitude when I remembered John whispering that he'd arranged for Luca to spend the night at my in-laws so I had the evening free.

And even though I knew it would hurt, I'd remember Maddie's hand in mine through it all.

CHAPTER THIRTY-EIGHT

Maddie

At half past nine, the crowd dispersed from the brewery. Fireworks started at ten, so everyone left with well wishes and slices of pie on paper plates to go watch from wherever they'd planned to view.

Aidan tugged me out the door and down the stairs, then craned his neck up to view the night sky. Seeing the stars on almost any night was just one more thing I liked about Silverton. We were high up enough that even the lights from the parking lot didn't obscure the brightest ones.

"I'm hoping you'll come back to my house and watch from the back yard, unless you'd rather go to the garden?"

John had told me Aidan wouldn't want to be anywhere but alone with me—John had assured me with a wink and nod that he'd absolutely want to go to my house. But I didn't want to pull him away from his friends, and though Aidan was quiet about it, the crammed room made it clear he had a lot of them.

He was quiet about it, but he engendered a kind of devotion in the people he interacted with. I felt it myself, and even if I hadn't been in love with him, I'd admire and regard him highly.

He gave me a perplexed look. "You think I'd say no to that?"

I pressed my lips together to keep from smiling obnoxiously big. "I don't want to take you away from the party. I wouldn't blame you if you wanted to—"

"The only thing I want tonight is more of you."

My stomach flipped. "Good. Me, too."

The drive to my house was tense, but in a delicious, anticipatory way I didn't mind. When he pulled into the driveway and parked, nerves fizzed through my body. He held out a hand when he opened my door, and I took it. Warm, slightly rough from the work he did, even with gloves, and large enough to make mine feel delicate.

Once inside, I dumped my purse on the kitchen counter and rustled around in the fridge to find what I needed. I set them on a small tray I'd positioned earlier and held it up with a raised brow.

He grinned and looked adorably bashful. "You really didn't have to."

He had to be referring to the small chocolate cake I'd gotten for him. The party had been fun and the food and beer and even the pie were delicious. But at some point in the last month and a half, we'd talked about favorite desserts and he'd said chocolate cake from the Silver Ridge Resort's restaurant had become his dream dessert since the time he'd had it the year before. I couldn't resist the chance to give him something I knew he'd enjoy.

Aidan was a man who didn't need things. He didn't have a running list of *stuff* that seemed like good presents. He didn't want luxury travel or a fancy car. These were things I could give him, if I wanted, but I suspected it'd make him uncomfortable more than excited. I had yet to date a man for whom that was true, and though I wished there were things I could give him, it was a relief.

Everyone wanted something from me. Except him.

"I hope you have room for it," I said, lifting the tray and heading for the door to the back deck.

He gave me a mock disappointed look and took the tray from me, so I held the door for him and followed him out.

"I'm thinking the deck is the best option for a good view. They won't be above us this far out, but we should see them that way, right?" I pointed toward the horizon where the sun had slipped away in the last hour.

"Yep. We should see them pretty well."

We spent a few minutes opening champagne, filling flutes, and slicing cake. His ecstatic groan when he tasted his first bite had me grinning like a maniac.

"I don't know why this is making me so happy," I said, shaking my head at the absolute, fizzing joy slipping through me. And it wasn't the champagne.

He flashed his eyebrows as he finished swallowing. "I think you delight in things that make other people happy."

I thought about that before responding. "I'm not sure I'm that selfless."

He shook his head. "Maddie, you're incredible. And you don't have to be selfless. I love that you're a strong, determined woman. But you're also extremely mindful of others, even with all that hulking ambition." He nudged my elbow with his.

I chuckled. "I think you're getting confused. I'm

mindful of *you* and always have been." *Because I'm in love with you.* "It's not like that for everyone."

His eyes bore into mine. "You're like that with Luca. And Dahlia. I know for a fact you are with Juliet and Anthony. I suspect you are with most people who are close to you."

I gripped his upper arm, enjoying the curve of his bicep under my fingertips. "Well, maybe. But I can easily say I've never met anyone who does as much for the people he loves and his community like you do. You're an amazing man, Aidan, and I'm so glad to know you."

He bent and pressed a soft kiss to my lips. "Thank you for being a part of tonight. It was a dream to start my fortieth year with you." He took another giant bite of cake to punctuate the thought.

"I'm glad I could be there." I felt the tremor in my words, so I cleared my throat. I didn't want to break down and sob over his birthday cake. *That* wouldn't be much of a memory for him, nor for me. "Is it as good as you remember?"

I took a bite of my own as his jaw flexed and I marveled at how attractive I found everything about him, even, evidently, the way he chewed a piece of cake. But *wow*. It really was good. Rich, but not so rich it felt like eating clay. Fluffy cake with layers of frosting that was somehow creamy and darkly chocolate at the same time.

I sighed an "Mmm" and felt his gaze on me. We'd turned off the porch lights since the fireworks were due to start in a few minutes, but the moon and stars were bright enough that we could clearly see each other.

When I turned to him, his eyes were on my lips. Before I could speak, he took my mouth with his and utterly devoured me. The kiss ignited every cell in my body and in the minutes we indulged in the pleasureful press and slide, nip and pull, lick and taste, I lost all sense of up and down. It wasn't until the loud pop and spray sound of the first firework that we pulled apart.

"Better than I remember," he said, a dark chocolate-style richness to his voice that made my toes curl.

We watched an impressive display of fireworks in the distance snuggled together, leaning on the banister. My chest felt like it might burst with each *pop!* as the reality of my feelings for Aidan swelled in time with the explosions.

By the time the night was dark, we'd finished our glasses of champagne and the cake. We stayed out under the summer sky pricked with stars I'd never seen in New York, legs twined together on a chaise lounge, and talked until close to midnight. After cleaning up, I slipped off to the bathroom, and when I emerged, Aidan held his keys in his hands and my heart sank.

I wasn't ready for our time to be over—not tonight, not ever...

"I should probably go." His gaze slipped over me, then shifted to my eyes.

I grabbed his hand and walked him to the front entryway. I didn't want him to go, but I certainly didn't want him feeling like he couldn't tell me no, either. I stopped next to the stairs before we reached the doorway.

"You can go. But you could also stay." My hands gripped both of his, and I hoped he could see I wouldn't be upset if he left, but I wanted him to stay. I couldn't say I loved him. The knowledge that I would leave and that would only hurt him stopped me short of that. I wasn't sure I could handle telling him and then leaving. Plus, I didn't want it to seem like a manipulation or a line. I just wanted him close.

The air charged like it so often did when our gazes locked. He swallowed, his throat bobbing, and nodded. "I'd like that."

A grin split my face, and I let go of one hand and guided him upstairs with me. He'd been upstairs, been in my room, even sat on the side of my bed. Had that really only been last weekend?

But he'd never been there like this.

CHAPTER THIRTY-NINE

Aidan

Surreal. That was the feeling that'd hung around my shoulders all day. I wished I could've stayed with Maddie and lived out the sensation with her, but instead, I'd left her bed, her house, and had been thrust back into the stark reality of the rest of my life.

It wasn't exactly that Maddie was sectioned off from the rest of my life. It was more that I'd attempted to cordon off everything having to do with my in-laws and the tree farm in my mind so I didn't have a panic attack over the frustration and worry. But as Rich nodded thoughtfully, I could tell what he was going to say.

I'd known the man for over twenty years, and I could see the rejection coming long before his lips shaped the words.

So here it was. The surreal feeling of going from what had been one of the best nights of my life and a perfect morning to this crashing, burning pile of frustration and disappointment.

"I think this is an offer you should really consider taking some more time with," Sandra, our very patient agent, said.

Rich's frown deepened. "I just don't know."

He'd already delayed this moment. We'd taken far too long, considering it'd been weeks since these offers had come in. We'd had one meeting with Sandra and, bless the woman, had gotten nowhere. He'd claimed he needed time to consider all the angles, whatever that meant, and now here we were. Stuck again.

My blood pressure spiked, and I crushed the exasperation as best I could. "She's right, Rich. This is an incredible offer, and the guy seems great." We'd talked with him on the phone last week. He'd been enthusiastic, assured us he'd always wanted a tree farm. He had no plans to "bulldoze and build a strip mall," which was Rich's ultimate nightmare. But still, Rich couldn't get behind it now, and it was a reality of my own making.

If I'd been honest from the beginning with Rich and simply told him that Viv had always planned on suggesting they sell *or* that I didn't want to buy it or take it over, this would have all been solved.

"I'm sorry, Aidan. Sandra." He stood, hat in hand. "I'm just not ready to move forward."

And with that, he left out the back. Sandra was still sitting there, so I couldn't very well run after him. But I did owe her an apology because she'd come in on what might've been a holiday for her otherwise and it'd all been for nothing. *Again.*

"I apologize. I didn't expect him to dig in his heels like this so late in the process."

She gathered her things and slipped her bag over one

shoulder. "Don't worry. I'm not sure if he'll get there, though. Maybe this isn't the right time?"

Her compassionate expression made my heart twist. Was she thinking about Viv? She'd been in this town as long as any of us, so she knew our family's history. Could she be thinking eight years wasn't enough time before making a big change like this?

I thanked her as she departed, but my mind circled back to the thought that it had been long enough. Certainly for me, anyway, and I wanted it to be enough for them. Viv wasn't here, and what they didn't know was that if she was, she'd be pushing them to sell. For that matter, they would've sold it years ago if she'd had her say.

Instead, here we were. Stuck. What a miserably familiar place to be.

There were things in my life that made me feel less stuck in place, though. And despite the bad news of Rich blowing out of here like his tail was on fire and my clearly ruining Sandra's day with this pointless meeting, though she tried to hide it with kindness, I had Maddie.

I couldn't stop the grin that overtook my face even as I sharply elbowed all thoughts of her imminent departure from my mind. We'd started yesterday in a kind of rough place, really, and mostly because of me. But in the end, she'd forgiven me and I her, and we'd moved forward together. A team. And it'd felt so good.

I mean, waking up in her bed was definitely a far better starting place for a day. So right, in fact, it was silly.

In order to enjoy the weekend, I planned to face Rich and finally force myself to tell him the truth. He needed to know where I stood, and then I'd know, too. Maybe I was crazy for thinking that was the hold-up—maybe he had some other reason he didn't want to sell. It seemed so stupid for one simple conversation to be the holdup on all of this, but I was old enough to know darn well discussing the sale of a man's legacy as his dead daughter's husband wasn't exactly a simple conversation.

I knocked on their front door just as I heard their RV's engine start up. They both waved from the giant front window, so I went to talk to them there.

"I need to speak with you sometime soon," I said, no preamble because they were clearly eager to leave.

"We're off to Bear Lake this weekend, but we'll be back Tuesday. I'll talk to you then."

And that was it. They pulled out and sailed up the road toward the canyon, where they'd begin the winding path toward their vacation spot. It felt a lot like avoiding the subject, but what could I do? I couldn't even call because first, no one in the family made phone calls and drove anymore, and second, he wouldn't have reception for at least two hours.

So? I'd start the weekend. I now had a date to come clean with Rich, and maybe I'd have some success psyching myself up for the job, even running it through with Maddie if she'd let me, before I did. And if it went as badly as I expected, she'd be there for me after.

Speaking of, Maddie's name popped up on my phone. A thrill of anticipation hit and I eagerly answered, ready to move on from the trash part of the day.

"Hey, how'd your call with work go?"

She was silent a moment, at which point all that anticipation shifted into something darker, heavier.

"I'm leaving."

My mind froze at the words. Was this news? We always knew she was leaving. In a few weeks, I'd deal with that, but for now, I—

"I thought I had another week, but they want me back Monday."

Shaking my head but unable to find words, I jogged toward my truck. *This makes no sense. This makes no sense.* Finally, I came up with a response. "A week? Monday?" Not exactly proof of intelligent life, but still something. It did the job of prompting her response.

"I was always leaving early August, but they've called a vote. I have to be there Monday, so I'm leaving this weekend."

"What? Wh—what?"

She released a bitter laugh. "I'm leaving Sunday morning."

CHAPTER FORTY

Maddie

Luca was bouncing off the walls—or he would have been if there were walls.

The day after I found out I had to leave this Sunday and not the next, we joined a big group at a river—or what Utahns apparently called rivers—for a river float that afternoon. Before lunch, we'd all climbed onto inflated tubes and held onto each other's handles so we were linked as we floated. Now that we'd reached the end of the float and had a few minutes to rest after lunch, Luca ran laps around a circuit of the rope swing that swung out over the river, dropping into the water, swimming furiously to the side and scrambling up the bank to get in line and do it all over again. I hadn't seen him so energized, and if my heart didn't feel like it'd been put through a shredder, I would've loved it.

As it was, I had no real desire to do anything but attach myself to Aidan and not let go until someone pried me off.

John seemed to recognize the tension between us—or surrounding us. I guessed Aidan had told him about the change of plans. He'd taken Luca under his wing as he often did and followed right behind him on the swing and climbing the bank with the others as though he were another preteen and not a fully grown man in his thirties.

This let me cling to Aidan's hand without letting go. He seemed to need the contact, too. Occasionally, he'd cast me worried glances. We tried our best to chat with the others, but I'd let my friends here know about the change, and they were clearly giving us space. Maybe they could see the mess of emotion written on my face.

Historically, I wouldn't be worrying about the meeting on Monday. The board wanted me present. Great. A frustrating change of plans, and I generally dictated my own schedule, but I'd been out for nearly eight weeks and away from the city for longer. I got it. Or... normally I would've.

But I could feel the problem growing on a cellular level. Would this be some kind of no confidence vote where they made clear that my sabbatical and the ensuing media circus had brought negative attention to the company and they were ousting me?

Somehow, I didn't think so. I wasn't one for false bluster, which was part of what made me excellent at my job and very good under pressure. I knew my worth, my capability, and I usually had good self-awareness. The fact that this all seemed opaque to me and yet I couldn't bring myself to hunt down anyone who'd give me an insider perspective should've sent alarm bells through me.

But my heart and mind weren't doing what they were supposed to do. They were sliced open and bleeding out. They were in a gruesome tango of grief and anger over losing an entire week with Aidan, and a weighty sense that going back Monday would lead to my ruin. Call it dramatic —I would if it wasn't my life. But I'd felt this before in some small way—not the bleeding heart part. I'd felt it with Korry Taggart. In the spring, I'd known something was coming. I'd sensed that it was all going to come to an impasse, and sure enough, within a few weeks of that feeling haunting me like a shade, Taggart held me at gunpoint.

There would be no violence Monday. I could count on that, at least. But beyond that small guarantee, I wasn't sure. And if I didn't believe they'd be voting me out, why did it all seem so brutal?

"All set?" Aidan asked.

Ah. Aidan. Of course.

He was the reason. Because leaving Aidan to return to New York would be brutal in the starkest sense.

Our phone call had been heavy, and he'd come to me immediately. He'd walked right into the house, come straight to me, and wrapped me in his arms. His handsome face had worn worry and sadness, and I *hated* that I'd put them there.

But by degrees, he'd released me. Almost as though I could feel him making a decision of some kind, though I didn't know what, exactly. When he'd leaned away to look into my eyes, I'd seen determination there.

"We'll soak in every second."

My throat so tight it nearly strangled me, I'd nodded. "Okay." I'd only managed a whisper.

We'd clung together a few minutes longer before his phone buzzed and Luca asked if we were still going to the movies. We'd had such a fun weekend planned—movie night, river float, and a long-awaited tour of the tree farm on Sunday.

Now we'd have to cancel Sunday. But I'd told Aidan I

didn't want to change anything else and risk having my last weekend here spell out disappointment for Luca. So we'd gone to the movie and tried to slip into the fiction. We'd said goodnight when he dropped me off, and I'd spent most of the night staring into the darkness, wishing he were there, not able to string together coherent thoughts.

A day later and now we sat watching Luca and John and a host of others fling themselves off the rocks into the river and race to do it again. We hadn't talked very much, almost like the news of my early departure had stolen the words from between us.

But as we watched the scene play out and I glanced around, noting friendly faces I'd come to recognize and many of whom I'd learned to care for in such a short time, my heart twisted and squeezed in my chest as though someone was wringing it out.

I must've made a sound because Aidan turned to me. "You okay?"

I nodded, feebly trying to convince us both, but suddenly, I had words. "I'm not sure I'm ready to go back. I mean, I *know* I'm not ready to leave you, but I feel..." How did I even verbalize this? I shook my head, frustrated.

"You can tell me. I know you need to mentally prepare and that the biggest change here isn't about *me*. It's about you returning to work after a traumatic experience." He tightened his grip on my hand in a reassuring pulse.

I wanted to laugh and cry at his words. Why had I found him here? So far from my real life? And why couldn't my real life just wait a little longer to invade?

Fair to say I'd not only been in a dream here. I'd been in hiding—first from a genuine threat and then from the danger of returning to the soporific version of life that seemed like another world right now.

But I tried to explain because I needed to work through this, and drowning in my thoughts inside my own mind wouldn't help. "The last few months, I convinced myself that all I needed was this break. I've had it scheduled since January when things got more intense with the stalker, and I was actively scared and stressed and just—"

Aidan's arms came around me and held me. Safe. Warm. Loved. I pulled in a breath and continued. "It was a nightmare. I was scared, and then angry at being scared. So I made this plan because I'd always wanted to be here—to take a chance at finding you again, honestly, and to enjoy this place because I barely got a glimpse of it the first time."

His hands smoothed down my back, tender and reassuring, but he still didn't speak.

I took a deep inhale and pressed on, needing to explain this to someone other than my own rattled mind. "I promised myself I would be better. That by the end of this break, I'd be ready to get back to work. I've always been motivated by work, and not feeling that has been the weirdest combination of a relief and a heartbreak. I don't know if that even makes sense."

"None of this is simple. You went through a traumatic time—actual trauma. Having someone stalking you is traumatic. And that's not even including what you experienced when he attacked you." His voice came out sure and insistent, like he wouldn't tolerate me hedging.

"It was. And even though I've been telling myself this would be enough time, I'm scared about going back. I've changed in ways I never anticipated, and I don't know how that's going to fit with my old life."

I willed him to tell me to find a way to stay, or have something to say that could speak to this feeling that going back was a mistake. He held me a while longer before he sighed lightly and pulled back.

"I don't know what your life at work is like. But I remember you talking about it when we first met—you loved it. I also understand that this might've really changed you—everything this year. And I think it's okay to be scared. If I didn't do things that scared me, I'd probably never get out of bed."

Shocked, I studied his face. He meant it. "That can't be possible. You're so self-assured."

He huffed a laugh. "Most things I do scare me."

"How is that possible?"

A small smile pulled at his lips. "For the first few years after Viv, it was like anything I did, I was terrified of leaving Luca an orphan. I refused to drive for a full eighteen months. Like, I wouldn't drive, wouldn't get in the car. After that, I became more and more fearful. That was a lot of what I worked on in therapy, and I was able to slowly get off medication a few years back. But I still feel generally inept and unprepared for everything. I've just learned that hiding out and keeping everyone at bay won't change that, so I might as well go ahead and do it—whatever *it* is."

I felt the grin despite the tears that had moistened my eyes. "I like that." My eyes widened. "Well, to clarify, I *hate* that, but... I appreciate having a little mantra and knowing it's not so abnormal that I would feel scared but still do the thing I need to anyway."

He kissed the back of one hand, then the other. "You are most definitely not alone. And even when we're apart, you will always have a friend, and an ear, in me. You know that, right?"

There went my throat again, filling with concrete. My jaw ached from how I crushed it closed to keep from sobbing all over his shirt. I couldn't say what that meant to me and how it also broke my heart, so I nodded.

He'd always have me, too. My friendship, though I couldn't imagine how I'd actually give it to him from across the country, and I knew without a doubt, my love.

CHAPTER FORTY-ONE

Aidan

I'd stayed strong all day. I hadn't lashed out when Maddie suggested we go to Scoop for dessert after our dinner at Guac. I hadn't let loose the tantrum I wanted to throw at how the seconds kept ticking by without my permission.

But now, as she let us into the house she'd bought but wouldn't occupy in less than twelve hours, I felt utterly weak. I wanted to beg her to stay, but that wasn't what either of us needed. In fact, the image of her pitying face letting me down as I cried and told her I wasn't sure how my life would look when she left was one of the primary tools I used to keep the words locked inside me.

I would not ask her to stay.

She didn't need that pressure from me. Everyone pulled and pawed at her, grasping for something to have. Something she could do for them. Something they could gain.

And I would never be like that with her, both because it would destroy what we'd built and because I didn't want anything but *her*. I didn't want her money or house or wealth or reputation or business acumen or connections. If anything, those were hindrances to our lives and that'd become more than clear in the last day.

But as she tossed her keys onto the counter and pulled me up the stairs with her, I knew I couldn't let her leave without at least a little honesty. The mood in her room as she lay down on the bed and tugged me so we were nested together was nothing short of utterly somber. We'd promised each other we'd make the best of the time we had left, and yet neither of us had the heart to pretend like this wasn't the last time we'd lay like this. The last time we'd come home together. The last time we'd spend a day making memories, being a part of something *together*.

"Maddie," I said in a quiet voice, as though speaking too loudly would change something.

She slid her hand up and down the arm that I'd hooked around her belly. "What?"

I inched back and, with a firm hand on her hip, urged her to roll and face me. Her eyes were wet, and she brusquely wiped away several tears.

I shook my head, heart aching, and just... said it. "I know we've only spent a few weeks together, but I need you to know... I love you."

She pressed a hand over her mouth and blinked away tears. Her hazel eyes were brimming again almost instantly, and I hated that I knew they weren't elated. There was no joy in the confession.

"I'm sorry. Maybe I shouldn't have told you, but if I've learned one thing in this life, it's that we don't always get a second chance. With you, I did. Somehow, we've stolen these weeks together. I'll forever be grateful for this time together, but I know enough not to expect a third chance. You don't have to say anything, but I needed you to know."

She nodded and moved the hand that had covered her mouth to cup my face. "Thank you," she whispered. She must've sensed that same breakable quiet I had.

Then she dropped her head into my neck and I held her close, savoring and wishing. Cursing and begging. Wondering and waiting.

Before long, she relaxed against me completely. Her mind had been running much like mine had, but she bore the burden of trying to move back to the city, back to her *life*, as a changed person. I knew a little bit about attempting to reenter one's life after it'd been split wide open. I didn't know what it was like to have someone nearly take my life, but I certainly understood a brush with death in many senses.

I wanted to wake her and talk more. To make love again. To tell her everything would be okay and she was strong enough to handle anything. But what she needed was rest, and here was one small thing I could give her.

We woke with a start at the sound of her alarm. Four-thirty in the morning had come quickly. She rolled away and padded to the bathroom while I worked to get my eyes to open all the way. I hadn't actually planned on staying in the bed with her, but I hadn't been able to pull myself away. Even at the price of my eyeballs feeling glued shut thanks to my super dry contacts and the hungover feeling gnawing at me thanks to so little sleep, I'd stayed.

It was only now, as I took in her room, that I realized she'd already packed. Or at least, she had a large suitcase tucked against the wall next to her door.

When she emerged from the bathroom, she was fully dressed, face adorned with minimal, perfect makeup, and a kind of efficiency cloaked her.

"Do you need help packing?" I asked lamely.

"No. I packed most things last night and someone will come do the rest this week," she said, not meeting my eye.

She must've packed while I'd slept. Knowing that pricked at my sensitive skin, driving home how our lives were already diverging despite it being such a small thing. "Okay. Let me grab this for you." I took the bag, desperate for some way to help her. I could understand staying focused on the task at hand. I felt as emotionally spent as I could recall being any time in the last few years, and she had to be, too.

"Sure. Thanks." She slung a large handbag over her shoulder and we moved to the ground floor. Her phone pinged and she glanced at it before shoving it into an outer pocket on her bag. In the kitchen, she collected a few things —a small water bottle, her sunglasses, a string cheese from the fridge—and shoved them all into another pocket.

Too soon, we were moving toward the door. She was opening it and assuring me her security team would be here in twenty minutes and they'd take care of locking up once the housekeepers did something she called "closing" the house.

Closing it. How perfectly final. What an ending.

All night, I'd held her and wished this wasn't an ending. But here we were, descending the steps to a waiting town car. Why would she drive, anyway? She wouldn't be back.

Each thought came barreling toward me, battering my body with the truth.

The driver hopped out and greeted her. "Ms. Reynolds."

"Hi. I'll be just a minute," she said as he took the suitcases from me and tipped them into the trunk.

"Take your time," he said, and slipped back inside the car.

Now my heart was pounding, clogging my throat with pressure and a closing of its own. Now my mind was scrambling for something to say. Anything to say.

"I love you, Maddie. Thank you."

That was all. All I could say that came close to encompassing the enormity of what I felt for her, the way she'd changed me.

Thank you for letting me love you. Thank you for showing me this was even possible.

Another thought thundered to the forefront, so demanding I had to clench my jaw against letting them loose. *Stay with me. Come back as soon as you can. Why don't we try long distance? Are you sure you even want to go back?*

"Thank you, Aidan. I've loved every minute with you." Her brows pinched together like they held her tears at bay.

I coughed out a weird laugh tinged with grief and scrambled for something to say to keep from breaking down completely. "Even the part where you were nearly delirious with fever?"

One side of her beautiful mouth slid up into a pleased smile as she nodded. "Even then. Because you were with me."

She was trying to kill me. She'd leave here, her legacy

murder by verbal heart-stabbing. Damn, but this hurt. "It was my pleasure."

She pressed her lips together and leaned up and wrapped her arms around me and squeezed. I returned the hug, knowing it would be our last. Working to memorize the feel of her once again, the clean, slightly sweet scent, the slip of her cheek against my jaw.

Abruptly, she pulled away and kissed my lips with a quick, brutal press and reached for the door.

They were all right there. The words. The pleading. *Don't go. Stay with me. I love you. Please, please come back.* But the last thing I wanted was for her to feel any part of this had been just another person taking from her. So I said the only thing I could think of then, the prayer I prayed even as I spoke the words.

"Stay safe, Maddie. Please."

She shut the door. The car pulled away.

And she was gone.

CHAPTER FORTY-TWO

Aidan

Forty-eight hours after she left and twelve hours after I'd texted her goodnight, she responded. I'd tried to send the message early in case she'd gone to bed early, but I didn't hear back. So far, our interaction had been minimal and only messages. I hadn't wanted to press for a video chat or even a regular call. She'd left, after all.

And yet, despite her absence, my mind still orbited around her existence. Out of sight was most assuredly not out of mind. It did nothing but send more anxious thoughts through me—had she landed? Was her apartment in New York ready for her? Was she feeling okay? How had the first day gone?

I'd sent some of these and she'd responded to all of them. We'd exchanged messages on and off Sunday afternoon and a few late afternoon Monday. But later, as they'd tapered off, I'd sent a simple good night. I hoped she'd slept well.

And though I'd wondered if it was pushing it, I'd said *I miss you*. Like a fool, I continued to hang my heart out.

Though, no. I didn't want to think that way. I loved the woman, and though I wouldn't keep pressing that, I wanted her to know. Even if I couldn't ask her to stay, I wanted her to know she'd made an irrevocable impression here, and she wasn't forgotten simply because she'd left.

But no answer had come last night, and when I felt my phone buzz first thing, it hadn't been her. It'd been John, the most morning person of all morning people, checking in on me with fifteen memes about healing from heartbreak and a goofy smiling photo of himself where he'd scribbled a mustache and villain eyebrows on for Luca.

What an idiot. Good grief, I loved him.

I'd tried not to betray my bad mood, but it'd crept in more persistently as the hours ticked by and I didn't hear from her. Rich and I were meeting in ten minutes at the office, and I'd gone home for lunch just to get my mind right.

Unfortunately, as I was walking back, I got her response.

"I miss you too. I think it's best if we don't message as much. It's too hard."

I swallowed against the rocks in my throat and responded immediately. *"I'm sorry. I didn't mean to make anything hard for you."*

Thankfully, or maybe not, she responded just as fast. *"You're wonderful. Never apologize. I wish I was stronger. Take care."*

I stared at the phone, wondering whether there was

anything I could say to that. Her words felt final, like a door shutting.

Pain arced through me. It'd come in waves the last few days, mostly sneaking in when I finally let myself think about how much I missed her. Otherwise, since it'd only been a few days, I could pretend she was still here and we were both just busy. But this did it. Door closed, locked.

"Aid, good. Let's go ahead and start," Rich said as he stomped along the path between his house and the office.

I exhaled slowly in an attempt to get a grip on the moment and not drown in the wash of disappointment, regret, and hurt brimming in me. "Sure. Yeah. Let's do it."

It was fitting, this timing. Telling Rich the truth after years and years of avoiding it—breaking his heart in the wake of breaking my own—how perfectly awful.

He filled a mug of coffee from the carafe that'd been sitting on *warm* for hours, since I'd started it this morning, then took a seat at the round, six-person table. One leg was shorter than the others and had wobbled since the first time I'd come in nearly two decades ago on my first visit.

"So, what's on your mind?" He sipped from the mug.

I cleared my throat, reminding myself of all the reasons I wasn't going to shy away from the truth this time. *This time*, I would say the words I'd shoved down in order to avoid hurting him. This time, I would allow myself this honesty, for both our sakes.

"I understand you've been hesitant about selling the farm."

He nodded, slow and deliberate. "Yes, I sure have."

Willing him to say more—perhaps the part he'd been avoiding telling me for all these years—I waited. But he'd come prepared to listen, and ultimately, I didn't need him to say anything. This was my show.

"I need you to know that I feel strongly you should sell. And in case there's a part of you that wonders if I'd like to buy it, I have to tell you, I can't."

His brow furrowed and he pressed his lips into a familiar frown. "I wouldn't have asked you to buy it, Aidan. I wanted to give it to you. You and Luca."

My heart squeezed. It was more than I'd imagined. It made me want to hug him and shake him. Even so, I sifted through all the tangled thoughts to find the right one first. "Thank you. Truly, Rich, that's so generous and thoughtful. But I can't do that."

He waved me away. "Of course you can. You know more about the business than I do by now. You're managing it beautifully, and Luca has practically grown up here."

I nodded. "Yes. That's true. But I've got my own business. I'm sorry to say it, but I've lost sight of that. I should've said something years ago, but I didn't want to hurt anyone."

His frown deepened and he was quiet for a moment. As a patently contemplative person, his silence didn't surprise me, but my stomach had tied into knots. And before he could speak again, I rushed to explain myself, hoping I hadn't upset him too deeply.

"I wish I felt like this was where I was meant to be. I'm sorry. I know I should've spoken up sooner, but you've had so much pain to deal with, and I didn't want to cause you any more by disappointing you or... failing you." The words were out now, floating between us, little shards of glass raining down all around the worn-out table.

He reached for me and patted my hand. "Oh, son. You couldn't disappoint us."

I swallowed hard.

He continued. "I know you've got your own dreams, but

don't you think you might shift it, just a little, to include the farm? I know how you love the trees. You and Viv have so many good memories there."

Low blow. But I respected him using all his resources. And I hoped he'd respect me using all of mine. I pulled out a document with a bright green plastic cover and slid it across the table.

He eyed it with a flicker of wariness and what I knew had to be pain, opening it with just his thumb and index fingers. Viv had always loved a colorful presentation. "What's this here?"

"Viv was going to give this to you. She was working up some other plans to go with it—ideas for what'd come next. But this was the start." My heart practically fluttered, it pounded so fast. Here was overkill for my point, a kind of weapon I hadn't entirely planned on using. Though, perhaps to my shame, obviously I'd had it ready.

He thumbed through the pages, frown drawing down all the more before he tripped his chin up, his eyes following a few seconds later. "She thought we should sell. Even then?"

I nodded, gritting my teeth at the surprise laced with pain.

"She was that unhappy?"

"No. Please don't think that. But she saw how it was wearing on you and Martha. She wanted you to have time to travel and do all the things you'd talked about. She wanted Thanksgiving leading up to Christmas to be fun instead of so crammed with long hours and back-breaking work." And she wanted to be my admin and help me expand my business, but I didn't need to spell that out, I guessed.

He took a slow breath, his focus pinned on his daughter's last project for work. Regret and guilt snaked around my chest and squeezed.

"I'm sorry I didn't tell you sooner. I'm so sorry I kept it from you, but I just couldn't bring myself to. And the longer I waited, the more it felt like it might seem like I was using her to get what I wanted. That's not what this is. I'm only trying to make clear that what I want, and what she wanted, are similar if not the same."

He cleared his throat and took a swig of his coffee, that troubled, almost grim look seeming to ease by degrees the harder he stared at the folder. Finally, his gaze found mine.

"You've honored Vivienne so well. You've loved us, cared for us, and kept this business afloat." He sniffed, banishing the faint tremble of his voice. "I admit I love the idea of this place being passed down from one to the next of us, but my legacy is in you and Luca. So's Viv's. You may not be my boy by blood, but you joined our family a long time ago, and you're ours."

He smiled, and I let out a watery laugh-sob. My heart ached and twisted with a potent mix of grief and elation. "Thank you."

He shook his head slowly, a faint smile on his face now. "No, son. Thank *you*. Thank you for being patient and so careful of our feelings. But now it's time for you to live. And it's time for us to sell this place so you—so we all—can do that to the fullest."

We stood at the same time as though choreographed, and he stuck out a hand to me, which I took, then pulled him in to hug him and pat his back. "Thank you for taking care of me and Luca, too. We couldn't have—" My voice broke, every emotion surrounding us crowding in and pressing on my chest.

He nodded, eyes teary. "I know. I know. We couldn't have done it without each other." He patted me once more, then leaned away, sniffing hard again. "And now that we're done with the waterworks, tell me what I need to do to get the deal done. If you're not taking it, I suppose this guy out of North Carolina's as good as anyone else."

I wiped my cheeks and exhaled, chuckling even as I felt like weeping for joy and relief and a glimmer of wishing Vivienne was here to see me and her old man crying at each other. Of course we'd cried together in years past, but there'd been a dramatic pause as we'd steeped in the work of surviving.

And as we sat and reviewed the offer and all it would mean for him, his posture perked up and his leg started bouncing. His excitement over the reality of truly retiring and having that nest egg accessible seemed to finally hit him.

And when I left, I had one thought repeating in my head. I'd finally been honest and, instead of prioritizing someone else's feelings or doing some mythical, unobtainable version of the right thing, I told the truth even if it meant hurting them a little. Not in a brutal way, but in the way that needed to be done. And it'd turned out better than I could imagine. I had a feeling Martha would agree once she heard about his plans for a cruise around the world.

If I'd trusted him a little more, I would've said this all years ago. If I'd been willing to be vulnerable and open with him, to risk disappointing him, to confront the shame of not wanting what he did for my life, we might've come to this place so much sooner.

And that thought circled my mind again and again but with a turn. What if, instead of worrying so much about pressuring Maddie, I'd just asked her to stay? Asked her to try long distance? Asked *something* of her, and trusted her to respond honestly?

CHAPTER FORTY-THREE

Maddie

Anthony narrowed his eyes at me for the nth time today as I pressed my lips into a thin, sickly version of a smile.

"I appreciate that. Thank you so much." There came the smile again. It'd been a fixture on my face the last month. I didn't know how else to cover the reality that had sunk in ever more persistently by the day since I'd been back.

I'd been waiting for it to click back into place—that feeling that had fueled me for years. The satisfaction. The grind and the pleasure that stemmed from it. That *Working Woman* inside me, ambition personified.

No luck. Not even close.

I hadn't been fired. They'd simply had an end of month meeting they wanted me there for before we launched into the end-of-summer and rounded the corner to Q-4. All I could think was how unimportant it was and how disrespectful of my time it was to make it seem like they *needed* me here during planned time off a solid month-plus before the next quarter began.

I'd worked tirelessly for this company, and they couldn't give me twelve weeks off? I'd taken what amounted to less than four weeks of vacation in the last four *years*. And on top of that, it wasn't like I was on a joyride through the French wine country. The first three and a half weeks were spent literally running from a stalker, and the last seven?

My throat locked up and I nodded into the phone, squeezing out an "Mm-hmm. Sounds good. Talk to you soon." Hanging up before I moved, I turned my desk chair toward the glass windows behind me to escape any more of Anthony's scrutiny.

"Okay, it's time to have a talk." His voice was almost pleading.

So much for evasion. "About?"

When I turned back, he stood with a hip popped out and arms crossed, and my heart sank. I'd fleetingly hoped he might mean something work-related, but the look on his face had a pre-emptive *"Don't even try."*

"I think you and I both know what about, but one second." He tapped out something on his tablet, smirked, then swiped a finger to answer a call. A familiar voice came on the phone.

"Is she ready?"

I stood. "Is that Juliet?"

He pursed his lips and raised his eyebrows. *Crap.*

"Yes, my dear friend, it's Juliet. And it's time to have a chat."

I squinted at both of them. Anthony stood facing me, holding Juliet's face on the tablet toward me. My pulse had started racing the second I heard Juliet's voice because that meant real, actual trouble. I couldn't put her off. Anthony I could sometimes avoid, and I had done for the last week since he'd been asking me if I was okay every five minutes. I loved the man for his protective friendship and loyalty, but I wasn't about to discuss the pit in my stomach or the general sense of loss I felt.

Except now, apparently, I was.

"I'm fine. I know I'm... different. But it's just been a lot. I'm still getting back in the groove."

Anthony brought the tablet up so he could give Juliet a look, then swung her back toward me.

"Honey, I'm not sure you're fine."

I sniffed, wholly uninterested in sitting down in the feelings that'd been crowding my mind every second since I left Silverton. Since I left Aidan.

Aidan. Just the thought of his name sent an ache pulsing through me so sharply, I pulled in a breath to ward against it. "I was stalked. Held at gunpoint. I've been away from working and being back is... different. I promised myself I'd be ready, but I don't think I am. I needed that extra week. Maybe I needed another month. But I'm not going to do any good by sitting around drowning in the feeling of failure to bounce back from something I couldn't control."

Juliet's luminous blue eyes looked sad. Not pitying, but sad for me. "I'm sorry. I'm so sorry you went through that. I'm so glad you're safe."

Anthony nodded. "Yes. If I could watch the video feed of Wilder Saint taking out that horrible man on a loop, I would."

A reluctant laugh crept out at that, and Juliet grinned. We had seen the video footage of the takedown, but I hadn't watched anything else. I hadn't wanted to see or hear the fear in my voice, in my body. But watching Wilder full body attack Taggart, disarm him, and knock him out? Yeah, that'd been sweet.

Still, their agreement that I'd been through something didn't end the discussion. I felt the giant *BUT* hanging in the air around us and waited for it to come. But I didn't want to. I wanted to delve into this as much as I wanted to read the accounting department's summary of the second quarter.

"So? See. You agree. It was awful. That takes some time. I haven't been working. It's been a lot of catch-up, and a lot of getting back into the routines of things. I'm used to the quiet of the mountain and not the city noises now. I'm still... finding my way back to breathing fully oxygenated air."

Juliet gave me a rueful smile and a look that told me I knew better than to think that was case-closed on this little intervention.

"And Aidan? Have you talked to him?"

There it was again, that pain. *Aidan, Aidan, Aidan.* His name echoed through my mind, rattling the cage of my chest, and utterly battering my heart.

"Not much," I said, willing her not to ask anything more. "E-mailed with Luca a bit." Before I left, he'd mentioned a big showcase that happened every fall and how he wanted to do some kind of presentation on the stock market. We'd talked about it a lot, and I didn't want to just abandon him. It wasn't fair to him that I couldn't stay in Utah, that my life was here. And it was a small way I could help that didn't excoriate my heart. So we'd been talking back and forth every few days. Nothing huge.

Before Juliet spoke again, Anthony approached and handed me the iPad. "I'm going to give you two a minute."

He exited swiftly, the giant office door shutting softly behind him.

I propped up the tablet with Juliet's face staring back at me on my desk and sat down in the chair. "It hurts."

Her frown deepened and I could practically feel the empathy wafting off her and through the screen. If she were here, she'd hug me. Thank God she wasn't because that would definitely make me cry.

"I'm sorry. I just wonder if you'd feel better staying more connected to him, not less."

I sighed. "We kind of tried that the first few days, but it was brutal. Awkward." Painful. Miserable. Made me want to charter a flight back to Silverton immediately and never leave again.

She looked truly befuddled. "You told me he told you he's in love with you."

I shut my eyes against that. "He did."

"How is it awkward talking to him? You got so close. Quickly, yes, but in some ways it doesn't feel all that fast considering when you first met."

I tsked. "It's not like we were dating all that time."

"No, but you were thinking of him. *Wishing* for him. And then you had him, and I dare say he turned out to be as good as you imagined. Smart, interesting, handsome as all get out, and bonus, he's an amazing dad to an awesome kid. Oh and also, he loves you and thinks you're amazing and wants nothing from you—he's not about to ask you for business advice."

I snorted. "Definitely not, though Luca kind of does. In fact, our only real disagreement was when I *did* offer some. But in his usual Aidan style, he was amazing about that, too."

She grinned. "And so?"

I waited, but she didn't say anything else. "So, what?"

"So why are you not with him?"

Despite the feeling that she'd just hit a giant gong above my head, I glanced around like the fake audience to our conversation would agree she was nuts. "Um, because I live more than two thousand miles from him? Because he didn't seem interested in that. He didn't..."

Saying that aloud would hurt too much, so I swallowed it down.

But never one to let me off the hook, she prompted, "He didn't *what?*"

My chin wobbled, but I firmed it and took a long sip of water. "He didn't ask me to stay."

"Oh, honey," she said, worry and care for me broadcasting clearly. "Of course he didn't."

"What does that mean?"

She gave me a soft smile in that way she had that showed me she cared about me, but was probably going to say something I didn't like. "How could he? You were always going to leave Silverton, right?"

I nodded, gritting my teeth against the welling emotions threatening to overwhelm me.

"I'm guessing he didn't think asking would do anything. You hadn't mentioned anything long term. You got together *knowing* you'd be parting when you left. Not a wait and see."

"But what if he didn't want that? What if this was just a fling, or... I mean it wasn't a fling, obviously, but what if he needed it to be short term? That he wouldn't want to commit to someone long term and long distance anyway?"

She shrugged. "Well, you'd only know that if you talked about it. But I think if he told you he loved you and really did all the things you said he did, I suspect that if he thought he had a chance at more with you, that you'd entertain staying in Silverton, he would've asked you to stay."

That hit me like a shot, and I sat back in my chair. Someone hollered her name, and she apologized profusely for having to go and made me promise to text her later. I agreed to the terms before she disappeared, but as soon as the screen went dark, doubt crowded in.

Or should I say *more* doubt. Because I'd had doubts every second of every minute I'd been away from Aidan. And honestly, not just Aidan, but also Luca. Dahlia and Sarah and the girls. Silverton. Sadie Miller's cinnamon twist bread, if I'm being honest.

I didn't feel right here. It felt like I was wearing someone else's suit. Someone else's life. And it had been someone else's—the woman who'd left here before Christmas. The *Working Woman* who knew nothing of what would come. Who'd tried to work in LA, then moved every few weeks, once Taggart's letters found her, forcing her to flee or be found. A woman who hadn't seen the *nothingness* of her life flash before her eyes. A woman who hadn't fallen in love with an amazing man.

Or, more accurately, the *best* man.

And in the small town I'd hardly stepped foot in during my first visit, I'd begun to feel at home. Dahlia, Sarah, Quinn, Calla, and Sadie had folded me in so generously. John had become a friend, too. And Luca...

My heart seized at the thought of Luca. He'd hugged me tight, then backed away, his eyes glassy, when John told him it was time to go. He hadn't seemed hurt or angry, just resigned. So like his father, and maybe that was what left me feeling restless and angry myself.

Luca's e-mails had been a welcome point of contact, and yet painful. A reminder of another person I'd hurt, a person

I was letting down, and a person I missed more than I imagined I could.

Why hadn't Aidan just asked me to stay? I'd asked myself that a thousand times in the last few weeks. Despite not wanting to believe it, Juliet's statements came back immediately. *"How could he? You were always going to leave Silverton, right?"*

I'd certainly arrived there with the plan. And I'd convinced myself, even after I'd realized I loved Aidan and was rapidly falling for his son, that I could still leave them. That I could walk away and feel thankful for the time I'd had with them, but return to this life. Wake from the dream of mountain peaks and sage breezes and the best people to real life.

This life that felt so dreadfully empty and cold.

But who was I without this? The implications of my leaving would be huge, especially after a long break. My actions influenced an entire workforce, not just myself. I couldn't do things on whims.

Is it really a whim if you've been thinking about it for years?

My heart clutched at the thought. At the truth of it.

I'd been wondering about a different life since my first visit to Silverton. It was part of why I'd hidden my name from Aidan. It was part of why the fantasy of flirting with a handsome local had been so delicious. That *what if?*

And if I was being honest with myself—if I'd finally cut the crap and decided to get back to one thing I did know about myself and shoot straight, I'd have to admit it.

I'd bought a house there. I'd sought out friends. I'd formed a relationship with the first man I'd ever imagined a real future with.

And I hadn't done that by accident.

What was left of that version of me who'd penned *Working Woman*? She felt so far away. Or maybe the better illustration was how far I—this new version of myself—felt from her. I'd changed fundamentally. It'd started creeping in before that first stop in Silverton. It'd grown more intense seeing Nate marry the love of his life and turning right to dealing with the book tour and ensuing danger with Taggart. But maybe more than anything, it'd broken open completely upon staying in Silverton and falling in love with the place and the people and the version of myself I was there.

If I hadn't already lived through something unbelievable, making a life-changing move to upend what I'd worked for tirelessly would seem downright foolish. But hindsight was twenty-twenty, as they say, and I was looking back with a microscope on hand, turning over every tiny piece of evidence that led to this surety.

I wasn't this person anymore. I'd become someone new —was still becoming her.

I paced my office and gazed out at the view of the park. Beautiful fall colors beginning to tinge crisp leaves. A blue sky with fluffy clouds and the familiar shapes of the skyline. All of it too manicured and cultured. None of that wildness, the jagged heights of the mountains, the pines dotting up the slopes until they disappeared at the tree line. No little main street. No girls' night. *No garden.*

Too much missing here. Too much to miss there.

But if I was really considering this, I needed to be sure. I had to know without a doubt, and I had an e-mail to send.

CHAPTER FORTY-FOUR

Aidan

Maddie's message came on a Tuesday, almost exactly seven weeks after the last one. Weeks and weeks of nothing at all, and now, one short, confusing, mind-altering note.

"I'm going to be in town in early October. I'd love to see you."

Early October. Why would she come up out of nowhere to say she was visiting? And why did my heart start cartwheeling around about it? Didn't it know it was too old for that kind of thing?

John caught my scowl and inevitably poked at me. "What's that look for?"

I only blinked at him. He narrowed his eyes. "Wait. What's up?"

He kept things lighthearted as a habit and I'd argue, a shield against some things he didn't like to deal with, but he'd been there for me. Through the worst moments of my life years ago and many of the ups and downs since. And though losing Maddie had been nothing like the loss of my wife, it'd still hurt. Deeply. In a way that changed me.

And that hurt and change still felt new. I didn't really remember how to deal with someone who was still alive, as messed up as that sounded. How could I stand to know she was out there walking around, living her life? How did people handle that?

When I thought about it, really drilled down to the fact that I'd loved her and let her go—hadn't even fought her leaving—the more like a coward I felt. Who does that? Who just lets the woman he loves *walk away*? So what if our lives didn't fit in *any* way? So what if I had nothing to offer her and I couldn't move to be with her because I would never endanger the stability that living in Silverton with relatives and friends who'd known us all our lives, and had known Viv, too, provided us.

All that aside, how could I let her leave without even saying I wanted to try... something. Anything.

I'd convinced myself it would've been too much. Maybe it would've, but would it have changed anything about this moment if it had? If she'd still left, or stayed away, I'd still be here, by myself, trying to feel less miserable than I did.

"Maddie said she's coming to town in October. Wants to see me." I avoided his gaze, but my eyes jumped back to him when I heard him grunt.

"Yeah, like that's happening." He crossed his arms and leaned back in his seat.

"Why wouldn't I see her?" I asked, just the thought of missing a chance making me feel wretched while the thought of seeing her and saying goodbye again, or feeling the stark change I knew had taken place between us in the last months come between us in person, had the same effect.

He studied me, clearly perplexed. He glanced around at the nearby tables as though to make sure no one was listening. They were packed this morning—good for Sadie. The popularity of Rise and Shine and her Loaf of the Month club had only grown in the last year.

That said, I didn't want people listening in, and they absolutely were. Fortunately, it was mostly locals who were both nosy and less likely to sell a story about me and Maddie to the papers.

"You wouldn't see her because she's been acting like Silverton got wiped off the map the day she blew out of town. She's been acting like nothing really matters all that much except her own convenience, and like you should do whatever she wants." Face hard, he frowned at me like I should know better than to even think of it.

"True. But I think—"

"No. Seriously, no. Why would you do that to yourself?" His visible frustration seemed to multiply.

I nudged my coffee cup a few inches away, frustration and a familiar twinge of embarrassment hitting. "I suppose because I love her."

His jaw flexed and he stood, reaching out a hand to me. I took it and he pulled me out of my chair, brought me close, and patted my back with his other hand. The familiar gesture had turned conciliatory, as though he wanted to make peace, but didn't have the words to allow for it in this situation.

Part of me understood his anger. I felt a bit of it myself. Where was my self-respect? Where was my pride?

But that's the thing about love. It doesn't prioritize

pride. It shouldn't be the cause of self-disrespect, of course. But that wasn't an issue here.

Yes, Maddie had pushed me away, but we'd never planned out how things would look. We'd said only "we'll talk," and presumably then she realized it was too much for her. She had the bigger transition to deal with, the trauma to unpack, the identity to settle into. I had merely kept on going in my daily routines, but without her. It had been challenging, but I understood that what she faced when she left was monumental.

What kind of person would I be if I didn't see that she might have reasons for her silence? I didn't assume she had feelings for me the way I did her. In fact, the silence between us confirmed that she didn't fairly effectively. But it didn't make her unfeeling. I didn't like that she'd had to wall herself off from life here, but again, she'd been through something life-changing, and then she'd had to return to her old life as if it hadn't happened.

I couldn't pretend I didn't care she'd be here. There was no part of me that wanted to play that game. And as John and I slipped outside and left the bright yellow walls of Rise and Shine, I knew I wouldn't.

"I wish you'd consider that seeing her might be bad. But if you're really still in love with her, I guess I get it." Hands in his pockets, he looked about as aggravated as he ever did.

"I appreciate you—"

"You know what? No. Because here's the thing. You're the best. The actual best person I know. And I refuse to accept that this woman disappears, no contact, no nothing, and suddenly waltzes back in here for... what? A weekend fling? We both know that's not what you're interested in and she's got to know that, too. I don't want you miserable after she leaves, and she *will* leave. I didn't take her for a cruel person, but this seems needlessly in-your-face." His eyes raked down the street, then circled back to me. "Sorry. I know you love this woman. I just... I love *you*. And Luca. And I don't want you hurt anymore."

Well... *damn*. Fair points, all around, and I couldn't ignore them. As much as I wanted to see Maddie and no part of me believed she'd purposefully hurt me, his words sent caution into my veins like an IV. The glow of possibility cooled with forced circumspection, and I nodded, patting his shoulder to reassure him I'd heard him.

"Thank you for caring so much. Thanks for loving us. And thank you for your opinion. I probably shouldn't trust my instincts all that much with this situation."

He sighed. "No, you have good instincts. I just don't trust *her* all that much. And I'm happy to be the naysayer and bad guy who gets proved wrong, trust me. But just... go easy, okay? I know you're going to see her, and the more I rant and rave about it, the more I get that you practically have no choice. Just... keep your expectations low."

"Thanks."

He grinned. "Of course." His eyes flicked behind me. "And now, if you'll excuse me, the she-devil is coming, and I have no desire to get reamed for merely existing."

She-devil? I turned, and *ah*, should've known. Dahlia tapped away on her phone without looking up until she nearly ran into me.

"Oh, shoot. Sorry. I shouldn't be so absorbed in this thing, but I am dealing with a bride." She widened her eyes.

She'd regaled me with many a story about bridezilla brides. "Fall's a nice time to get married in Utah. That'll be pleasant."

Every trace of amusement fled her face. "Yeah, but having baby pink tulips in November? *Pricy*. And not because I'm trying to make an extra cash, but rather because getting sustainably produced tulips in early winter is just not really a thing that can be done without a higher price point."

"That's frustrating," I said, wondering if the client just couldn't understand the general concept of seasonal flowers and out of season things cost more.

"It is. But also... and this is a thing I don't typically say to out-of-towners because they show up thinking they know, but also because I don't often have the issue but... baby pink tulips in November?"

The horrified look on her face was so stark, I cracked up with a genuine chuckle. "I can't even imagine."

"Right? You promise when you get married you won't make me use baby pink flowers in some fall or wintry scene?"

My heart swooped down low, then splattered on the ground. Why that offhand comment made me pause so dramatically when similar statements from her in the last few years I'd known her hadn't fazed me a bit? Well, obviously. But also, *ouch*.

"I'm unlikely to marry again, Dahlia, but I solemnly swear I won't ask for anything pink." *Would Maddie even like pink? She didn't seem like she would, but it would depend on the season. Plus I—*

With all my might, I shoved those thoughts away. I couldn't be thinking about Maddie's preferences for wedding colors because we were through. John had made a compelling argument about why I need to avoid her once she arrived. Yes, I'd see her, but no, I wouldn't walk into the room expecting... anything.

"Are you excited to see Maddie? I've missed her! I'm so glad she'll be back."

Dahlia's words shook me from my promises to myself and I must've looked shocked because she rushed to explain.

"I'm sorry. Should I not have said anything? I knew because she asked me to do flowers for the party at her house next weekend and the rest of the girls were invited, so they know."

I just blinked back at her, stunned by the realization that Maddie had been in communication with her friends here and not me. This entire time, part of what'd soothed the burn of her total disconnect had been the thought that she'd needed to. She'd needed to focus solely on New York and life there, and not to worry about things here.

Me. Silverton. Her friends here.

But turns out, it'd only been me she'd shut out. Me and my son, who I suspected had also fallen for Maddie the first day he saw her and they gabbed about *Lord of the Rings* for an hour.

Dahlia's brows pinched and she squeezed my wrist. "Oh, Aidan, I hope I didn't—"

"No. No. Not at all. I've got to run and get Luca, but I'll see you soon."

And in the meantime, I'd straighten myself out. I'd be ready to see her—to be friendly and kind, and then leave. To walk away knowing this chapter of my life, this hope and love and vision that had kindled in my heart despite my best efforts, must be snuffed.

CHAPTER FORTY-FIVE

Maddie

Quinn Darling, as usual, gave no quarter.

"I just want to hear you say it out loud so we know for sure." Her arms were crossed where she leaned against the marble of the kitchen island, eyes glinting with that skepticism I'd come to appreciate.

"It's not that we aren't glad you're here. It's just that..." Dahlia glanced around at Sadie, Sarah, Quinn, and finally, me. "He's been sad."

Pain lanced through me. "I know. I have, too. Believe me when I say, I have struggled. But I've had a purpose for all of this. And I'm taking an insane risk. But I know it's right."

I'd just needed the time to get everything ready. I'd needed time to decide if my idea was in fact as wild as it'd felt when the thought had crossed my mind. After that, I'd needed time to make sure that getting farther into my routine wouldn't suddenly change how I felt about leaving Silverton, or my friends, or Aidan.

Over two months after leaving, I didn't need to guess anymore. Nothing felt right, and I'd known with a clarity I'd only previously had with business acquisitions and wine selections that I couldn't stay there. The Maddie Reynolds that'd returned to New York was a changed woman who didn't want to change back. Maybe that was the point—she was Maddie, not Madeline as my New York world knew me. Not just the formalized version, but how I saw myself and what I wanted, what I'd been through.

I'd worked for a decade and a half to get where I was, but the threat of being shot and the breath of an unhinged man on my neck had been enough to shake me from any sense of doubt.

It'd taken months after that, and in the process, I'd fallen hard and fast for the man of my dreams. I'd literally dreamt of Aidan Wallace for months before seeing him again in Silverton, and somehow, I'd walked away.

Every second I spent away from him felt wrong. Every evening I wasn't chatting with Luca, every night I wasn't sleeping by Aidan's side, every morning I woke up and saw buildings instead of Silver Ridge Peak was wrong.

So I'd come back. And maybe I'd approached this messily, but I'd needed the time to test myself. To really see if forcing myself back into my old routine would change me *back* to the Maddie before. The only thing I knew I couldn't stand in all of this was if *I* was the one who didn't actually fit here and I ended up hurting Aidan and Luca more than I already had.

And Quinn, Sarah, Sadie, and Dahlia could evidently see the truth on my face. Sarah clapped and Sadie grinned.

Quinn nodded, appeased for now, and Dahlia gave me a beautiful smile that was absolutely hiding something.

"What?" I asked, not liking the *something* hiding there.

"A week or so ago, I accidentally mentioned that we'd talked. That you'd been in touch. And he seemed... kind of devastated by that."

My eyes shut and I exhaled the anxiety climbing into my throat. I had worried that my silence would ruin things —would strangle his feelings for me. And though devastation sounded like he probably did still care, I didn't want him to feel that because of me.

"I have so much to make up for. And I appreciate you all being here and working with me to start the process."

Sadie spoke up from her seat on the couch. "Calla's feeling pretty exhausted and they're thinking the baby may arrive a little before her due date, so she's not straying far from Wyatt, but she said to tell you she's glad you're back, especially if you're not going to run away, and that she supports you for doing what all intelligent, successful women do, and getting yourself a Silverton man." Sadie's cheeks brightened and she slumped back in her seat like just getting the words she must've promised to say out was a relief.

I chuckled, wondering if it would work out like I hoped. I'd envisioned this grand gesture—me riding back into town on my shiny white horse and swooping in to save Aidan. Well, not save *him*, but save *us*. Save us from the absolute madness of being in love with each other and not being together.

I'd spent years alone. Years searching. Years wondering whether I'd ever feel a fraction for someone else that Nate felt for Ariel or, based on everything I'd seen, what the Saint men and Julian felt for their partners.

"Well, okay. I guess we better go get ready so we can get back here and you can start on phase one," Quinn said, twirling her keys around her fingers and catching them in her hand.

Nerves fizzed through me, but I nodded. "Yes, please. See you in a bit."

They all departed with encouraging smiles and farewells, all promising they'd be back by seven at the latest. Juliet sent me her fifth *"Have you seen him yet!?"* message as I was shutting the door behind them, so I dialed her quickly.

"I have to go to bed soon or I'll be a mess tomorrow, but I have to know. Have you?" The urgency in her voice made me miss her fiercely.

I'd spent the last few months missing. Missing Aidan. The mountains. My new friends. My oldest friend. My brother and his wife. My nephew. My *freedom*. I'd grappled with all this thinking, bemoaned the "poor me" nature of it, but finally decided that all of this—the months of longing for a change, the axis-tilting nature of being stalked and found by someone so unhinged, and then finally finding someone I wanted a life with—all of it added up to one conclusion.

It was time for a big change. A more abrupt and lasting change than I'd ever made, and yet one I knew with the same certainty I had about most other decisions I'd made in my life, that it was the right one.

I'd planned to ease back in. I didn't expect him to greet me with open arms, but I'd invited him here tonight for this party and he'd agreed to come. He'd see what I meant, and he'd realize it eventually, and I wouldn't give up.

This time, I wasn't going anywhere.

Luca finished his presentation and beamed right as applause began. He was up on a stage, elevated above the audience, and I was clapping and laughing and honestly, a little teary-eyed. It was so good to see him and amazing to hear him deliver such a cogent, interesting presentation. He'd shared a lot of the details over email, but this was even better than expected.

I'd spotted Aidan the minute I walked into the room, but I didn't want to distract him or Luca, so I'd slipped back behind the raised seating, into the shadows, to watch. By the end, I'd edged forward, into the light, and as though thinking about him seeing me made it happen, Aidan's eyes found me.

My breath came in a rush. *So handsome.* I hadn't let myself look, but there was no denying it. He was just stunning, even if he did look two parts confused, one part perturbed to see me. He made his way through the milling crowd that had broken when Luca finished since his was the last presentation, and finally reached me.

"What are you doing here?" It came out accusatory.

My heart raced and raced. "I—"

"You made it! I didn't know if you really would!" Luca's arms wrapped around me and squeezed, released, and he beamed up at me. "What did you think?"

With a quick glance up at Aidan, I smiled back at Luca. "You were amazing."

The crowd shifted and bumped against us. Aidan's eyes were boring into me, and as much as I wanted to talk to him and explain everything, there was no chance we could do that here.

"Where are Gig and Doodle? Did Grandma and Grandpa come?" Luca peered around Aidan toward a small group of people who were all chatting amicably.

"They are. They'll want to see you, but—"

"Please, go talk to them. I'll see you later?" It was so much less than the begging I wanted to do, but I knew we wouldn't make any progress here. Plus, this moment was for Luca, and we didn't need to ruin it with the tension between us.

Aidan's brow dipped low, but he nodded.

Relief, and not for the first time tonight, hope whispered through me.

Everyone arrived on time. The caterers buzzed around the house from person to person, sharing delicious tiny bites of food. Dahlia's flowers were gorgeous, spraying from the banisters, large vases, and any place I could think to stuff them.

But Aidan hadn't arrived yet. And the closer to eight o'clock it got, the more nervous I became that maybe he wouldn't show. I'd still make my announcement, but I wanted him here for it. He'd said he'd be there, and I had no reason to doubt him, except for the fact that I knew I'd hurt him by leaving and cutting off communication. I couldn't take that back.

When the doorbell rang at ten to eight, my breath caught. Everyone else was here. Dahlia nodded, signaling she'd get the door. Anthony would've done it, but I'd let him off the hook for tonight since he hadn't been ready to leave the city so soon after being nomadic for so long.

The low tenor of men's voices registered through my nervous pinging thoughts, and I took off toward them. What had I been thinking, letting Dahlia answer for me? I'd been waiting to see Aidan for weeks—months at this point. I wanted nothing more than to run to him, and though I recognized the need to tread carefully now, I'd been a fool to think I could stay calm when he was down the hall.

My breath caught at the sight of Aidan's profile—his hair looked freshly trimmed but still long on top and his beard was still that dark mix of black, gray, gold, and red. His gaze moved between his cousin and Dahlia like he couldn't quite understand them. He wore a faintly confused expression, if I was reading him right, and just as I registered that, Dahlia's words pulled my attention to her.

"I wasn't trying to be unwelcoming, John. I simply didn't realize you were coming."

John scowled. "As if I'd let him come here alone like some kind of—"

"We're sorry we're late, Dahlia. If you could just show us in, we'll be fine..." His words faded out at the end, softening as his gaze found me. He swallowed hard and dipped his chin. "Maddie."

My heart twisted and leapt and probably attempted a back handspring if the rioting in my chest was anything to go by. "Hi, Aidan."

He looked so good in his button-up rolled at the wrists and jeans that looked worn but still nice. He was achingly handsome, and it'd been so long. The blip of a meeting earlier had been so fast, it hardly counted, especially since I'd known all along that would only be a glimpse. We wouldn't talk the way we needed to—the way I hoped we would tonight.

In many ways, coming to this point felt longer than the

time between our very first meeting and returning to Silverton, and yet the actual time passed was a fraction. Still, that draw toward him, the magnetic feeling, filled every inch of the handful of feet creating the distance between us.

"Maddie. Hey. Thanks for having us. I'm curious about this *announcement*." John stepped between us and held out his hand as though he'd sensed the push and pull between me and his cousin.

I shook his hand, sensing the forced formality and noting the little pinch at my heart. He and I had been friends when I'd left, or so I thought. But I couldn't fault him for coming here with suspicion or at least skepticism in his eyes.

"You can hold your horses and wait like everyone else. Let's get you a drink and let them talk a minute," Dahlia said, reaching for John's arm and tugging at him.

The strangest thing happened then. John physically jolted, his cheeks reddened so quickly I would've thought something was wrong, and he jerked enough that Dahlia pulled her hand back, practically cradling it, while John gritted out a, "Fine." And off they went, no longer touching, John trailing behind Dahlia and leaving no small amount of that odd energy behind them.

"I still have no idea," Aidan said, shaking his head after them.

It was easier to joke about them than confront everything between us now, wasn't it? So I forced a laugh and a small smile. "Who knows."

He nodded quickly, and the air thinned. The shift that so often happened when we were alone stalled out and instead of that magnetic draw, it was as though one of us had reversed. There was resistance, and instead of launching myself into his arms like I had more than once in my mind, I stayed glued in place, willing him to stay something more.

"Well, uh—"

"I'm just so—"

Those thin smiles drilled home the distance between us all the more. "Sorry, you go ahead," I offered, waving my hand between us.

"No, please. You go."

How pathetic that even that gentle reply was like agony to me. His politeness felt like a wall he'd erected, and I had no idea how to mount it. "I was going to say I'm glad you're here. Thank you for coming. I know it's been a while."

I cringed inwardly, wishing I'd said something better. But what was there to say after the time apart and the silence? I'd spend however long it took explaining it, and I hoped what I said in a few minutes would smooth the way.

"Thank you for inviting me. Please, don't let me keep you."

I blinked at that, somehow still shocked he was staying so formal and withdrawn when we were standing just feet apart. But why wouldn't he? I'd done nothing but build up the very wall that now stood between us since I'd left.

"Of course. Thank you. I'll... I'll talk with you after, okay?" *Please. Please say yes.*

He nodded, not looking right at me. "Sure."

Quinn hooked her arm through mine. "Ready?" she asked, fully ignoring everyone but me.

"Yes," I said, and with one last glance at Aidan, I went to take my place.

This might backfire spectacularly, but I'd never forgive myself if I didn't try.

CHAPTER FORTY-SIX

Aidan

My heart thudded a slow, heavy beat. It'd finally calmed after the initial rush of adrenaline at being in her house, smelling the scent of her space that was familiar and sent memory crashing through me, and of course, of seeing her. Hearing her voice. Feeling the heat, then the distance between us.

For the second time today, the first time in months, I'd had her within reach. She'd made no move to touch me, and despite every atom in my being crying out to take her in my arms and hug her, kiss her, remind her how much I loved her, I didn't.

John had drilled the response into me on the way there. *"You don't know what this is, and she's chosen to freeze you out. So you stay quiet and see what happens before you hang your big heart out there for her to shred again."* Based on all of our discussions thus far, I knew better than to counter his point.

He had a good one. She'd left me guessing and even with her return, hadn't told me anything of substance. There was also the fact that she'd been in touch with Luca —almost the entire time she'd been in New York. What did that mean? Why was I both a little envious and low-key destroyed over that discovery?

But as though my body was bracing itself to receive whatever news she'd deliver, everything went from high alert, intense, and mentally chaotic to that slow, steady beat right as she stepped in front of the crowd I hadn't bothered to look closely at.

"Thank you all for coming tonight. I'm sorry for the last-minute nature, but I wanted you to hear this from me first."

My stomach flipped, then sank. *Hear what?*

Maddie continued with a small smile. "I'll be doing an official press conference Monday, but again, I wanted this to come from me, in person, and allow you all to ask any questions you have."

Her eyes flicked to meet mine, and dread sluiced through me. What questions would this raise for me? What would this announcement, which would later require a press conference, mean?

Somewhere in my gut, I feared it might mean she and some East Coast pedigreed heir named something like Warner Huntington The Third or something equally stiff planned to marry. It made no sense given everything I knew, and yet it was the only thing I could think of that would merit this kind of in-person announcement.

"Come on, just tell us!" Quinn hollered from somewhere, sparking good-natured chuckles through the crowd.

Maddie's smile sparkled with humor, and a luminescence lit her up. Though wasn't she always a little like that in my eyes? Even now, even after months apart and nothing but a few texts between us, she drew me in.

"Fine, fine. The big news is, I'm moving to Silverton." Her gaze found mine again. "Permanently."

Everything in me froze, including my brain. Her words buzzed around in my head, not landing long enough to really make sense. People clapped and chattered indistinctly around me, and someone hugged her, tearing her eyes from mine.

"Well... that's certainly news," John said, patting my back from where he stood next to me.

I couldn't see her face—couldn't understand anything, though my heart had taken off in a sprint.

"Yeah, sure is," I mumbled, turning for the exit.

It didn't make sense, but my only impulse was to leave. I didn't want to stay here in the crowd and congratulate her. I wanted her to myself. I wanted to understand the choice— needed to. Why, after so little communication and interaction, was she moving here?

The foolish, perpetually hopeful man I'd once been hadn't learned his lesson, because here he stood, gulping in air from Maddie's front porch, possibility gobbling me up bit by bit like flame held to paper.

She was moving here. Permanently.

For me.

The thought struck before I could keep it, and I hated it, and loved it, and wanted to hide from it all at once. I couldn't even express how much I wished that were true, how deeply the longing for that to be reality took root. I steadied myself on the stone wall of her house and the cool, rough granite brought me back to the present just as John stepped outside.

"You okay?"

I looked around, hardly seeing the porch or front steps. Was I okay?

I nodded, words coming slower than the action. "Yes. I… yes. But I have to go."

He narrowed his eyes. "Pretty sure she'd like to talk with you since she made such a big deal of you being here," he said, eying me with no small amount of concern.

"I know. But I'm not doing that here. I'll talk to her soon. Tell her—"

The front door swung open again and a small group spilled out, Maddie just behind. Her gaze found me in an instant.

"Thanks for coming even though you had other obligations tonight as well, you guys. I appreciate your support. See you soon," she said, holding a hand up in farewell even as she focused on me.

They must've been leaving early. Maybe it wouldn't be so obvious that I was fleeing if others had to trickle out, too.

My heart beat so fast, I could hardly feel it. This had to be some kind of irregularity, but between the news and all the raging hope clamoring through me, I couldn't speak. I cursed myself inwardly for not being up for talking. As much as I wanted this to mean something for us, it didn't make sense that she'd made this move for me. And I couldn't ignore or suspend the hurt, even if I did understand where it came from originally.

"I—congratulations," I said, descending the first, then second step without looking.

"Thank you. Can you stick around for a few?"

Those hazel eyes just about slayed my escape plan, but I needed time. I'd never been one to act quickly or on impulse. I wasn't the kind of guy who assumed things. Heck, I wasn't a guy who dated millionaires and lived in a delusional world where I believed I might have a shot at her even after we'd essentially broken up.

Except lately, I had been that guy. And *that guy* wanted to take her in his arms and kiss her, hold her, claim her. But this guy, the guy that'd been living in reality and getting nothing from her the last two months? He needed a damn minute.

"Sorry. I made plans and I'm his ride. Plus Luca... you know how it goes, Maddie. We'll see you soon, yeah?" John hooked his arm around my neck and hauled me with him as though he could sense the part of me that wanted to stay and figure all this out now. His excuse made no sense, but I was grateful for it nevertheless.

"Okay. Drive safe," she said, but we were already crossing the street, in the car, pulling away.

I willed myself not to look back. If she'd already gone inside, it'd feel like too much of an ending. Like she'd made this choice and this announcement based on factors having nothing to do with me. And if she was still there, I'd feel yet another heart-wringing twist. I'd want to turn back. I'd have one more piece of evidence that this meant something to her —that I did.

It was all nonsense. Her staying or going back inside didn't tell me anything. Even so, I lost the battle with myself just before the road curved away and her house fell out of view.

Sure enough, she stood there looking after us, watching our slow progress as we wound our way out of the neigh-borhood.

"She's still there," John said, as though he'd noticed right when I did.

"Yep." My voice came out raw.

He drove on for a few minutes as my mind whirled with

variations on the theme of *what does this mean?* John's words interrupted my baffled thoughts.

"You get that she's back for you, right?"

I jolted and shook my head. "We don't know that. I don't know that. Plus, you were the one who tried to convince me not to even see her."

He made a scoffing sound. "If I hadn't been there, I might see how you can feel unsure. She did a number on you without even trying, and this could be the world's biggest game play of all time. But it's not."

I studied him. No longer uptight or defensive like he had been on the way there, his posture was relaxed and he seemed certain. A sigh escaped me and I scrubbed my hands over my face.

"You have no idea how much I want that to be true," I admitted.

He chuckled. "Yeah. Pretty sure I *do* know. And I'm telling you. The way she was looking at you—during the announcement, even before. And after, at the door... woman's got herself a fever and the only prescription is Aidan Wallace."

I groaned and rolled my eyes, which he wouldn't see but would know. "That was awful. Please never speak like that again." But I laughed, too, a slip of relief inching into the anxiety, confusion, hurt, and longing.

"Seriously, you should go back later. Talk to her."

Nerves activated the instant he suggested it. "What do I say? 'Hey, just wondering if you're moving here for me even though we haven't talked in two months?'"

He thought about it a moment, then shrugged. "Why not?"

I sighed again. "Whether or not you believe it, I do have *some* pride left, you know."

"Of course you do. But you're also in love with this woman and she's just made one hell of a grand gesture."

Had it been a grand gesture? Can it be if it isn't directly stated? Or was I the idiot who was second-guessing everything?

I'd let her go. I hadn't wanted to. I'd wanted her to stay, and I hadn't said a damn thing. I'd thought I was doing the noble thing, the *right* thing. But every minute without her felt wrong, and not even getting to talk to her was worse.

It hadn't worked for me. And if John wasn't wrong, it hadn't for her either. And if I ever wanted a chance with her, I couldn't keep running away—couldn't keep pushing down what I wanted in favor of some idea I thought was best.

I needed to say what I wanted and let her respond. I hadn't asked her to stay and yet she'd ended up back here anyway. Wasn't that enough of a sign?

CHAPTER FORTY-SEVEN

Maddie

Aidan knocked quietly three hours later. I'd been shocked to see his text come hours after he'd left. He'd only stayed about ten minutes after arriving earlier and had clearly had no interest in lingering and talking.

As someone who generally did things well and often right the first time, I'd screwed up countless times with Aidan. I hated that this whole thing had gone sideways and definitely didn't result in him getting the message I'd thought I was sending.

I'd watched John's car slip down the road with a tight chest and aching heart. Dahlia and Sarah had retrieved me and assured me it'd take time. And they were right. I'd known this wasn't going to unlock everything between us, but I hated that I'd missed the mark so thoroughly that he'd essentially run away. I'd shocked him and not in a good way. *Way to go, Maddie.*

But after the last of my friends trickled out and the catering staff slipped a tray of leftovers in the fridge, I'd checked my phone and seen the text. *"Can I come over to talk when everyone's gone?"*

Off to the races, my heart galloped in my chest as I responded, praying it wasn't too late. He'd sent the message an hour earlier. But soon enough, those little dots popped up and he was responding, saying he'd be here soon.

I paced the living room and practiced what I'd say for the thousandth time, and then came the knock. I sprinted to the door and pulled it open, heart tripping at the sight of him. He hadn't changed, but his demeanor had. That part of him that'd felt untouchable before, like he'd slipped on a mask or coated himself in something protective and distancing, was missing.

"I'm sorry it's so late," he said, that voice pouring over me like mulled cider.

Paired with the chilled fall scent walking in with him, my senses were overwhelmed. Still, I found my voice, more than ready for this moment. "I'm just glad you're here."

He followed me inside and I stopped near the bar of the kitchen island, not sure what to do with my hands. They wanted to reach out and touch him. They wanted to pull him toward me so I could press my lips to his. They kind of wanted to strangle him for leaving without more than a few words earlier.

"I'm sorry I left so quickly. I..." He cleared his throat. "I was surprised."

"I know. And I have so much to say. So much I owe you."

He was shaking his head before I finished. "No. No, Maddie. You don't owe me. You never have. I just wasn't sure what this all was."

He ran a hand through his hair in a way that made me want to do the same but also clearly betrayed the nervous energy running through him. Aidan had a calm vibe that rarely seemed edgy, and yet I could feel all kinds of things radiating from him.

"I do. And what you think this is, it is. I'm leaving my company. I'm changing my life. I talked so much about wanting freedom and a fresh start, and I'd convinced myself I just needed a little break after all the madness and I'd be ready to go back. But being back..." *being without you...* "wasn't right."

He nodded. "I'm glad you figured that out. I'm sorry you have such a big transition ahead—it's a huge change. But I'm so happy for you that you figured out what you want."

Ugh, this man. My heart absolutely glowed with love, and I couldn't wait any longer to spell it out for him. I closed the distance between us and took his hands in mine. "I did figure it out. I don't want to be in New York."

He nodded. "Good."

My heart pounded relentlessly. "I want to be here, in Silverton."

His response this time came out a little gruffer. "That's... very good news."

"And I... I love you. And I want to be with you."

His smile dawned slowly, his face transforming from handsome to something practically celestial. "Thank God."

Then his lips were on mine and we were crushed together, all the time apart obliterated by the ravenous kiss. His hands were in my hair, at my back, mine were on his neck, under his shirt. It was as though our bodies needed to make up for lost time as much as our hearts had, and yet I had more to say. I pulled back after a few minutes, afraid we'd get lost in the reconnection and miss some of the things I had to say.

With one more kiss to his lips, we stood with my arms around his neck and his hands at my waist. "I'm so sorry I disappeared on you."

He exhaled softly. "That's not my favorite thing that's ever happened."

I laughed. "Yeah. Mine either. I—" I shook my head, disappointed in myself even though I'd made peace with it. "I was so convinced that if I shut off everything about Silverton—especially you and Luca—then I'd do what I needed to do. I've spent so long in work mode, and I felt so far out of it. But it wasn't just that I'd taken a break and was struggling to get back into it. I changed this year. Like, *really* changed, and I couldn't get myself back."

His brow furrowed and I registered I hadn't explained the silence, so I continued. "I'd talked myself into the idea that I'd be ready to go back by the end of the summer. When I left and it felt like I'd ripped out my heart and handed it to you, I decided that cutting out communication between us was the answer. That if I had enough distance, my head would clear and I'd be able to do my job again."

"But that didn't happen?"

Emotion crept up my throat at his tender, concerned expression. "No. Because you still had my heart. And maybe in the past I've been able to handle that—only my mind in the game. But after everything that's happened— my brother's wedding and meeting you and the stalker and falling for you... I didn't want to. I'd found what I'd spent years looking for, and suddenly I'm okay just leaving it behind? Never mind I couldn't manage to cut off communi- cation with Luca because... I just couldn't. It didn't make sense. "

I rolled my eyes at the idiocy, but he pulled me closer and pressed a kiss to my temple before speaking.

"I need to apologize, too. I was so convinced you had to go and I had to stay and that was the way it should all go, I didn't even ask you."

"Ask me what?"

"To stay. To be with me. To try long distance. *Anything.*"

An ache filled me, and the only way to alleviate it was to press a kiss to his jaw, then his cheek, then his mouth. When I pulled back, his expression matched my feelings exactly.

"I don't know when I convinced myself that I had to give you up, but I did. And I'm sorry."

I chuckled. "You thought it was the right thing to do, didn't you?"

He squinted. "*Maybe.*"

I tucked away a smile. "I wondered. I mean, I'd always planned to leave, and it snuck up on us, but part of me had hoped maybe you'd say something. And yet another part of me was relieved I didn't have to say no. But I'm guessing you knew that, somehow, and decided to make the decision for me and not say a word."

"Are you laughing at me for trying to save us both the agony of you shooting me down?"

I couldn't contain my grin or the love multiplying by the second for this man. "No. I'm just enjoying the fact that you are who you are, and I love you."

He sobered and bent to touch his forehead to mine. "I love you, too, Madeline Reynolds. And I'm so glad you're home."

CHAPTER FORTY-EIGHT

Four Months Later

Aidan

S ix months after Maddie had officially rocked the tech world by resigning her position as CEO of her company and moving to the small, nowhere town of Silverton from the Big Apple, I'd decided it was time.

Our lives had folded together seamlessly since she'd moved back. *Oh wait.* No.

Our lives had been headbutting against each other since the moment she got back into town and we got serious about what a long-term commitment was like. She'd never been in a relationship that lasted longer than a few months, and she'd definitely never dated a single dad.

Luca loved her, loved us together, and generally had no

issues, other than that he'd hit full pre-teen mode on me around Christmas and become moody and reluctant any time he talked to me. This, I regret to admit, made *me* moody, and at times, reluctant. Poor Maddie got to deal with us both.

The beauty of it was, she did. And she did it well. She didn't seem scared by our moods or the way we'd go quiet when upset. She'd coax Luca out of his shell and she'd soothe my bruised, frustrated dad ego.

But it took a while before our schedules synced since she had meetings all over the country to resign this position on that board or whatever else. I'd been naïve to think her resignation of the CEO position meant she would have time. She still traveled, took on a larger role at a non-profit she'd started years ago, and like seventeen other things. At one point when I'd seen her two days out of fourteen and had grunted out something about not ever seeing her, she'd sat me down and we hashed it out.

All of it.

My fears—that she didn't need me. She'd end up leaving. She didn't actually want to be here and I was holding her back. That I wasn't doing enough for her.

Her fears—that I could never love her like I had Viv. That Luca didn't want her around. That she wasn't doing enough to bring value to our relationship.

But we saw it. Both of us had a similar illness—my need to do the right thing, the honorable thing, and her need to produce and achieve. They coalesced in this surprising but perfect way because, just like we had years ago upon first meeting, we understood each other.

She explained she loved work, but she loved coming home to us. I thought about asking her to move in right away, but she'd made clear she wanted to be engaged and then married, that she knew it might sound old-fashioned but she didn't care.

And ultimately, neither did I. I just wanted to be with her, and though we'd both expressed long-term commitment, we'd been taking it relatively slow.

But the time had come. I was done waiting, especially since I'd realized I had nothing else to wait for. We'd had every discussion. We'd done everything we needed to do to feel ready. But I'd gotten hung up waiting for her to give me the signal until I finally realized she wanted *me* to be the one to make it happen.

So tonight? I planned to do just that.

I'd debated a long time about this. What kind of proposal would a woman like Maddie like? I didn't have a private plane to fly her off to some gourmet meal, and she'd surrendered access to the corporate jet with her job. But knowing her, that wasn't what she wanted. Or at least I hoped I hadn't missed the mark too completely with this plan.

It would've been handy if it'd been summer, but I couldn't wait another four or five months. February in Utah could be brutally cold, but miraculously, I caught a break with a fresh blanket of snow under a sparkling night sky.

It wasn't fancy, but it would be right.

I looked up as Maddie slipped out the door. "Luca is so into that new series. He's going to be devastated to wait for the next book."

Nerves bounced around my gut. "Sure is. Yeah."

She tipped her head to one side. "You okay?"

I huffed, my breath showing white in the chill of the evening. The black diamond sky overhead made it feel like the stars were close, watching. "Yeah. I'm more than okay, Maddie."

She smiled. "Good, because I—"

She sucked in a breath as I took her hand and went to one knee in front of her.

"I've been waiting for you to let me know you were ready. Like a fool, I've been sitting around, biding my time until I felt certain you wanted this. Until I realized that everything you've done since you got back has shown us that. And I know I'm ready."

"Okay," she said, nothing but a whisper.

"Madeline Reynolds, I love you. I don't know why I've been given a second chance to love an amazing woman, but I have and I want it. With you. I can't believe how lucky we are that you landed here over two years ago on your failed vacation."

She chuckled at that, and my heart surged, glowed, nearly burst. "I love your ambition. I love the way you treat the people around you. I love that you've worked so hard to redefine what you want and who you are after something awful."

She shifted on her feet, restless to just stand there, I could tell. My smile flashed and she grabbed my hand with both of hers and pulled it up to her lips.

"Maddie, I love that you have let me be the man I am— someone who loved deeply, and lost. Someone with a child and a whole host of obligations. You've found ways to enjoy those parts of me I struggle with instead of trying to change them or making them a project. You've let me be a whole human, and I can't tell you what that has meant to me."

"I love you so much," she said, voice shaky.

"Guess I better get on with it, huh?" Our breaths swirled white between us. "I want our lives to be more than the fantasy we shared years ago. I want us to work together, to struggle and succeed, to love each other and Luca and whoever else comes along like crazy. Will you marry me?"

She was smiling, crying, and nodding before I finished. "Yes. Of course. Yes." She dropped my hands and cupped my face, stepping close, and bent to press a kiss.

The frozen deck bit at my knee where I kneeled and the snow underneath was melting through, but I wouldn't trade this moment. I kissed her back, elation and relief and a shudder of nerves washing through me. She broke away and pulled me to standing.

"Can we go inside now?" she whispered against my lips.

We laughed together again. "Yes, please. I think my toes are numb."

EPILOGUE

Three Years Later

Aidan

Jessica Juliet was born on December twenty-second at twelve minutes after two. A day later, the last of our visitors were filtering through, sneaking in a visit before we were discharged. We'd told them all they could see us back home, but when asked if we wanted them to come, we'd both said a resounding yes.

Martha and Rich had brought Luca first thing yesterday afternoon. Once he'd had a moment, Martha peeked her head in, claiming she just wanted to see. But Maddie had waved her in, insisted she and Rich come all the way in, and had set the new baby in Martha's arms. "Meet Jessica Juliet Wallace."

I don't think anyone had a dry eye. Well, except Luca and Jess. Because as fate would have it, Maddie had always wanted to name her daughter after her best friend, and it just so happened she shared a name with Viv. Vivienne Juliet Templeton had been honored in the name, too. When Maddie realized the connection, she'd worried I would be upset, but it felt like a tribute. A way to fold in Viv's memory with this little girl who would never know her, but would, in this small way, still carry a piece of her.

Rich had looked up from my daughter's tiny face and said, "Beautiful."

And Maddie had glanced at me before saying, "Thank you. She's excited to meet her Grandma and Grandpa."

Martha's soft, "Oh," and Rich's throat clearing told us how much that gesture meant. But how could they have doubted? They'd accepted Maddie immediately. And as they'd assured me, they considered me their son.

Only family visited, but we had messages from all Maddie's friends. Juliet had Facetimed from some far reach and John was waiting until we were out of the hospital before he and his wife met Jess.

But today, we had a few more visitors while we waited to be discharged.

"Well, I'd say this is an excellent product." Nate Reynolds, Maddie's brother, grinned down at Jess and ran a just-washed finger over her eyebrow.

Maddie chuckled quietly. "I agree. I think her market value's going to be incredible."

Nate nodded sagely. "Definitely. Real growth potential here."

They kept up like this while Ariel and I listened and laughed. I'd met them at our wedding a year after she'd first arrived back in Silverton. I liked them both immensely, and watching Nate and Maddie banter back and forth about nonsense was always supremely entertaining. It gave me insight into her in a way hearing about Nate never could've.

After a few more minutes, he whispered something in Jess's ear that no one but she could hear, then returned her to my arms.

"What'd you say?" I asked, knowing he did this with his own daughters, too. Ariel had told us at some point that Nate had snuggled their newborn girls on his bare chest, bonding with them as Ariel recovered, and she'd seen him talking, whispering. When she asked him what he said, he'd claimed he was sharing promises with them, mostly about doing whatever he could to love them and care for them.

I'd taken the note, and Jess and I had had a similar conversation hours ago.

Nate grinned. "I told her how lucky she is to have a mom and dad like you two, a big brother like Luca, and an uncle like me." His smile flashed larger and everyone laughed.

"Pardon me but it's my turn and I believe you're supposed to relieve the sitter soon, aren't you?" Annette Reynolds marched into the room like she owned the place—her usual approach.

"Yes, Mother. We'll get going." He rattled off something in Italian, to which she snapped back just as quickly. Ariel's bright blue eyes caught mine, and we shared a look we often did. Something to the effect of, "What can you do with these people?"

Maddie chuckled low behind me as I adjusted into the seat next to her bed. "He said she has to be nice to us and not pester you about Luca."

I stifled a laugh. "He's a good man."

She pressed her lips together, likely staving off tears.

She'd been frustrated with how easily she cried lately, not because she didn't want to cry *ever*, but because, as she'd put it, "all this blubbering makes it hard to say what I'm trying to say."

After a moment, she cleared her throat. "He is."

Annette hugged Nate, then Ariel, and they waved as they snuck out, off to relieve the sitter who'd taken up at our house and was watching their girls.

"Now, tell me how my perfect granddaughter is doing," she said, taking a seat on the bed at Maddie's side and running an affectionate hand over her face. It was a gesture I couldn't have imagined when I'd first met her, but their relationship had grown in ways I didn't think Maddie or Nate could've envisioned either.

Maddie's departure from New York had shaken Annette in the oddest way. Instead of fury or judgment, it seemed to soften her. It was as though that shift in Maddie's focus had done the same for Annette. And she'd grown on me over time, too. It didn't hurt that she doted on Luca, and though she pestered me about sending him to language camps and getting him tutors, she was genuinely a lovely grandmother.

"She's been hungry. I'm guessing she'll be rooting around for another meal here soon," I said, handing the bundled baby over to her grandmother.

"Good. She's a tiny one, but that never stopped the Reynolds girls, did it?" Annette winked at Maddie.

Tears hit my wife's eyes in an instant, and my heart ached with love. Annette held Jess for a while until she got restless and surrendered her to Maddie for a feeding. I'd forgotten, or maybe erased, the challenge of breastfeeding from my paternal memory, but like everything she did, Maddie was determined.

Once the baby had settled, belly sated and snoozing again, I snuggled into the space my wife had made for me in the bed. We'd be discharged any time now, but of course that meant sometime today and never anytime soon. So we rested together, knowing the days ahead would be wonderful and challenging.

Her head on my shoulder, she exhaled. The sound told me she was steadying herself, likely crying again.

"What is it, love?" I asked, keeping my voice low and smooth. The baby wasn't hassled by hospital announcements or talking. You were supposed to make noise so they could sleep. And yet, every instinct in me said to protect this child's sleep at all costs.

"I'm just so full. So full of love and happiness, I'm not sure I know how to handle it." She knit our hands together, and I leaned to press a kiss to her head.

"You don't have to do it alone, Maddie. Share it with me. And we'll share it with Jess and Luca. Your mom and our children's eighteen pairs of grandparents and all of our friends."

Her eyes glistened with tears as she looked up at me. "Okay. I can do that."

I shook my head, perfectly understanding the sentiment of feeling so full I might burst. "I love you. So much. I never dared dream of this."

"I love you, too, Aidan. Let's never wake up."

Thank you for reading Aidan and Maddie's story. I hope you loved their love story as much as I loved writing it! Don't miss John and Dahlia's romance in Almost Ready.

Home With You: The Rambler Battalion, Book 4

All of You: The Rambler Battalion, Book 5

ACKNOWLEDGMENTS

Thank you to the many people who listened to me agonize over this book. For some reason, Maddie and Aidan's book hit at a challenging time in my writing life. The whole process felt almost like writing a first book rather than a twenty-fourth for some reason, which was... instructive.

But that's the beauty of writing, I think. We learn things with every book we write—at least I do. And through the refining process of writing this book, I've learned quite a bit about myself, my process, and that I shouldn't ever start a book during my kids' summer break again, hah.

Thank you to Zee Monodee, my amazing editor, who so patiently helped me find the heart of this book and do the best for Maddie and Aidan.

Thank you to Amanda Cuff, my proofreader, for being so patient with me as I missed more than one deadline—gasp. Thank you, truly, for your patience and grace.

Thanks, as always, to Amanda, Ashley, and Genny, my amazing beta readers, for sharing your thoughts and letting me trial run my various what-ifs for how the book begins. I think we made the right call.

Thanks to all the readers and bookstagrammers and booktokers who've been so supportive of the series thus far. I hope you've loved Maddie and Aidan.

Claire Cain lives to eat and drink her way around the globe with her traveling soldier and three kids, but is perhaps even happier hunkered down at home in a pair of sweatpants and slippers using any free moment she has to read and cook. Or talk—she really likes to talk. She has become an expert at packing too many dishes in too few cabinets and making houses into homes from Utah to Germany and many places in between. She's a proud Army wife and is frankly just really happy to be here.

You can also join Claire's facebook reader group for exclusive content and fun: https://www.facebook.com/groups/clairecain/

Website: http://www.clairecainwriter.com

E-mail: Claire@ClaireCainWriter.com

Newsletter sign-up for new releases, exclusives, and freebies, including a free book:

http://www.clairecainwriter.com/newsletter

amazon.com/author/clairecain

bookbub.com/authors/claire-cain

instagram.com/clairecainwriter

facebook.com/clairecainwriter

goodreads.com/clairecainwriter

pinterest.com/clairecainwriter